MOON

Moon

Ann Larrabee

SANTOS BOOKS
EVERY STORY SACRED

First Printing, 2025

Published by Santos Books, Elizabethtown, PA 17022

ISBN: 9798992412864

To my mother and grandmothers--the strongest women
I knew.

Contents

1

The Alarm Goes Off

On the morning of her forty-fifth birthday, Moon groaned out of bed as she always did, limped to the bathroom pushing the cat who was trying to trip her out of her way as she stumbled along the narrow, cluttered hallway—and barely made it in time. *'What a disaster if I hadn't,'* she thought. The cat had no comment on the subject. *'I have enough mess to clean up as it is without adding more, and I would be late to work on top of it,'* she mused as she stared at her reflection in the mirror above the sink. Her hands dripped water and soap residue, but she made no effort to rinse or dry them. She stared at herself as if uncertain who this person was. She felt as though she was looking at a stranger.

'That's not me, is it? What happened to me?' she wondered. *'I had brown hair, not whatever this is. It isn't brown, it isn't grey, it isn't really anything. I had lips and cheekbones. Now everything is...gone. I have pouches of fat and wrinkles; I can barely find my eyes. They used to be my best feature: big and brown: people said they glowed. What happened to me? Where did I disappear to?'* The cat's comments had more to do with breakfast than with Moon's identity issues. Sad and confused, she turned away from the mirror.

"I hear you! You will get fed as soon as I get dressed!" Moon rinsed and dried her hands, thinking longingly not of the cat's breakfast but of her own choice of coffee and donuts on the way to her job. She navigated the dark hallway back to her bedroom, deciding which clean pantsuit she should select for work. '*Add laundry to the list,*' she sighed to herself as she put on a simple navy polyester outfit with red trim, the last one in the clean laundry pile. The cat made one final attempt to trip her before it raced to the kitchen to oversee food preparation.

Moon's apartment was too small for her, too dark: too cold in the winter, too hot in the summer. It was in the middle of the first floor of a building of twenty such units built sometime in the 1930s, across town on Prescott Street, just a few blocks south of the central business district. Moon had moved there after her divorce, filled it with cheap Salvation Army furniture and housewares, things she didn't care about, and a few things Geordie hadn't wanted, mostly sentimental mementos left over from Moon's childhood. The building was a major code violation, the apartments were tiny, cramped, inconveniently plotted, poorly maintained. Every week something developed a mind of its own and "went on holiday" (as Moon would say about things that broke down, jammed up, or fell apart). Mostly it would be something simple that Moon could patch together herself or smack into compliance. When she chose to. If she chose to. Calling maintenance was useless unless talking to an answering machine was the highlight of your day. At first, Moon had made the effort to keep things repaired. She did try. But bit by bit she too gave up. Now there were doors missing from cupboards, the toilet worked erratically, the window in the bedroom leaked air and water (Moon had installed double curtains packed with insulation to block out sun, wind, and rain.) There was something funky growing under the kitchen sink (Moon suspected mushrooms, wondered if they could be a source of income, abandoned the idea), 'Ah, Home Sweet Home'.

Moon herself was too large for the apartment. Once a woman of only slightly over average weight, she had put on fifty pounds in the last five years. Barely able to fit in her chair at work or get out of her chair at home, Moon bewailed her increased size, ate some ice cream to comfort herself, and bought more clothes. Her closets exploded with ill-fitting shirts, pantsuits, yoga pants, sweatpants. She no longer considered buying dresses or skirts, although she had invested in a few muumuus for her days off. Moon hated the apartment, but she hated to think of leaving it so, except for work or shop-

ping, she didn't. Craving company of some kind, Moon had soon taken in a stray kitten, though she would have preferred a dog. Pets weren't allowed in the apartments, but the management generally looked the other way when it came to cats.

It was not a good fit. Moon kept the cat because it was company, the cat stayed out of sheer maliciousness. After five years they couldn't stand each other but neither was willing to admit it. 'Kind of like my marriage', Moon thought.

Moon left her bed unmade, her nightgown hanging over the edge of the open clothes hamper in the corner, its ripped hem dragging on the floor. She didn't bother to look at herself in the dresser mirror as she brushed her shoulder-length hair into a low ponytail, fastened with an old rubber band. She scooped up her purse from the chair next to her bed after finding it under a pile of shirts and pants that hadn't made it to the hamper and fished her loafers out from under the bed where the cat had dragged them.

'*Breakfast,*' she thought as she left the hallway into the kitchen/living room. The cat agreed, but as soon as Moon had scooped food into its bowl, the cat stalked off, distaining it. Moon sighed. This was the usual morning routine. The cat always ate as soon as she left for work, but its rejection left her as depressed as the early morning reflection in the bathroom mirror.

Moon collected her keys from the bowl by the door lest she accidentally lock herself out (as she had done many times before, the cat declining to let her back in) and slipped on a small pile of letters in front of her apartment door.

'*Why can't they just put them in the mailbox?*' she wondered before remembering that the mailboxes were mostly broken, still on the Super's List of **Things to Be Fixed Before the Tenants Complain.** Two birthday cards: one from her daughter and one from the Ladies Guild of her church, a shopping flyer….and a letter from the owner of the apartment complex. '*Probably complaining about the cat again.*' She didn't notice similar letters in front of other doors. Coffee and donuts were calling before work!

Donut Junction was offering their famous summertime special: Orange Juice donuts, so Moon celebrated her birthday with two, washed down with a Vanilla Cappuccino. The day was Spring-time warm, clear and bright, perfect for May, just the right kind of day for a birthday treat. She arrived at her desk in the bank just in time to briefly review the day's loan requests before the main doors opened. Moon had been employed at the Tri-State Bank since high school, working her way up from teller to assistant loan officer. She liked it. It wasn't overly stressful, she knew most of the people in town well, certainly the ones who had accounts there. She liked most of her co-workers and got along well with her boss. On quiet mornings, she spent her breaks gossiping in the basement lounge with two of the secretaries, discussing the latest Hollywood rumors as well as their own small-town scandals. They didn't socialize after work. Moon was divorced and both secretaries had a string of boyfriends complete with romance woes. Moon didn't feel she should offer advice: her own marriage hadn't turned out so well. So, she commiserated but held her peace. *'Let them mess up their lives on their own,'* she thought. *'They don't need my help.'*

The break lounge was a former storage room, emptied out when records were computerized and stored offsite with records from other branches of the bank. It consisted of a couple of vending machines that were filled monthly, an old metal waste basket and newish plastic recycle containers, a sink for wash-ups and counter for a coffee pot, a table and chairs generously donated from the kitchen of the bank president when his wife remodeled their home, a couch in case someone wasn't feeling well and a tiny bathroom. One of the secretaries had installed a First Aid kit for emergencies: it remained unused, but its very presence was a comfort. Once a dull institutional light grey, the break room had been repainted some years before as an art project for the high school and still boasted some stylized murals on a light blue background.

Today the gossip centered around one of the bank's biggest clients who was currently defaulting on his loan. *'Glad I didn't approve that one,'* Moon congratulated herself before she realized that the client was the owner of her apartment building.

'Oh, rats,' she thought, remembering the letter. *'I bet it wasn't about the cat after all.'* She waddled back to her desk, retrieved the envelope from the desk drawer where she had tossed it, unthinking, that morning, and slit it open with her official bank letter opener.

We regret to inform you.... Her apartment building was to be sold, and she was being given notice to find someplace else to live. *'Rats!'* She had thirty days. *'Happy Birthday, Déjà vu.'* Five years ago, the same thing had happened: her divorce had sent her to the cheap crowded apartment she now shared with the mad cat.

Moon stared at the letter, then at the pile of loan applications still on her desk. She felt cold, frozen in time.

"Hey! Isn't it your birthday today? Why are you at work? You should be out partying, celebrating." one of the secretaries she lunched with was passing her desk. "Tell them you have a headache! Go treat yourself! Don't waste a birthday at work!"

'She's right,' Moon thought, *'I shouldn't be here. I should be home, while I still have one.'* She shoved the letter into her purse after locking the rest of the paperwork in her desk. *'Tomorrow,'* she thought.

Moon left word with her boss's secretary that she wasn't feeling well and was going home, which was such a rarity for her that it was accepted without question. By the time she reached her apartment she really did have a headache. Moon greeted the cat who ignored her, took some aspirin, and cried until the sun went down. Her celebration supper was a hot dog, some baked beans followed by some aging chocolate ice cream from the freezer.

"Might as well use it up, less to move when we do go," she told the cat who didn't care.

She forced herself to wash a small load of laundry, took some more aspirin before drifting into an uneasy sleep.

The next morning was no different except that it was no longer Moon's birthday. The morning alarm changed nothing. Now, instead of thirty days to figure something out, she had twenty-nine.

"Something has to change." she told the cat as she dished up the food for the cat to ignore. "I can't find myself in the mirror, and pretty soon I won't have a mirror to not find myself in. Something has to change!" On a whim, she picked up the phone and called Sue, her pastor's wife, her best friend.

"I am in desperate need of a coffee date! Can you meet me for lunch at the usual place?"

All morning Moon fought to keep her mind on her work. Loans for homes, loans for college or trade school, loans for cars and RV's, loans to get out of debt, loans to help build credit: it made her head hurt again. Or maybe it was the effort it took not to break down in tears. She felt trapped in a time warp, five years gone, but once again she was being served divorce papers, and an eviction notice in one document. She remembered holding back the tears that day too, stumbling down the street until she found a newspaper with apartment listings.

Her 'new' apartment certainly hadn't been the nicest, but it was available. It was shabby, dark, old, but it was close to work and cheap. She had been too depressed to care about it more than that. She had a Chevy sedan that she rarely drove, not wanting to waste money on gas and having nowhere she really wanted to go. It usually sat in a secluded corner of the parking lot. Now the building would be sold. Would it be torn down or used for something else? Why couldn't she just stay where she was? And what about the cat??? So many questions with no obvious answers. She hoped desperately that Sue could help her navigate the mess she was in.

The Downtown Diner was a remnant from the 1950's, once a popular nightspot for cocktails as well as dinner entrees and business lunches. It was now a daytime eatery featuring traditional breakfasts and midday soup/ sandwich combinations. Years ago, it had been a favorite of the high school kids allowed off campus, famous for its burgers, shakes, and pies. It was still Moon's "go to" spot for comfort food and understanding waitresses—the perfect place for lunch. Two blocks from the bank, three from the church, tucked between a men's clothing shop and an antiques store, it was a cozy place of deep comfortable booths, bright al fresco tables with shaded seating on the back patio: a rendezvous spot where Sue and Moon chose a patio table to take advantage of the warm Spring weather.

"I have no idea where to turn or what to do—I feel like I've had a five-year hangover," Moon admitted over a rib-eye sandwich dipped in French onion soup. "It feels like I just woke up when I read the eviction letter. Even though I hate the place, it still feels like a betrayal! WHY is this happening to me?" Sue shuddered supportively, remembering the earlier crisis.

"Well, and what have you done with your life since then?" she asked, pushing her Caesar salad around her plate. "You've been in a holding pattern since Geordie moved on. Think, Moon. Maybe this is your clarion call to get on with it while you still can."

"And do what? Where? How? I now have less than thirty days to find somewhere to live or the cat and I will be sharing living space out of the trunk of my car!"

"Then that's the first thing you need to focus on," Sue mused. "You can't do anything else until you have someplace to live. What sort of place do you want?"

"What do you mean?" Moon stopped chewing and started to pay attention.

"Do you want another apartment, bigger, the same size, or maybe a flat, or a house? Do you want to stay here in town, move somewhere else, what? Define your goals, then we will figure out how to get there!" Sue was becoming animated, but she kept her voice low, private.

"I want a place to live, other than my car," sulked Moon. "I really don't want another apartment like I have," she mused. "Maybe a flat would be nice but—you know I am tired of being surrounded by neighbors on the other side of my walls who complain about every little thing I do or fight and scream at each other. I want some privacy. Truth? I miss my house. I miss my garden. I miss my kitchen and the sunlight on the sink when I washed the dishes. I miss hanging out my laundry. I miss my old life," Moon started to cry.

Sue ate in silence. She understood how badly Moon needed to work through this. A lot was still unprocessed from the divorce when Moon had buried herself in her job and tiny apartment rather than deal with her losses, always hoping that it was only a bad dream and that she would awaken back to her home and family. Her home was gone, her ex-husband had moved on, and her daughter hardly had time for her, so caught up was Joy in her own husband, career, and social life. Sue knew better than to offer any suggestions yet. Moon would figure it out on her own—she just needed an ear right now.

On her side of the table, Moon was in torment. "*What DO I want?*' she thought. '*What do I really want? I want to be happy again. What was I like when I was happy?*'

"Happy," she announced to Sue as she dried her tears on a napkin. "I want to be happy again. I want to look into a mirror that belongs to me in my own bathroom, and see ME, not some old lady that I don't recognize."

"Okay! That's a good beginning," Sue encouraged. "Now, how do you get there?"

"I don't know. First priority, I guess I need a place to live," announced Moon. "I don't want an apartment, I'm tired of feeling like I live in a rabbit warren. I want a house."

Sue decided to push a little. "Can you afford one? What price range? What amenities? How big? Where?" She stopped rearranging her salad and reached for Moon's hand across the table. "Allow me to be the Devil's Advocate."

"And you a preacher's wife," Moon laughed. "Ok. My credit is excellent, and I work at a bank, but I don't fancy a 30-year mortgage unless I have no other option. I want to stay here in Jefferson. I like this town; I like my job. I guess I could investigate foreclosures, rentals, or maybe rent-to-own. I could, should, call a realtor anyway to see what else is available. I have twenty-nine days to figure this out! I may have to settle for an apartment, but it will be better than---NO! I am tired of *'settling'*. It's all I have done for the last five years." Moon looked at Sue. "May I borrow your cell phone? I still don't own one," she admitted ruefully.

Sue considered for a moment, then shook her head. "I'm going to do you a favor...and say 'no' this time. I think it's about time you started taking more responsibility for yourself. Either call from work, wait until you get home, or go buy yourself a cell phone. They aren't expensive and you don't need to buy a contract, just pay as you use it. At least until you decide if you like having one. Try some new things out, Moon, be adventurous. Don't just wallow where you are, afraid to move forward. That's the only way you will find out what makes you happy now."

Moon looked sulky, then smiled. "You always give me good advice, shame on me for not taking it more often. But I don't want anyone at the bank up in my business so I will call from home for now. And lunch is on me." She grabbed both checks before Sue could move. "My birthday, my treat, my present to myself. Done."

Moon considered buying a cell phone as she walked back to the bank. It would be handy but also an added expense and Moon wanted to make certain she could afford a house if she could find one. In addition, she preferred her landline: what if she couldn't afford both? *'One step at a time,'* she thought. She needed to find a realtor as soon as possible.

Back at the bank Moon checked the break room for a discarded copy of the daily newspaper. She found one, tossed aside on a chair next to the vending machines. Moon folded it neatly, tucked it into her tote bag before returning to her desk. During quiet times, between clients, Moon jotted down phone numbers from the For Sale ads in the paper and from the phone directory she kept in her desk.

By 4 pm she had a list of 6 possibilities. No clients were waiting to see her, so she clocked out a little early. Back in her tiny apartment she ignored the cat who was ignoring her in return. She didn't bother to change out of her work pantsuit even though it was stained with spilled coffee. Instead, she plopped down in front of her phone and began calling the realty numbers on her list.

The first had no apartments or rentals of any sort, no rent-to-own, only upscale townhouses in a nearby development. Moon was familiar with the subdivision having dealt with mortgage loans for some of the properties. Unless a multi-millionaire suddenly proposed marriage and offered one as a wedding gift, Moon wouldn't be living there. One down. Moon took notes (just in case), put a check mark by the number, moved on to the next.

"Leave your number and a brief message, we will return your call at our earliest convenience." Moon regretted not buying a cell phone. Briefly. She didn't leave a message. No way to return her call when she was almost never home. The same was true for the next two. The fifth sold only commercial properties. The sixth realtor patched her through to one of their agents who was with a customer but promised to call back within the hour.

"That's the best I can do for right now," she assured the cat who was still ignoring her, undoubtedly plotting her demise immediately after dinner. "We will see what happens next."

Moon heaved herself out of her chair, collected oddments of clothes on her way to her tiny bedroom to be washed, hung up, put away---or thrown out in the case of an old shirt that the cat had vomited something up on. '*Yuck!*'

She veered off to the kitchen area to dispose of the shirt, shuddered at the state of counters.

The scene was...indescribable. There was food on the counter, dirty dishes, more dirty clothes, unidentified stuff in boxes. The garbage was overflowing. Never very fresh smelling, the kitchen area was worse than usual. Moon stopped, overwhelmed. She felt a powerful urge for a nap. She dropped the shirt in the garbage before going back to her chair.

"When I was a girl," she told the cat, who didn't care, "one of my favorite stories was about a group of monkeys who lived in a tree in the jungle. Every time it rained, the monkeys would huddle together, cold and wet, telling each other 'We cannot continue this way. Something must be done!' But when the rain stopped and the sun came out, the monkeys all went out to play, forgetting about how cold they had been. They played and played until night came and the rain began to fall. There they sat, shivering in the tree, muttering to themselves, 'We cannot continue this way. Something must be done!' The pattern repeats day after day and the monkeys never do fix the problem. I think I have become a monk..." the phone rang at the same time someone knocked on her door. '*And it pours,*' thought Moon.

She opened the door for her next-door neighbor before answering her phone.

"Tomorrow morning? O... kay. I work at the Tri-State until noon, would lunch maybe work for you?" Moon held up her hand to ask for quiet as her neighbor was chatting loudly with a purring cat. "At the diner? Perfect. Did they tell you what I am looking for? Great. I will meet you at noon. Thank you so much!"

"Yes? What's up, Sissie?" she asked as she flopped back into her chair. The chair creaked alarmingly; Moon ignored it.

"Did you get a letter too?" Sissie asked the cat. "What <u>will</u> we do? Do you have someplace to go?" The cat continued to purr, rolling over to expose its belly for a scratch. Sissie obliged, much to the cat's delight.

"What are <u>you</u> going to do? Do *you* have somewhere to go?" Moon asked. "I'm still a bit in shock."

"Why would you be?" Sissie was surprised. "Most of us have known about this for months. That's why they stopped fixing things. Haven't you noticed that Maintenance doesn't answer the phone anymore?"

"To tell you the truth, no, I don't even call them about stuff. I haven't bothered for a long time," Moon shook her head. "It makes sense, though. Why bother if you are only going to lose the building. So, where will you go?"

"To my daughter. I don't want to but I guess I can stand it at least for a while. I'm getting too old to live alone, seventy next month. It's high time. She lives out in the country. I can have my cat."

"You want to take that one too? I don't know where I will end up and it would be easier knowing it has a home." The cat purred ecstatically.

Sissie scooped up the cat and cuddled it. "A going-away gift? Oh, yes! That way I will always remember you. And they get along so well together, the cats do. She comes over often after you go to work—gets out through the broken window in your bedroom."

'A going-away gift to remember someone you don't really know?' Moon thought. *'You just want the cat. Why didn't you say so? I would have given her to you long ago.'*

But would she have? Possibly. Possibly not. The cat, however much it despised Moon, was at least a live roommate.

Sissie stayed for a while longer, hinting at snacks, before leaving with the happy cat. Moon continued to occupy her chair, thinking and remembering, until she fell asleep, dreaming of her former home.

The cat speaks: "I was only a few weeks old when I was scooped up out of a box left on a street corner, so I barely remember anything before I lived here. It's not a bad place to live, I guess, as places go. I'm just not happy here. The person who lives here doesn't like me much. I mean she feeds me but only if I nag about it. It's not like it's great tasting food, I get much better next door, but it's okay.

Nobody really talks to me here—they talk to themselves mostly. I try to get attention by getting right in front of them, but it doesn't matter. I'm no more valued than the old chair in the big room, or the unmade bed in the little room in the back.

And it smells bad here. Sometimes it smells so bad I can't keep my food down. Then it smells even worse.

There is a hole in the window above the bed. There is stuff in the hole to keep out the drafts, but it won't keep me in! As soon as I am alone each day, I squeeze out the hole, walk along the ledge to the next window which is always open and there I am welcomed. There is another cat living there, they have really good food and treats, they like having me around. They play games with me, nap with me, I often wished I didn't have to go back to the other place.

Still, I go back each day, eat the food put out for me, try to connect somehow with the person living there. What's the use? They obviously don't want me, I would be better off somewhere else, somewhere I am needed and valued.

I am done, finished with this place. I am no longer going back to those stinky rooms and that crazy person. They can talk to themselves for the rest of their life for all I care. I am free! Some deal was done and now I belong with the cat next door, and I am never going back! I am free!"

Moon woke to the phone ringing sometime after eight the following morning (wrong number) just in time to grab a quick shower, dig out a clean pantsuit (cream colored with tiny brown embroidered flowers on each collar), and order a latte and donut on her way to work. She plopped into her chair exactly at 9:30, feeling better than she hadm for quite a while. Maybe it was the leftover glow of the dream, maybe it was the feeling that things were changing. It seemed that more than a page of the calendar had changed. Something different was in the air, something fresh and promising. The good mood stayed with her all morning, overflowing through her client meetings into lunch. The real estate agent understood exactly what Moon was going through. She was already meeting with several of the apartment's residents, most of whom merely wanted another cheap place to live. Apartments, especially inexpensive or rent controlled were nearly impossible to find in Jefferson. Moon was presenting her with a quite different challenge, which made her more than eager to help.

"We have a few smaller homes for sale that *might* be in your price range but rent-to-own is also rare. Could you put any money down? Is your credit good? Do you own other assets?" The list went on, Moon forced herself to pay attention, but it was becoming extremely difficult. She felt her good mood starting to slip away from hope to despair, as she listened to the realtor's discouraging news. She was almost ready to consider settling for another cheap apartment, when she heard the agent say, "I will print off a group of possibles, I can drop them off at the bank or would you like to stop by for them in an hour or so?"

"I will stop by." Moon perked up a bit. "I have some other errands and I'm not due back to work anymore today."

"Excellent. We will see you in an hour or so." The agent gathered her papers, took one last long gulp of her coffee before leaving, presumably for another appointment. Moon sat staring off into space for a while before finishing her own coffee.

'How do I go about getting a house of my own,' she mused. *'I don't have anything to offer for a down payment. No collateral except my car. MY CAR!!'*

Moon collected her bag, left money for her lunch and hurried back to the bank. She needed to see one someone about her car, the car she really didn't need and never drove. *'Why didn't I think of this before?'*

Back at the bank she cornered Lacey Burnham, who also worked as a loan officer. "Is your son still looking for a car? Would he be interested in buying mine? It's nothing special, just a late model Chevy, but the maintenance is up to date, and it runs well. I don't drive it much at all—and I could use the money," Moon whispered the last part.

Lacey considered. "I think he bought one, something sporty, you know men, but his girlfriend is also looking for a car, something more sensible. What would you want for it?"

"Three thousand," said Moon firmly thinking *'but that's negotiable.'*

"I will talk to her. May I send her over this weekend if she is inter-ested?" Lacey nibbled her pen thoughtfully.

"I will be at my apartment all day Sunday and my car is parked out back," Moon didn't allow second thoughts to deter her. "I have a file *'somewhere'* with the maintenance records. I will dig it out."

"No need," Lacey replied airily. "If you take it to Crosstown Motors for servicing, and I know you do, they will have all the records."

'Everybody in this town knows everybody else's business,' thought Moon sourly, but she smiled brightly and determined not to let anyone at the bank know what she was up to.

"Why do you want to sell it," asked Lacey, curiously. "I hardly ever see you drive it."

"That's pretty much it," Moon admitted. "I don't really need it any-more."

"Why? Did you lose your license?" Lacey eyed her speculatively.

"No, I didn't lose my license." Moon tried to keep her temper under control. "I just don't need the car, or the expense. Everything is in walking distance in this town."

"Yes, well you could do with more walking," Lacey commented, turning back to her work. "I'll have Sherle come by tomorrow to look at it."

Moon gathered her things and went home, stopping by the realty before the grocery store on the way. She bought a microwave dinner, a slice of pie for dessert and a small packet of flavored coffee. That evening, over dinner, she looked through the papers the realtor had left for her.

Tiny, two-bedroom houses were priced in the hundred-thousand-dollar range. Moon wasn't upset about the size, but the cost was out of reach. Moon went over them several times, but nothing seemed to be what she wanted. Carefully she put the pages in her phonebook, tucked in a drawer by the kitchen phone. Maybe things would look better tomorrow. Moon stripped the sheets off her bed, made it with clean ones, showered, and opened a package with new pajamas her daughter had bought her for Christmas a year ago. Moon had never taken the effort to open them: her old ones were good enough. Now the old gown was in the garbage and Moon felt…fresh.

2

The Countdown

Moon overslept her alarm the next morning, waking up feeling better than she had in a while. The bedside clock said 9 o'clock; Moon remembered that someone might be coming to see the car later this morning. She limped to the bathroom, avoided the mirror, didn't miss the cat at all, threw on a muumuu while anticipating coffee. She was in the middle of brewing a pot when someone knocked on the door.

"I'm Sherle," the intense young blonde at the door in rock concert tee shirt, blue jeans and sandals introduced herself. "We were just out back looking at the car—could I test drive it?"

"Sure." Moon went to fetch the keys from her bag by the recliner. "Park it in the same space when you are done," she asked. "Bring me back the keys. We'll talk then." Sherle took the keys without a word. Moon crossed her fingers.

Back at her cluttered, dirty kitchen table Moon poured herself a cup of coffee and set the realtor's folder in front of her. One by one she went through the offerings again, though nothing had changed. The cheapest of homes were still too expensive. She put the papers away and thoughtfully sipped her coffee. *'Patience,'* she told herself. *'It doesn't all have to be settled today. But it would be nice... While I wait, I can do some cleaning and packing.'*

She tied the old garbage bag shut, tossed it in a corner of the kitchen to be taken out later, and began filling a fresh one. For the next hour she bagged trash, washed dishes, filled boxes with unwanted items to go to Salvation Army resale or the church jumble fund raiser. *I'm not moving things I don't want anymore!' she thought.* By the time Sherle brought the keys back the kitchen was cleaner, barer, but not much improved. *'I won't miss this place'.*

"Three thousand? Seems a little steep, but I like the car, and it runs okay. Is a cashier's check, ok? I can drop it off later." Sherle was as business-like as Lacey. *'No wonder they get along so well,' Moon mused.*

Moon went back to cleaning and sorting. She toted bags of garbage out to the dumpster behind the apartment, stopping with an empty bag to clean out her car. A remnant of her divorce, formerly Geordie's 'winter beater' because he wouldn't ruin his beloved second-hand BMW in the sludge and road salt, it had never truly felt like "hers"—merely what Geordie thought she should be driving, especially since she had been entitled to one of the cars in the settlement. It was good enough, but not *too* good. Someone else's opinion controlling her life for the past five years. The choice to sell it was hers alone, it buoyed her self-esteem immensely.

Back in the still-tiny but cleaner kitchen of her apartment, Moon sat down at the old Formica-top table with a piece of paper and the stub of a pencil fished out of the 'junk' drawer and began figuring. She listed her checking, savings, CDs. pension fund, insurance value and lightly penciled in the three thousand from the sale of her car, not counting on it until she cashed the check. Even if she liquidated everything, there wasn't enough for a down payment on one of the houses in the sheaf the realtor had sent her. Could she pick up a foreclosure through the bank? Assume the remains of a mortgage? Would it be ethical, or would it be like insider trading? Could she talk to her boss about it, or would it be all over the bank's gossip in a matter of hours? Should she go to another bank, or would that make it worse? Moon's head began to ache again. She checked her medicine cabinet, found the last of her aspirin, and tossed the empty bottle in the recyclable bin, washing down the pills with the dregs of her coffee.

Nearly a week gone and what did she have to show for it? A clean kitchen, the potential sale of her car, a new home for her cat, but still no place for Moon to go. She sat down in her chair in the living room, surrounded by more debris and clutter. Feeling overwhelmed she closed her eyes and drifted off.

The apartment was dark and cold when she woke, disoriented, hungry, confused. No cat to pester her, she almost missed it. Almost. Painfully she pushed herself out of the chair, thinking about lunch. Or supper. Either would do. There had to be something that hadn't gone bad left in the kitchen. Somewhere in the back of her mind she remembered that it was Sunday. Sue would be calling tomorrow to find out how Moon was, how much progress she had made, why she hadn't come to church even though Moon seldom attended services outside of Easter. She found the kitchen light switch before she could trip over the cat that wasn't there and stopped, surprised again at the cleaner kitchen. *'My other kitchen always used to shine,'* she thought, *'it used to be a place of welcome. I remember Sunday dinners for Geordie and Joy, how much fun they were to put together. I remember Grandma's Sunday dinners! I'm... too tired to cook now.'* The old wall clock that had been her mother's kitchen clock, one of the few things she had been allowed to keep from the divorce because Geordie hated anything that had belonged to her parents, informed her it was past eight p.m. Time enough to throw a load of laundry in so she would have clean clothes for tomorrow. Moon loaded up her pantsuits from the bedroom, fixed herself a sandwich and baggie of chips, (she could buy a soda from the machine in the basement) and trekked down the back stairs to the musty laundry room with its coin washers and dryers. Moon picked up a newspaper left on the table to read while her laundry washed and dried. It didn't pay to leave clothes unattended. They disappeared. Moon had lost all her nice sheets several years ago thus learning her lesson.

'I miss my own washer and dryer,' thought Moon as she glumly chewed her sandwich. Slowly her needs were beginning to take form

in the back of her mind. *'If I had my own home again, I could have a washer and dryer maybe. I could do wash without having to worry about having the right change or coming back to find it gone. I still wonder who took my sheets...'*

Back in the cramped, cluttered bedroom Moon took the time to hang up her pantsuits instead of dropping them in a heap on the chair. She set one, a dark rose with white eyelet trim, hanging on the door and chose shoes and undergarments to go with it. Several pairs of panties were tossed into the trash—mostly holes and tatters. Just before falling asleep, Moon felt like she was finally waking up.

Monday morning. Moon loved Mondays. She loved the promise of a fresh week. She ordered a black coffee instead of a latte on the way to work and bought a banana from the fruit vendor.

At the bank, she stopped at Lacey's desk with the car keys.

"Did Sherle talk to you about the car? Does she still want it?"

Lacey was on the phone, so she held up one finger to stall Moon until she finished, as she reached into her desk drawer. "I had them cut the check first thing this morning. You'll need to clean your things out of the car and give me the keys when you are—oh!"

"I cleared my stuff out already." Moon handed Lacey the keys and title. "I will call Crosstown Motors now and tell them to release all of the maintenance records to you or Sherle. There won't be a problem. Sherle can pick up the car anytime she likes. I appreciate this, Lacey.

"Not a problem. It seems to be a win-win..." Lacey's phone rang, and the workday began. Moon tried to decide if she felt sad about selling her car as she began advising her own clients. She immediately realized that she didn't, that she felt freer, less burdened. During her break, she deposited the check before she could misplace it. She called Crosstown, arranged for the transfer of records, fended off a salesman trying to sell her a new (expensive!) version of her old car, before joining the ladies of the secretarial staff in the break room.

The most interesting gossip still centered on the default and sale of Moon's apartment. One of the secretaries belatedly realized that

Moon lived in those apartments and Moon's hopes for privacy were dashed.

"This is terrible for you!" "Where will you go?" "Do you have something in mind?" "Is there anything we can do to help?'

"It's okay. It's been a long time coming. I mean, the place is a dump." Saying it out loud resonated something within Moon. It *was* a dump, and it *was* a good thing that she was moving on!

"I haven't finalized any plans yet," Moon admitted cautiously. "I'm looking at a lot of options right now."

"You're running out of time," Lacey remarked from the doorway. "THAT'S why you wanted to sell your car!"

"Oh, Moon, what will you do without your car? How will you get around town, get to work?" the secretaries were all avidly concerned.

"The same way I have been all this time: walk! I hardly ever use the car, it just sits. I could use the money, someone else could use the car," Moon said shortly, seething at Lacey's comments.

"Is it still for sale?" one of the secretaries inquired. "I could put out the word for you."

"Thank you, honey," Moon smiled gratefully, "but I already sold it. Now I just have to decide where and when to move."

"Better get shakin'," Lacey shook her finger playfully at Moon. "Available apartments are going fast because of the default. Word is they are tearing the old complex down and building new housing for seniors. You might qualify but I doubt you'll be able to afford it; you won't get the subsidy because you're still working." Lacey breezed off down the hall leaving Moon sitting in stunned silence, feeling like she had just been slapped. Her face glowed as dark as her pantsuit and her thoughts frozen. '*Bitch.*'

Embarrassed and as shocked as Moon, neither of the secretaries could find their voice, neither said a word when Moon pushed herself up from the table and stalked back to her desk. Fortunately, there was a client waiting for her. Moon assumed a bright smile and greeted him warmly. She could focus on work and worry about her living situation later.

Moon didn't have much appetite for lunch for a change, but she needed to get out of the bank and away from prying eyes. Out of habit she walked the two blocks to the diner, tucked herself into a booth toward the back and ordered a BLT and a diet Coke. Glumly she chewed the sandwich and considered her options. It looked like a home of her own was probably out of reach, so she really should start looking at flats and apartments before it was too late. Moon mentally kicked herself for not paying attention sooner. Even Sissie, who wasn't on the short list for Nobel Prize winners had seen the future of the building early enough to form an exit strategy. '*Where was I all this time?*' Moon was again leaving things until the last minute, to her chagrin. She paid her bill, left early, and stopped in at the realtors on her way back to work.

"Nothing really fits—out of my price range mostly," she told the agent. "Anything cheaper? Anything at all?'

"I will see what I can find. Stop by later on your way home after work; I will try to have something for you. Don't worry. We'll keep looking."

"Thanks. I am running out of time," Moon smiled ruefully. "I'll see you after four."

No one said anything to Moon about her living situation. Only her clients spoke to her at all. After work, she collected another sheaf of papers from the realtor, fixed herself a t.v. dinner pried out of the back of the freezer, and began looking through the offerings. Most of them were once again too expensive for her. There were a couple of duplexes listed for rent, that she set aside to review again later although it really wasn't what she wanted. The very last sheet made her stop and stare. It was a single-family home, a tiny bungalow several blocks away, close to the edge of town. It was old, almost a hundred years old and sadly in need of repair. Two tiny bedrooms, kitchen, living room, dining room, one large bathroom and a bedroom/pantry off the kitchen. No second floor, just an attic, but it had a full basement and a bit of yard front and East side of the house. There was no price listed, just the words CALL ME below the specs. Moon made a mental note to do just that the first thing in the morning as she washed the few dishes she had used. Before going to bed, Moon cleaned and straightened the living room. Two rooms done, the apartment was beginning to look more like living space and less like a flophouse. She set three bags of garbage aside to be taken out in the morning when she left for work and crawled, showered and exhausted, into bed.

"This one interests me, but there is no price, and the others are still just out of reach for me," Moon pointed to a photo of the little bungalow as she sat across the desk of the agent instead of spending her lunch hour at the restaurant. "How much are they asking for it, and could I see it if it is in my price range?"

"Strictly speaking, it isn't for sale," the agent shuffled her papers until she found the one that she was looking for. "Here... It is part of an estate and can't go on the market yet, not until more of the probate is settled. But it can be rented out: we may be able to set up a contract that applies the rent to the purchase price when the legal stuff is all settled. It is likely to take at least a year, maybe longer, before all is done, but all parties have agreed to honor the contract if the house doesn't stand empty. They are asking $700 a month rent and a purchase price to be set later but it probably won't be above $50,000 because of the shape it's in and the size."

"The rent is acceptable, it's only a couple hundred more that I am paying for the dump they are selling out from under me, but I would want the purchase price set before I sign the contract in the event that they decide to jack the price up later. And I want to see it first before I make any kind of decision. Has there been any other interest in it?"

"Not really. I only heard about it last week and I haven't shown it to anyone. It hasn't met anyone else's needs. Bigger, newer homes or apartments have been the best sellers for the past year. When would you like to see it?"

"Are you available later today? I will be done by four or four thirty at the latest."

"I can do that," the agent replied. Stop by and we can ride over together."

Moon drummed her fingers on the desk. "Yes, that will work. I don't have a car so that will work out nicely." Sherle had been by some time the day before: the parking spot was empty. Moon was already wondering how she was going to get around if the house worked out. It was several blocks farther to work, laundromat, grocery, other places so close to her current apartment that she took them for granted. Had she been too hasty in selling the car?

"Excellent! Then when you are done, I'll give you a ride home." They shook hands and Moon went back to work, stopping only at the taco stand to order one supreme taco and a diet soda to eat at her desk while she did some calculating. She was careful to tuck a napkin into her collar to protect today's pantsuit choice: a black and grey linen with silver accents, another Christmas gift from Joy that Moon hadn't yet worn. It made her feel...jazzy.

3

Progress is Made

Moon tried to keep her excitement under control over the next week. The little bungalow was exactly what she hoped it would be: spacious compared to her apartment but small enough that she wouldn't be overtaxed keeping it clean (she hoped). She had rather gotten out of the habit of being what her mother had called "house proud". *How could anyone be "house proud" about the tiny dump she lived in?'* she thought. But she knew there was more to it than that. It was time to end the mourning period of her marriage. Nothing was ever going to bring Geordie or her old life back. Joy had even let it slip a year or so ago that Geordie was engaged to be married to the woman he had been seeing.

No, she was delighted with the house and had told the realtor that she would sign the papers as soon as they settled on a final purchase price. She didn't want to run the risk that she would commit to the purchase at one price, do the repairs and updates that she wanted only to have the final price 'renegotiated' beyond her means and she would be forced out.

That seemed to be the sticking point. The children and grand-children of the previous owner couldn't seem to agree on a locked-in price and wanted to leave it open-ended until the rental period was over. All repairs would be Moon's responsibility but would be considered as improvements to be tacked on to the final cost. Moon wasn't having any of that, and time was slipping away. She now had little more than two weeks to finalize her plans. Many of the other residents including Sissie and the hostile cat had already moved out. The building felt emptier, more abandoned every day. If something wasn't settled soon, she would be reduced to accepting any dumpy apartment that was available.

Finally, the lawyers and the real estate agent had enough of the bickering, no one else was showing any interest in the bungalow, and there were bigger estate questions to settle so the price was fixed at $55,000 with monthly rent of $700. Repair costs would be split between Moon and the estate, any upgrades were to be paid for by Moon alone (she suspected that any "repairs" would quickly be considered "upgrades", and thus become her expense). The rental term was set for five years from the first of the month, after which time a balloon payment of the rest of the purchase price would be due. Moon signed the papers, handed over $700 to cover the first month's rent. Back in "the dump" as Moon now thought of her apartment, she took a deep breath and called her daughter to see if she could help with the move. That proved to be a big mistake.

"What do you mean you are moving?" Joy demanded. "You've had that apartment for years. Why give it up now?"

"Because the building has been sold, we've all been evicted. I hear they might tear it down. The point is I am moving; can you help?"

"Where are you going? You can't come here, there's no room and, well, things aren't going that smoothly for me. The truth is I may be getting a divorce as well…" Joy launched into her own tale of woes and Moon tuned her out, made encouraging noises now and then while jotting down names of people she knew from work or church who might be able to help.

"…so, you see you really can't come here, I'm sorry, but there it is," Joy finished.

"No, I understand completely, don't worry about it," Moon soothed. "I'll handle it. It will be fine. I have a place to go, I just need a little help getting my stuff there. That's all."

"You HAVE a place already? Why didn't you say so? Where are you going? That new apartment building on 6th? You can't afford that, it's hideously expensive and the units are tinier than yours!"

"No, no more apartments, I rented a little house over on Oak St. I just need to decide what to take and how to move it."

Joy's silence alarmed Moon because it always preceded an outburst of fear and anger. Her tirades were legendary: they often left Moon with headaches for days.

"You. Did. WHAT? Did you sign anything, can you legally get out of it? What were you thinking? Why didn't you call me? My God, Mom, what have you done?" Joy paused for breath and Moon stepped it rapidly.

"I found a place, I'm happy with it. I need to move. Phone number will be the same, address is 160 Oak St. Don't worry about me, I'll be fine." Moon hung up and went in search of aspirin to ward off the headache. The phone rang persistently, but she chose not to answer it.

Saturday afternoon Moon was dressed in comfortable jeans and tee shirt, drinking a diet coke and having a lovely old sorting fest when she was disturbed by someone knocking on her apartment door.

'Oh, leave me alone! I'll be out of here soon enough,' Moon thought. She shoved the cartons of things to be donated aside to make a path to the door, yanked it open to find Sue in the doorway.

"Why don't you answer your phone? I've been trying to reach you for days! I didn't want to bother you at work but that would have been the next step!" She pushed past Moon to get a better look at the progress.

"When were you going to tell me that you found a new place?" she demanded cheerfully. I happen to know one of the realtors and she mentioned it at Bible Study last week during coffee time. We are all thrilled for you, you should join us sometime. Is there coffee on, or should I make some?

"Bible Study is on Wednesday afternoon, and I didn't sign the papers until Thursday. I work weekday afternoons, as you well know, so don't give me any grief for not playing hooky from my job. And you will have to do without coffee, the pot is packed. One of the few kitchen things I'm not throwing out. It seems like everything in this apartment is past its shelf life, including me," she said sadly sinking into her chair. "I don't think I tossed the tea kettle and there might be some packets of English Breakfast in the cupboard. Will that do? There are mugs in a box on the table."

"Perfect," Sue said cheerily. "Milk or lemon?"

"Lemon in the fridge for me. If you want milk, I don't think it's gone off yet, it hadn't earlier when I had a bowl of cereal to use up the last of the corn flakes. I am trying to use up as much as I can, so I have less to move next week."

"Yes, I meant to ask about that," Sue's muffled voice came from the kitchen amid the sounds of sink and cupboard. "Do the stove and refrigerator go with you?"

"No, they came with the apartment, and I don't want them anyway. Older than I am and that's saying something. There is an old set also at the new place so I will be ok for the time being, until I can find something better. The big problem right now, now that I have somewhere to go, is getting there before they shove me out and change the locks!"

"And I believe I can help with that, but not until you bring me up to date on your new place, how you found it, and why you didn't pick up your phone. You need caller I.D, girl!"

"No, I, well maybe," Moon thought of Joy's calls, her unhappy rants. She joined Sue in the kitchen at the table. "We'll see when I get settled in. Which won't happen until I move! I found the place by calling a realtor the day after my birthday. You gave me the idea when we brainstormed over lunch. It was really the only offer I could afford. I don't want to live in an apartment anymore: I was happiest when I had my own house. I want to feel that way again, Sue. I look in the mirror and I don't see 'me' anymore. I lost more than just a husband

and home when Geordie divorced me. I lost me too. Or maybe I lost that during the marriage, I don't know. I do know I need to find that again. This is a start, but of course Joy doesn't think much of it—she already told me how foolish I'm being."

"Joy will someday learn that minding one's own business is a full-time job!" Sue declared. "She cares but she doesn't know how to show it, so she blusters and rants, and holds people at arm's length in the process. Give her time, she'll cool down. Now, on to the problem at hand: getting you moved. You are moving when, next Friday?" Moon nodded.

"Well, with the kids out of school we have been looking for a project for the youth group—something like "Help your neighbor." Willy Snow's dad has a pick-up truck that he is willing to loan us and will drive. We can take a few small things in your car. The kids can load and unload the truck, we should be able to do it in two or three trips."

Moon was stunned. "What do they get out of this?" she asked.

"The good feeling that they are helping someone in the community, in the church, who is truly in need, not to mention a break from the video games; and pizza or ice cream when we are all done! Do you accept the offer? Or do I have to go out and find some other needy old lady for them to help?

"Yes," gasped Moon. "I...yes! Except I don't have the car anymore. I sold it, to make sure I had enough cash to afford a house if I found the right one. I hated that car, anyway. Geordie bought it shortly after he bought his "dream car', as a winter beater and with the idea that when he left, he could pawn that one off on me and leave his precious BMW free and clear. I always suspected he had this all planned out!" Moon stopped for breath. "Rant over. Anyway, the car is gone. That's why I'm in such a flux about moving this stuff. I'll figure out how to get around later."

"Easy," answered Sue. "Bicycle."

"Oh, no. I refuse to be some fat woman pedaling her bicycle all over town!"

"You start riding a bicycle around town and you won't be fat for very long!" Sue peered at Moon over her mug and wiggled her eyebrows at her. Moon laughed.

"Okay. We'll see. First let's get me packed up and moved."

"More important, is the house ready to be moved into?" Sue inquired? "Do you need help cleaning? Can you get into the house before Friday?"

"I hadn't thought about it," Moon admitted. "I guess I planned to clean as I went along."

"Hmmm." Sue mused. "Much easier to clean first and plan where everything is to go. Could we go over Thursday after you are done with work?"

"I don't see why not. I will talk to the agent Monday and see if she can give me the keys. It will be fun to show you around." Moon grew pensive. "I love empty houses. I always have. So many *possibilities,* so many options. So many things it *could* become. I love the echoes of the floors without carpets and furniture, the windows without curtains. I like to listen for the stories the old houses always have, so many stories about people who lived there before: the families, the love, the fights. People live in happiness and sadness. It seeps into the walls and floors, permeates the whole house. I love to listen to an empty house before I start adding to it..." Moon drifted off into silence.

Sue stared at her. "I never knew that about you, and I have known you for forty years! Now I can't wait to see the house with you before your stuff comes over." She was silent for a while, looking around the boxed-up apartment. "Are you taking everything?"

"No," Moon replied. "I've already ditched a lot of stuff--threw it in the dumpster, gave it away. Some stuff I will just leave here, I guess, and replace later. Like that chair in the living room. I don't want it, I can't give it away, it's in too bad shape, and I can't lift it into the dumpster out back. I'll leave it here and if someone wants it, they can have it. The same with the mattress and box springs. I think after all this time I deserve a new set, don't you?"

"And new sheets to go with them!" agreed Sue.

"Let's not get carried away," laughed Moon. "The old ones are okay…"

"For rags!" cried Sue. "Moon, enough! This is your chance for a fresh start, and I am so glad you are taking it! But don't sabotage yourself, please. Where are you getting the mattress and box springs?"

"They have a sale at the furniture store always the first week in September—back to school and all. I was going to wait until then and try to get a bargain."

"No," decided Sue. "Even on sale you will pay several hundred dollars for a set. And they tack on a delivery charge, unless you want to bring them home on a bicycle you don't have yet. Let me check something." Sue took out her phone, opened the screen and clicked on an app. "What size?"

"I'm keeping my bed, so twin size. Firm."

"Pillow top?"

"Possibly. Not necessary."

Sue clicked on a few items and showed Moon the screen: a ten-inch-thick firm mattress for $179 and a steel foundation frame for $94. "Can you afford that? Shipping is free, straight to your address."

Moon gasped. "Yes! How did you do that?"

"Amazon. I'm a Prime member. I can purchase it. You reimburse me. And I can show you how to sign up to do this yourself."

"That would be very helpful." Moon admitted. "Show me now and I can order it. Do they have sheets too?"

Sue laughed. "Yes, Moon, they have sheets too. And mattress protectors. And pillows. Let's go."

Moon pulled her chair around next to Sue so they could both see her phone screen and Sue guided her through account set up and purchase of the things for her bed at the new house. They would all be delivered Saturday, the day after Moon moved in. The cost, excluding a year of membership, was less than what Moon would have spent on the mattress alone at the furniture store. She was flabbergasted.

"You can leave the old mattress and box spring here. They will dispose of it along with the other furniture you don't want. Just shove what you are leaving in the bedroom and close the door. The kids will take what is out in plain sight."

"Progress!" Moon cheered. "I feel like I am finally making progress! Finish your tea, grab a garbage bag and let's pitch some junk!"

"Deal," agreed Sue, "and I will load up anything you want to donate and drop it off for you!"

Getting back into the house proved to be no problem. The agent had the keys and was happy to give them to Moon a day early, along with copies of all the paperwork. Moon was free to go into the house any time she wanted. She was looking forward to seeing it again with Sue. She rescued an old folder from the recycle bin at work, relabeled it for the house's paperwork.

Joy had been trying repeatedly to contact her mother, but Moon managed to avoid the phone calls and dodge the visits to the bank and to her home. She was grateful that she didn't own an answering machine: Joy's opinion was obvious to everyone. The secretaries at the bank did everything they could to run interference for her and Lacey became so annoyed that she finally asked Joy to leave the property after Joy accused her of 'stealing an old woman's only means of transportation'. When Joy demanded the return of the car, Lacey called security to escort the girl out. Moon was cautiously thrilled.

"My goodness, has she always been that demanding? I always thought she was such a sweet girl," Lacey remarked over coffee in the break room.

"She was," Moon remarked sadly. "The end of my marriage was particularly hard on her. Geordie was so sick with cancer, then remission so he wasn't, then he left, and it all seemed to be my fault. When he got sick again, when the cancer returned and his girlfriend stepped in, well, the walls went up with me on the wrong side. Now Joy's married too, it isn't going as smoothly as she would like, I guess she feels adrift, so she reacts by pushing people around, pushing people away.

She doesn't understand what's going on with me—doesn't have time for me in her life and feels guilty about it. When the dust settles after Friday, she will be fine. Or, I hope, at least better."

"Well, I hope so. Heavens, what a scene! Have you spoken to her? Put her mind at rest about what you are doing, so she doesn't worry so much?"

"Ah, yes, that's the problem," Moon finished her coffee, looked longingly at the plate of peanut butter bars someone had brought to the breakroom for treats but that she hadn't sampled, once again decided not to, and pushed herself away from the table. Her pantsuit, her favorite one with the embroidered leaves on the cuffs and sleeves, wasn't fitting as well as it used to these days. Somehow the washer had ruined the waistband which was much looser around Moon's middle. "Joy isn't interested in listening right now, only in adding to the drama. It takes her mind off the things that are wrong. I understand it, even though my coping system is different. I am *great* at ignoring things. World Class!" she laughed. "If she comes back, show her out. Don't let her get into her spiel or she'll never let up! Now I need to think about buying a tape measure." Moon hurried back to her desk, counting the minutes until she and Sue could take a good hard look at the house.

Thursday after work, armed with new tape measure from the hardware store as well as notebook and pencil, the two women drove up to 160 Oak St. in Sue's station wagon, ready to begin turning the house into a home.

At first Moon wouldn't leave the front porch. She stomped on the boards, examined the color of the floor paint, measured the width and length, checked the sturdiness of the railings, and examined the ceiling. She noticed two eye hooks that she hadn't seen before and pointed them out to Sue.

"Porch swing, you think?"

"Oh, definitely," Sue agreed. "Just in time for a long summer of lemonade and people watching!"

"My thoughts exactly. Hydrangeas in front of the railing?"

"Absolutely! And you might think about a light of some sort for safety. That one by the door looks…inadequate."

"That's because it's nothing more than a bare bulb with a cap. I will want a bit more in the way of light out here. Maybe a motion sensor."

With that they opened the front door, noting that it opened silently on well-oiled hinges. The door itself was heavy, solid oak, with a frosted oval window in the center that let the afternoon sun into the hallway but kept outsiders from seeing into the room. The door fit snugly into its frame: Moon doubted that she would have much of a draft problem that winter.

The hallway was short but wide and opened into a spacious dining room with a large bay window that looked out onto a small yard bounded by a neat alleyway that ran along the north side of the house. Moon immediately measured the opening and jotted the numbers in her notebook along with some ideas for colors and styles. After all, dreaming was cheap. Moon didn't expect that the house would snap into perfect form immediately, but it would help to have a direction and some goals in mind. She didn't own a dining room table and chairs, but the *possibility* was enticing. As was the idea of indoor plants: geraniums, African violets, spider plants, and ferns. Impossible with the cat who would have dug up the flowers out of sheer spite, but certainly possible now.

Meanwhile Sue was admiring the built-in hutch with its glass doors that took up the south wall of the room. The glass was dusty and smudged, the shelves grimy with neglect and the woodwork needed polishing but, in its heyday, it had been splendid and would be again. Moon sketched the hutch in her notebook and took some measurements, before moving to the living room that faced Oak Street.

At least as large as the dining room, it was separated from that room by an archway and two polished columns that were attached to the walls by counter-like shelves. It was obvious that something like statuary or decorative vases had once sat there, now the space was empty and watermarked. Moon ran her hand over the surfaces, measured, and mentally planned a restoration project. She measured the double windows that overlooked the porch and the street, measured the hardwood floor thinking of an area rug (braided? oriental? A matching one in the dining room.)

"What are you going to do with the walls?" asked Sue. "The wallpaper looks awfully tired, not to mention outdated."

"I like the idea of wallpaper, but I think for the near future I'm going to steam it off and go with a neutral paint. Something creamy that will go with anything."

"I like that. It will open the rooms up to the light and bring out this glorious woodwork. We can rent a steamer from the hardware store and have this old paper out of here in no time. Once we see what we are dealing with we can prep the walls and go from there. Keep the measurements of the walls so we know how much paint to buy."

"I'm 'way ahead of you!" Moon was scribbling in her notebook. "I don't have much in the way of furniture anymore, not that I'm keeping anyway, just the bedframe, kitchen table and chairs and the glass front bookcases, and I think I want the painting done before I buy any more. Let's check out the bedrooms."

The smaller bedroom was just off the living room with two windows, one that looked out onto the porch and one that faced south to an old grape arbor. Moon measured, made notes and moved next to the larger of the bedrooms.

It was directly east of the first bedroom, connected to the dining room by a short hallway that also led up a flight of stairs to the attic. Like all the other rooms it had a nine-foot ceiling, unlike the others it featured a ceiling fan and light. Moon tried the wall switch with no results.

"Call the electric company first thing in the morning to get the power turned on," called Sue from the next room, a full bath that linked the bedroom and the kitchen.

"Already done, account switches into my name as of tomorrow morning. Phone too. There should already be power, could be a breaker or the unit isn't working. Try the lights in the bath!"

"Yes, we have power! You are probably right, breaker or bad unit. Maybe the wiring is disconnected somehow." Sue stuck her head in from the bathroom. "I'm going to get this room scrubbed while you make your notes. Meet you in the kitchen.

Moon finished her notes before grabbing a can of wood polish and an old rag that she recognized as being from the tattered night gown she had thrown away some weeks earlier. She barely remembered cutting it up for cleaning rags but was glad now that she had. By the time Sue was done in the bathroom, Moon had the main rooms swept, dusted, and the woodwork polished. There were scars and marks that would have to be taken care of later, but things looked one hundred per cent better. Sue was resting on the plinth between the dining and living rooms.

"That bathroom was ugh!" she declared. "I've never seen a divided bath like that before with a separate room for the toilet."

"Maybe it was added on when the privy moved indoors," Moon laughed.

"Well, be glad the windows are frosted, or you will be charging admission and earning spectator's fees! A window fan will fit nicely in there in the summer and there is an outlet just around the doorway. Have you seen the kitchen? We are going to be here *all night!*".

"Nonsense. With two of us it won't take long at all. How do the stove and refrigerator look?"

"Ugh, to put it mildly! Still, there's no limit to what soap and water-with-bleach can do. Let's go!" Sue heaved herself to her feet and they started in on the kitchen.

It was nearly ten o'clock when Moon finally returned to her apartment. She and Sue had cleaned, swept, dusted, washed, and polished everything they could. The little bungalow had finally been declared livable. They had even peeked into the attic and prowled around the full basement, found the breaker box and reset the tripped breaker. To celebrate they had treated themselves to a pizza, eaten on the front porch as cicadas and crickets called to each other and stars came out above them.

"It's an empty house," mused Moon, "but it already feels more like home than my apartment ever did. I really don't want to go back there but I still have a few last-minute things to pack and move around."

"Need help?" Sue yawned.

"No! Go home to your family! You have done more than enough for one day. I just have a bit of loose ends to tie up before the kids come tomorrow. Speaking of which, take the key so we can lock up and you all can get back in."

"Good idea. I'm too tired to think," Sue yawned again. "I would be crawling through a window, arrested by the police, and on the front page of the paper! I can just see the headlines: MINISTER'S WIFE LEADS LIFE OF BURGLERY!"

"Stop!" Moon howled. "We will be arrested for disturbing the peace! Seriously let's ditch this trash and get going. We have a big day tomorrow!"

But an elated Moon didn't fall asleep for a long time after the last of her packing was done. She sat in the old chair that she was leaving behind, going over her new house in her mind, making notes in her book, and dreaming about what the house might look like someday.

4

New Beginnings?

Moon remembered moving day when she was three. She remembered the layout of the house she lived in and the excitement (and fear) of watching her toys and favorite things packed up and loaded into a yellow truck with a big green ship painted on it. She remembered the nice men who promised to take good care of her things and bring them safely to another house she had never even seen. She remembered watching the truck pull away from the curb on its journey, filled with her family's treasured possessions. She remembered the long car ride all the way across the state, over a river, into another state that didn't look that much different from the one they left. She was tired, Daddy was driving, and she had her favorite toy kitties, so it was all...okay.

The new house was even bigger than the one they left, older, with a big yard. Once again, she had her own playroom and plenty of room to help Mother garden. Vegetables! She loved pulling the carrots up and brushing the dirt off them. She loved the bunnies and toads that came calling to her vegetable patch. And she loved the books that Mother helped her choose from the library. She loved learning the words and how they made the pictures come alive, rather than the other way around.

A few hours later Moon woke with a start. It was just the first light of day, and she was still sitting in her old chair, in yesterday's clothes. Painfully she pushed herself out of the chair, showered, bagged her dirty clothes to be washed later at the laundromat, and, in a clean pantsuit, left her apartment for the last time. Only two other units in the building were still occupied: a second-floor efficiency held by a student who would be going home from summer school that weekend and the manager's apartment. All other units were dark, empty, silent. Moon turned her back, walked away without a second thought.

It was still early. The bank wouldn't open for a couple of hours, so Moon headed for the Downtown Diner where she knew she could have breakfast, coffee, and time to read a book she had uncovered, buried on the top shelf of the closet. A thriller, another gift she had tossed aside, not wanting to spend the time reading even though it had always been one of her favorite things to do. So many things she *used* to love, like knitting and sewing, reading almost any book she could get her hands on, gardening, listening to music. What happened to her enthusiasm for all that? No energy for them after her divorce. No desire to do the things she used to be passionate about. Everything went by the wayside as she ate and slept away the past five years. Moon was beginning to recognize the depression that had locked her into her current existence.

She ordered black coffee and veggie omelet made with egg whites and a side of fresh fruit. Within a few minutes she was lost in the book, loving the word play, the adventure, the intrigue. When her food arrived, she barely noticed, so engaging was the story. She forced herself to put it down long enough to concentrate on eating her breakfast slowly, paying attention to each bite. When her plate was clean, she went back to reading her book, putting off the moment when she would have to pay the bill and go to work.

Lunch was spent in the break room in air-conditioned comfort: a sandwich from the new vending machine and a bottle of water while she caught up on some loan contracts before diving into her book again. Gossip ebbed and flowed around her, but no one bothered her until Lacey came in.

"So, when's the big day?

"Today. By the time I get off work it will all be done."

"Really? You hired a moving company? Shouldn't you be there to make sure they don't get 'handsy' with your things?"

"Lacey, the only thing I had worth stealing was my car and I sold that so, no, I'm not worried."

"Who did you hire if I may be so nosy? Someone with a good Better Business Bureau rating, I hope."

Moon considered Lacey for a moment. She knew Lacey would continue to press until she got some answers, but Moon was beginning to resent the inquisition.

She answered with slow, deliberate words, "My best friend, Susan Branwell, is the wife of the minister of our church, as you well know. She arranged everything for my move, and I trust her implicitly. So, you see, Lacey, everything is under control." *'I hope,' She thought.* Lacey merely shrugged.

Moon tried extremely hard to keep her mind off the excitement of moving into her new house. She paid extra attention to her clients and even tore up a loan application in favor of helping a middle-aged woman meet her financial needs without putting herself into a debt that would eventually consume everything she had. It was a surprisingly good day, all considered. The sun was shining on the first month of summer, Moon was getting a new place to live, her new bed would be set up tomorrow, and... WHERE WOULD SHE SLEEP TONIGHT? Moon was leaving her old ratty chair, lumpy mattress and sprung box springs behind to be disposed of by the apartment clean-up. She hated the idea of getting a motel room on her first night in her new home. She hoped the floor was comfortable!

Five o'clock crept up, Moon cleared her desk and set Monday's appointments in her locked drawer for the weekend. If she came in at all tomorrow it would only be if called to help the tellers. Now it was time to go home. Home. Moon had never called her apartment 'home' in the five years she had lived there. It had always been 'my apartment.' Now, for the first time since the judge declared her marriage over, Moon could honestly think about 'going home.' She gathered up her canvas tote bag and stepped out into the late afternoon sun. The walk to Oak St. would take about half an hour. She could have asked Sue to come and get her from work, but Moon wanted the chance to savor the moments alone before she arrived at her own front door. She wanted to enjoy the green of the leaves, pick up some garden ideas from the yards on the way, stop at the grocery store for milk and something for dinner. Her first dinner in HER home. No Geordie to complain about where she had put things away or the leftovers she served for supper. So-what if he hated casseroles. She loved them and she could make them, freeze some, have them for lunch or dinner another day. Just that thought made her happier. She bought a frozen dinner, some spaghetti and her favorite sauce with mushrooms and garden vegetables for a weekend meal, planning to do a full shopping expedition as soon as she had time to organize HER pantry. The small room at the very back of the house off the bathroom could be used as a tiny third bedroom or a large pantry/laundry room once plumbing had been added. How hard could it be? *Famous last words!*

Shortly after six o'clock, Moon crossed the threshold of 160 Oak Street and gasped in shock. There was her ratty old chair in the middle of her nice, clean, living room!

"What are you doing here? I stuffed you in the bedroom to be left behind!"

"And where were you going to sleep?" came a voice from the kitchen. "Planning on spending the night at Joy's? I didn't think so!" Sue hugged her friend. "Toss it out later, after you have replaced it or better yet, reupholster it or slip cover it in the meantime. Be creative!"

"Ha, ha! But you do have a point. The bedroom stuff I ordered won't be here until tomorrow so...thank you!"

"What are friends for? Now, dinner's ready, the kids went for pizzas with Mr. Snow, you're late, I'm late, so sit, eat, I will see you Sunday!"

"Wait! Dinner's ready? What did you do?"

"Made meatloaf, mashed potatoes, and glazed carrots. Enough for my family (who are eating it as we speak) and you. Yours in the oven keeping warm. You bought the pizza last night, my turn tonight. If you feel like some entertainment, I left you a new deck of playing cards on the kitchen table. I know how you *love* solitaire." Sue blew raspberries at Moon, just as she had forty years ago when they had been best friends in school. With a wave of her hand, she was out the door leaving Moon alone in her own living room.

'Cards? Meatloaf?' Yes, she could smell the dinner: warm, mouthwatering, <u>HOME</u>! Moon set her bag on the chair then thought better of it and installed it on its own hook in her bedroom closet. The wood floors echoed with her steps, but not as bad as yesterday. Her minimal furniture helped to soften the emptiness a little. She removed her sandals, lined them up on the floor of the closet, unconsciously imitating her mother's routine, selected a pair of holey socks from the clean laundry basket and padded quietly into the kitchen to enjoy Sue's cooking.

The table was set with her everyday silverware and a clean dish towel had been pressed into service as a placemat. The dinner was in the oven set to warm, the way Moon's mother and grandmother had done it for their husbands before the age of microwaves. The whole room smelled of comfort, of coming home after a long day at work. Moon almost expected to see her father at the table and her mother setting out the food on hot pads. Hot pads! Where would Sue have put them? In the bottom drawer of the oven, of course. Moon retrieved them, set the warm plate on the dish towel---and remembered the frozen dinner, in her tote, in her closet! She rushed back to get it, stuck it in the freezer and set the spaghetti and sauce on the counter. She didn't see the deck of cards until she was almost done eating.

It was odd for a deck of cards, more than twice as thick and each card was stuck to a piece of plastic. No, not a piece of plastic, a gift card. Moon started to cry when she realized what Sue had done: she had organized a housewarming 'card shower', 52 gift cards of $10 each, some for Moon's new Amazon account, some to the grocery store, several for the local department store, and some for a movie and popcorn at the local theater. Sue must have been collecting them from members of the church since Moon's eviction notice. The funny thing was that the gift cards were taped gently to the playing cards so the cards could still be used. *'Double your pleasure!'* she thought and started to cry again.

The living room was all indirect light first thing in the morning, the middle bedroom got some morning sun, prompting Moon to wonder if the front bedroom, though smaller, would be better for her. She was still hoping to use the back bedroom, the smallest of all, as a pantry and laundry room but it, along with the kitchen, certainly got the most morning sun through east-facing windows. Moon loved the morning sun and gloried in it after the darkness of her apartment. She would have many decisions to make in the coming months. In the meantime, the middle bedroom got enough sun, more as the day wore on, and Moon was too busy to notice. The bedding, mattress, and box spring that she had ordered online were delivered just before lunch, so Moon spent the afternoon putting together the basics of her bed. Once polished with a little beeswax and made up with the new foundation, mattress, cotton sheets, pillows, a blue and white patchwork quilted bedspread, the old maple four-poster looked much more inviting than it ever had in the cluttered apartment bedroom. Moon knew she would sleep well that night. She put away as many of her clothes as she could, storing the rest in boxes in the back room. Her dresser, rescued from a rainy curb several years before, fell apart when she tried to move it, so she had left it behind. A newish dresser, maple to go with the bed, would be one of her first purchases, along with curtains, perhaps a night table to go next to the bed. A small rug for the hardwood floor? Yes, keep it simple. The room's blue flowered wallpaper was in much better shape than the wall covering in the dining room and living room, so she decided to leave it alone. The list in her notebook was taking shape.

After putting the bedroom together, Moon started cooking spaghetti while setting up her kitchen. *'How did I cook with this stuff for five years,'* she wondered as she surveyed the motley assembly of pots and pans that she had brought. *'I didn't,* she thought, *'I lived on frozen dinners and fast food take out. Well, the utensils are good enough for now, but they will have to be updated as I update the kitchen.'* Another project for the list.

Moon unpacked the rest of her dishes, washed each one before placing them carefully in the cupboard next to the sink. She was of two minds about those dishes. Her mother had given them to her when she married Geordie, who hated them. She cherished the link to her mother, but she wasn't terribly attached to the dishes either, most of which were faded, cracked or chipped. Moon decided she would replace them when she found a pattern, she liked better.

She began a grocery list: oregano, basil, eggs, bread, cereal, milk, yeast, sugar, coffee, flour, cinnamon, cloves. The list got longer and longer. *'I wonder if the grocery store delivers. And <u>why</u> did I sell my car? I need a small chest freezer! Chicken, beef and pork from the butcher out on the highway, fruits and vegetables from the Farmers Market.* She felt so much the way she did as a happy bride, setting up her first home with Geordie. After supper, she sat on the porch steps, drank her coffee and watched the stars come out.

Sunday was a quiet day. Moon walked to early service because she had promised Sue she would be there. Sue was kind enough not to make a fuss over seeing Moon there, but her husband, Rev. Jim, shook her hand on the way out and remarked kindly "Welcome home." Moon knew he was doing more than merely telling her how nice it was to see her in church again. It was his quiet way of encouraging her to keep moving forward in her new ventures.

Moon walked slowly back to Oak St. from the church, taking the long way home. She thought about picking up some fast-food take-out for Sunday dinner, something she would have done automatically a couple months ago; instead, when she stopped at the grocery, she picked up salad ingredients, some skinless chicken to broil, a small bag of rice and a few oranges to squeeze for morning juice; it was all she could carry. But she did arrange for regular delivery of groceries for a very reasonable monthly fee as she placed her first order. That worry taken care of, Moon went home, had a nice long session with her new mystery novel followed by a nap and Sunday supper. After setting out her clothes for the next day, she again spent the evening on her front porch, chatting with her new neighbors, Ellen and Paul Crawford who lived across the alley.

5

Rough Road Ahead

The next few weeks were a time of adjustment for Moon, of getting used to her new home, and to her new schedule. She still walked to work, rising earlier, leaving home earlier. Rising earlier proved not to be a problem. Moon soon learned that an early morning freight train passed two blocks away from her house, and the whistle that sounded when it approached the crossing was better than any alarm clock. She also learned to anticipate and enjoy the moment. She grew to savor the early morning hours before leaving for work: the rising sun through the east windows of the house, the smell of coffee brewing and bacon frying, the unintentional call and response of train whistle and mourning dove, the taste of iced fresh orange juice, the heat of the dishwater as she washed up before leaving. She often packed her lunch now, only rarely going to the diner except to have lunch with Sue between her church committee meetings. She threw out several pairs of shoes that had become painful to wear, bought a sassy pair of flats to keep in her drawer at work, and a good pair of trainers with plenty of support to walk to work in.

So, all went well for the first couple of weeks. Until one Saturday morning when Joy showed up at the new house with her station wagon piled full of junk: mostly the things Moon had left behind.

"You need to pay more attention, Mom," she called out as she began unloading boxes of Moon's cast-off trash. Her former home was finally scheduled for demolition before the end of the year, with plans going forward for upscale condos in its place.

"You left half of your stuff behind! What? Were you having a senior moment? Do I have to get someone to watch over you to make sure you take care of yourself?"

Moon hurried down the back steps to intercept Joy and quiet her down.

"Joy! What do you think you are doing with that trash? That was left behind on purpose! I don't want it. It's junk, broken, useless! Don't even *think* of unloading that here!" she hissed. She didn't want the neighbors to see her in a shouting match with her daughter.

Joy had no such problem. She stared at her mother, then began berating her, getting louder and louder as she wound herself up.

"I don't understand what's going on with you. First, you don't tell me you've been kicked out of your apartment, then you hint that you want to live with me. When I say 'no', you throw your money away on this dump that you can't afford, and you run off leaving half of your stuff behind: things we gave you over the years, things that belonged to Grandma and Grandpa. I thought you spaced out when Dad kicked you out, but you really *are* around the bend now!" Joy was in full rant mode now. "Look at you! You aren't taking care of yourself at all anymore, your clothes are starting to hang funny on you, not that they ever fit too well, to begin with. You don't answer my calls, you avoid me all the time. And what do you expect me to do with this stuff? You left your mattress back there too and I have to unload all this before I can go back and get it for you! What the HELL are you sleeping on, anyway? The floor? WHAT WERE YOU THINKING!" Joy paused for breath as a squad car pulled up. Moon hadn't said a word. She backed away, embarrassed, shocked, and hurt at the anger that was spilling from her daughter's mouth. One of the neighbors must have called the police to intervene.

"Take it to the dump, Joy," she said quietly. "I don't want it. It's junk. You had no right..."

"No right?" Joy was off again. "I have no right to look after my own mother when she can't take care of herself?" she screamed.

Two uniformed officers were getting out of their black-and-white, talking to a couple who lived across the alley. They were gesturing toward Joy, obviously complaining about the altercation.

Moon felt sick. She had just started getting to know the families that lived in her neighborhood. She was terrified that this would taint the budding friendships she was hoping to build.

The officers were coming her way now. She didn't move, she didn't respond to Joy's accusations. She knew anything she said now would just make it worse, so she sat down on the back steps and waited.

"Problem?" the older officer asked Joy politely.

"No," Joy replied shortly. "Nothing I can't handle as soon as *she* comes to her senses!" She gestured toward Moon, still sitting quietly on the back steps, and began unloading the boxes again.

"Not now with that!" the officer blocked Joy's progress. "I want to know what's going on here first."

"Nothing that's anybody else's concern," Joy hissed, dropping a box. Something inside it sounded broken. "This is between my mother and me, so you can go about your business!" She turned to get another box from the car, but again the officer blocked her path.

"I said 'not now!'" he repeated. "When you start screaming at people and disturbing the peace of the neighbors, then it's no longer just your business; you've made it everybody else's as well. Now, why don't you lose the attitude and tell me, quietly, what's going on."

Meanwhile, the younger officer was asking Moon some questions: was she okay, who started the argument, who owned the house, who all lived there? Moon answered as best she could, telling the officer about the bankruptcy, mass eviction of all the tenants, her rental of the house, Joy's disapproval. She had the oddest feeling that she knew him from somewhere but just couldn't place him. It wasn't that important, so Moon let it go and focused on getting herself out of the scene that Joy was creating. The officer seemed sympathetic: he knew all about the emptying of the old apartment building. He and his older partner had chased squatters out of the building only two days ago. He called the realtor, confirmed Moon's story about renting-to-own the little bungalow on Oak Street.

"The stuff was all left behind on purpose." Moon whispered. "It was supposed to go to the dump with the rest of the junk when they tore down the building. Now it's here on my lawn—and I have no way of getting it out of here! I sold my car; I walk to work. I can't deal with Joy's issues right now. I don't want to fight with her, for me it's lose-lose!"

The officer smiled. "It's okay, I think we can help, here. Your neighbors said you weren't doing the screaming; it was all your daughter. They are worried about you."

He walked over to his partner who was still dealing with an irate Joy, held up his hand for quiet, and drew the older officer away for a conversation. Joy went back to unloading the boxes from her car, dumping them loudly on the ground to emphasize her disapproval.

"Ok, this is how it's going to go," the senior officer walked back over to Joy. "You are going to get your temper under control, pick up these boxes, and take them to the dump. Your mother doesn't want the stuff, and you are not going to clutter up her lawn with it. If you come back here and start screaming again, we will be back to escort you downtown to be our guest until you can calm down. Do you understand me?"

Joy tried to lower her voice, but she did not pick the boxes up. Instead, she renewed her effort to explain Moon's shortcomings to the cop. He wasn't having any of it.

"I *said* no more arguing, pick up the boxes and get them out of here!"

"It's not *my* crap, it's *hers*. I'm not going to deal with it. *She* shouldn't have left it behind! She can dispose of it if she doesn't want it!"

"She did. She left it at the old apartment. You had no business trespassing, collecting it from a condemned building without a permit and littering your mother's lawn with it. Pick it up and get it out of here or I will cite you on the trespassing charge and for dumping trash illegally! Now! Are we clear?"

Joy glared at the cop, picked up the boxes one by one, jamming them back in the car. As she got behind the wheel and drove away, she flipped her middle finger at the neighbors who were still standing by the alley, watching the whole scene.

The younger officer handed Moon his business card. "If she comes back, call me. I knew Joy in high school. She...wasn't like this then. She's become a very troubled young woman. I hope she works things out. I always liked her."

And Moon recognized him at last: Tommy Williams, who had hung around with Joy's crowd in high school, had dated both her and her best friend Gracie at different times before moving away his junior year. Joy had married someone else, Tommy hadn't.

Moon watched her daughter drive away with a sinking feeling, then went across the alley to apologize to her neighbors. Surprisingly, they didn't seem to hold her accountable for her daughter's outburst.

"She's a grown-up. She's responsible for her actions, don't you worry about it. We just didn't want to see you being abused that way. If you need any help, anything, you call us!" Ellen hugged her; Paul shook his head sadly but said nothing. Moon thanked them, grateful for their concern.

Her mood was somber as she walked back to her house. She needed something to do to cheer herself up, some sort of project to occupy her mind. Wallpaper! The hardware store was open, so she walked downtown and rented the steamer for a week. It was a bit cumbersome to lug the five blocks back home, but it was worth it,

Moon felt, as she set it up in the dining room and began steaming the old wallpaper off the walls. She kept at it through the afternoon and evening until nearly midnight, before she gave up for the day, fixed herself some soup, (creamy tomato with a grilled cheese sandwich) showered while the soup was heating, and almost fell asleep at the table. The bed felt heavenly, she nearly overslept, and missed church the next morning.

Moon dreamed of her grandmother's house that night: the smells of evening meals of chicken with herbs and spices, of lemon and beeswax furniture polish that grandmother even used on her wood floors. In her dream, she wandered through the house, now long gone as was her grandmother, touching favorite objects once again. She had loved the bookcases with the glass fronts (which she had inherited), the polished wooden table and cluttered desk with its fountain pens, colored inks, fancy note paper and envelopes, stamps, scissors, magnifying glass and evening newspapers. Sales and specials were circled in red pen, houses for sale that interested Grandma were marked in blue. Grandma always vowed that she would sell her house and buy something better; she even wrote out trial 'For Sale' ads for her own home when she went to see some of the more interesting available houses, but she never could part with the house she had lived in all her adult life. She clipped recipes and articles that caught her interest, sharing them among her children, grandchildren, and friends.

And Moon dreamed of music, the radio that grandma kept in the kitchen dancing to the tunes while she cooked on the big gas stove, as well as the phonograph/radio in the living room (what grandma called the parlor) that held all of grandpa's favorite records, still marked with the correct settings twenty years after his death.

Grandma's home had so many similarities to Moon's new house that things blurred in her dream, sometimes becoming the house on Oak St, sometimes Grandma's house as she remembered it from her childhood, sometimes her parent's house, still standing in another part of her town. In her dream she selected one of her mother's favorite books (sold at a yard sale, decades ago), took it to her favorite reading nook off grandpa's study only to find her-

self in her own living room, complete with a fireplace that didn't exist. She followed the smells of Sunday dinner and apple pie to Grandma's kitchen but wound up shaking out cotton rugs off her own back porch. She went looking for Grandma and Mother on her own big front porch but found instead the tiny front stoop and dark, dying evergreens in front of the house where she grew up.

She woke late, dazed, headachy, confused by the shifting dream settings. *'Probably inhaled too much old wallpaper paste,'* she thought. She took the roast from the fridge, tucked it into the oven with carrots and potatoes before walking to the Congregational Church. It wouldn't be ready for the noon meal, but by the time she had finished removing the wallpaper on the east wall between the dining room and kitchen, it would be lovely to have supper already cooked. A feeling of unease persisted all day, no doubt a holdover from the combination of the weird dream mixed with the argument with Joy the day before. Moon was confused: what to do about the walls, what to do about Joy, and what Grandma seemed to be trying to tell her. She finally put it all aside to concentrate on removing the old wallpaper, but it didn't resolve anything.

"How is your new home coming," Lacey inquired Monday morning as Moon passed her desk on her break. "Are you settling okay? Such big change from that little rabbit hole you used to live in!"

"What's your point?" Moon stopped and set her coffee cup on one of the coasters Lacey always kept out for drinks.

"No point, really," Lacey dodged, "Just that it's a big step. Like starting completely over. Almost...a second chance, to get it right."

"To get *what* right?" Moon wasn't sure where Lacey was going with this, but she knew from past experience that Lacey rarely handed out compliments.

"Well. I mean you made such a mess of your marriage, lost your home and your husband, and to be honest you have *really* let yourself go until lately, I mean they were even talking about asking for your resignation or moving you to a…ah…less…public…position…" she tapered off at the look on Moon's face.

"<u>Who</u> was talking about it?" Moon kept her voice level with effort.

"Well, you know, the bosses…." Lacey's voice trailed off again as Moon stalked away back to her desk. *'Bitch.'*

Moon felt sick and angry. She picked up her desk phone, dialed a number and spoke two words to the person who answered: "War council!"

"It's about time!" Came the reply, but Moon had already hung up.

"She is unbelievable! I can't stand her backhanded compliments! She acts as though she's being so socially correct but then there's that last little DIG. AND SHE'S USUALLY RIGHT! Well, at least partly," Moon finished softly.

Moon and Sue were on Moon's front porch again, in the swing Moon had bought (on sale) when she returned the steamer. They were sharing a thermos of coffee and cookies left over from the youth group bake sale that past weekend.

"So, why does it bother you this much now? You used to just chalk it up to Lacey being Lacey," Sue asked. "Lacey Frasier Burnham has been like this since she moved here in junior high school, remember? She came from some place out East when her dad was transferred in as a new vice president at Sherman Pharmaceuticals. Such a big deal. She tried so hard to fit in with the 'popular' kids but never quite made it, then she got that mad crush on Geordie, about the time he first noticed you, but of course he couldn't see her if you had given him glasses!"

"Oh, my!" Moon laughed, "I'd forgotten that! She tried everything short of running around in her birthday suit every time he showed up for some intermural thing. I suppose it helped that he was from another town, a different school, grade ahead of us; it made him cool and mysterious. Didn't do her much good, though did it? I think she married right after high school: A Marine Corps officer, they had just the one son before Corporal Burnham was killed on patrol overseas.

You know, I bet she still has a crush on Geordie. Funny, though, she had her chance when we broke up. Why didn't she make a move then? And why take it out on me now?"

"Who knows? Maybe she did and didn't have any more luck than before. Anyway, she can't help it, it's old habit by now. It's the way she learned to cope with an adolescent society that rejected her," Sue said sagely.

"Ooh, psychology 101," Moon teased. Sue had gone to college after graduation, Moon had gotten an associate degree in business from the Tech and stayed with her job at the bank.

"If you remember," Sue continued, "her mother was much the same. Always the snarky little backhanded verbal slaps meant to be 'helpful'. She was the terror of the Ladies Aid Society; I can tell you!

"The question now is 'What are you going to do now.' She does have a point: you have been given a gift, a second chance, and I see you are making some great changes. So, what's next?"

Moon munched her cookie. The stars were coming out early. It was her second-favorite time of the day. "Why does something have to be 'next'? Why can't it just be this?

"I had a dream the other night, after the fight with Joy. I dreamed I was back at Grandma's house as a kid, only I wasn't. It was Grandma's house, but it was also mine with a little of Mom and Dad's mixed in. And there was a fireplace in my living room!"

"Your mind is working overtime," Sue laughed "Maybe it's all that old wallpaper paste!"

"Yeah. That's what I thought, too. Do you think my boss was really thinking about moving me or firing me?" Moon leaned back on her elbows and followed the lights of an airplane across the darkening sky until it blended in with the stars.

"No," Sue said thoughtfully. "I think Lacey said that to rattle you. And it did. But again, she is right, you haven't been on top of your game for the longest time. I notice that you are eating better, walking more, have you stepped on a scale lately?"

"I...don't own one."

"Buy one. And a calorie counter. Or get one of those computer tablets and a weight loss app that tracks your calories and exercise. There are free ones out there. Your phone company offers internet sign up. You can get free recipes, music, books, and information. You already have that shopping website account: they have an app for that, too. The world has changed, Moon. We all need to adapt. Jim can help you set it up: he's particularly useful that way," Sue laughed. "But seriously, you called a war council, you haven't done that since just after high school when you were trying to figure out how to get Geordie to propose. I think you should have done it when things began to go bad with him."

"I didn't know they were, until they did!" Moon protested sadly.

"Baloney! You did so, we all did, but you are terrific at *not* seeing things. Like Geordie's new girlfriend, Joy's misery, and your own part in it. And because you didn't want to see it, you've been sharing a dump with a cat who hates you, eating yourself out of your clothes and generally turning into an old woman. It's no wonder you look in the mirror and don't see yourself."

Moon stared at her friend, astonished. Sue had always been honest with her, but she had never been this blunt before.

Meanwhile, Sue was on a roll. All the things she had wanted to say to Moon for years but had held back came flooding out.

"You could have called me any time and I would have come to help. Jim and I weren't that far away: one state over and his ministry was winding down there. He was so thrilled to be called to this church and it was homecoming for me, with my best friend waiting, but what did I find after moving in? Your marriage was in shambles, your daughter was stressed out right over the edge, and you were off in your own little world pretending that nothing was wrong instead of putting everyone and everything in their place! I wanted to shake you awake, but Jim told me that the best thing I could do for you was just *"be there, be supportive,"* to let it unfold, you would pull out of it on your own.

When you did, that's when you would need my help." Sue was crying now, years' worth of pent-up grief and frustration rolling down her cheeks.

"It has taken five years, *five years,* for you to wake up: I almost thought a couple of times that you might slip back into your comfort zone. But you didn't! You've let me help you move forward, and NOW I think you are ready to begin really moving ahead and fixing this thing! Oh, Margaret Olive O'Brian Newsome, I have missed you. You've been gone so long!"

Shocked at her friend using her full maiden name, Moon wordlessly hugged her friend, both cried for everything lost and found. After the emotion ebbed, she wiped her eyes on her sleeve and said, simply, "Thank you. And thank Jim, too. You've got a good man there, remember that and hold on to him."

"I do. And I am," Sue was wiping away her own tears with a Kleenex from her pocket, offering one to Moon as well. "I think first, if you think you are ready, we should set a goal, short term, and figure out the steps to achieve it. One victory at a time, don't you think?" Moon blew her nose, Sue laughed. "When do you get paid next?"

"Later this week. I was going to put some of it in an escrow account toward rent, buy a crock pot and some groceries, and set up auto pay for the electric bill. After a few months, I can get the budget choice and that will save money overall. I have also set up accounts for repairs and remodeling, and one for taxes."

"Hmm. Hold off on the crock pot until closer to fall. You may borrow mine if you really need one before that. Instead, go get your hair done. I think there's a gift card toward that: styled and colored. Maybe highlighted. Nothing drastic, but something to put some zip in your step. And two new outfits for work. That should do to start. We threw out a bunch of your clothes that you couldn't be seen in anymore, some others need to go, my friend. They just don't fit like they used to! It's time for some new things! Do you still sew?"

"I haven't for years. Geordie kept the sewing machine. He said, 'I bought it; I'm keeping it!' He probably gave it away or sold it later. I guess he sold a lot of the stuff he kept from the divorce to make his car payments."

"But wasn't that a birthday gift?"

"Didn't matter. His money, his property."

Sue sighed. "I never did understand that possessive attitude of his: everything was always 'mine, mine, MINE!' Well, we can work on that. How does hair and clothes sound for a first goal?"

"Doable," Moon admitted reluctantly. "Where do I get one of those 'tablet thingies' and how do I get it set up?"

Sue was already on her cell phone to her husband. "Moon needs a computer tablet, where did you get yours? Online? Really? That much?!? Oh, goodness, I didn't realize…well of course you need it for work. No, I'm not complaining. I just thought they would be cheaper. Okay. Hmmm. We need to do some rethinking here. Refurbished? Is that a good idea? I didn't think so. Oh, that's a good idea, I didn't think of that! See," she laughed, "that's why I keep you around! Yes, come get me. You can join us for coffee. We are on the porch! Love you, too.

Well, that was educational! I didn't pay attention to what Jim spent on his tablet because it was for work, it comes out of a different part of the budget and is partly reimbursed by the church, by an endowment program they have. His tablet is an iPad, one of the better versions, and cost just under $500. The Microsoft versions are even more expensive as are the laptops, closer to $1000."

"I can't afford that, not and put away money for the rent and taxes," Moon stated flatly. "That comes first. I won't risk losing this house."

"Of course. That's out of the question. Jim suggested 'refurbished' but that's always a gamble. There is another possibility you might want to consider and that's getting a new laptop from the rent-to-own store. The upside is that you pay for it on a budget plan, the downside is that it's more expensive over the life of the loan, and we are trying to conserve money."

"Not refurbished," decided Moon, thinking hard. "I want new. And I don't trust the rent-to-own for something like a computer. Maybe furniture or appliances, not computers. These cell phones do the same thing as a computer, right? And they are portable? How pricey are they?"

"Sometimes as expensive as the computers plus the cost of the phone service. I know you don't have Wi-Fi set up yet."

"Not yet. I usually use the computer at the library to look up things. Work is for work, and I've rarely checked my e-mail since we set it up. I've been too busy with the house."

"Okay, let's set the computer aside for the moment, but do buy a scale and maybe a calorie counter. If we must do this the old-fashioned way, then we will. Promise! Tomorrow?"

"Okay, war council over because here comes Jim. No men allowed," Moon called out laughing.

"I'm not loud," Jim protested, hugging his wife. "I'm quiet. Very. Quiet. And I *was* invited for coffee!" he protested. Sue stood to get him a cup from the house, but he waved her back down. "Can't stay, Sibling warfare at home. Did you get the computer issue figured out?"

"Not yet. Working on it. Meet me at the hairdresser's tomorrow after work?" Sue ordered Moon. "We can do some other shopping as well."

Progress Is Made

"**I** hate sitting in the beauty parlor, hated it since I was a kid," Moon paged slowly through her third magazine of hairstyles barely glancing at any of them. "This is all designed for people twenty some years younger than I am. And what's wrong with my hair anyway!" she demanded.

"It makes you look twenty years older than you are rather than twenty years younger," Sue replied idly. She was paying careful attention to her own magazine with an occasional penetrating glance at her friend. "Your hair used to be a dark coffee brown but maybe a shade lighter would look better, more youthful. Hair that's too dark brings out the wrinkles in your face."

"That's an old wives' tale," hissed Moon.

"Actually, it is kind of true," offered the receptionist. "Not the wrinkles so much as the changes in your skin. Really dark hair as you age tends to make you look 'hard' as though your face was set in plastic. Lighter colors freshen and soften your skin tones but don't go too light. You'll look washed out."

"That's good to know," mused Moon. "So, something like milk chocolate cocoa? With a few lighter brown highlights?"

"Good choice, or maybe with a few dark brown 'low lights' to add depth. Blended right it looks like you didn't have your color done. If you are having it styled, maybe a simple layered bob that plays off your facial shape. The simpler the better."

Moon and Sue looked at each other and nodded. "Show me," Moon handed the receptionist a stack of style magazines; she chose a simple, classic style that would highlight Moon's best features.

"Yes, yes," Moon agreed. "That's the one!"

"And with a little *understated* make-up, that's not far off how you will look," agreed Sue. "I mean it! Less is more unless you apply to Clown College! Some foundation to even out the skin tones, a little bronzer instead of blush to make your skin glow, some mascara to enhance your lashes, and lip gloss to shine!"

"Where in the world did you learn all this?"

"Theater. Costumes and Make-up. Remember, that's where I met Jim."

"Then, if that's how it turns out, it's worth it. Lead on!"

The Moon that walked out of the beauty salon ninety minutes later was a more poised, polished version of the one who had entered. Her back was a little straighter, her smile a little brighter. For the first time since her birthday, she started to see glimpses of herself, the real Moon, in the mirror. She knew she still had a long way to go but the essence was there again. She was starting to feel like the woman she had been more than a decade ago. The new surroundings, new pleasures, new friends, and now a fresher look, were beginning to work on the apathy that years of not having a reason to care had layered on her soul.

Sue took shameless advantage of Moon's good mood to herd her over to the department store. Knowing she wouldn't get Moon out of the pantsuits completely, at least not yet, Sue settled for a pair of coffee brown linen slacks and a coordinating sweater on clearance. She also talked Moon into buying a pair of Levi's jeans for the weekends and a light chambray work shirt to go with them while she herself selected a nice cranberry wool three-piece suit for fall Sunday services. She caught Moon eyeing a sewing machine in the appliance section and suggested that she make a note of the price. "We'll look around and see if we can get a better deal," Moon agreed. They also stopped by the health and beauty section and bought the scale and make-up, while Sue picked up supplies of her own.

Out on the street Moon hugged her friend good-bye and turned to walk home alone. She wanted time and silence to process these renewed feelings. Sue promised to call her soon, but Moon could tell she was already focused on the rest of her evening and the church meetings that took so much of her time and energy. That was Sue's center: her family and her church. Moon wondered idly what had happened to her own center, if indeed she had ever had one. At one time, she had believed that Geordie was her center, but a failing marriage had changed that and having a daughter hadn't salvaged it the way she thought it would have done.

Thinking about Joy reminded Moon of the painful scene outside her house a few days ago. She had not heard a word from her daughter since that morning. The silence was peaceful but worrisome. Maybe it was time to tie up some loose ends there. After she put her new clothes away, selected two of her newer pantsuits for possible 'remodeling', as well as two for the donation box, Moon took a deep breath, and dialed her daughter's number.

"What do you want?" Joy's voice was harsh, and it sounded like she had been crying.

"To invite you over for coffee this weekend," Moon forced herself to listen carefully to her daughter.

"I suppose now you want your shit back, well too bad. I dumped it just like that stupid cop told me to," Joy snapped.

"No, I don't want it," Moon said gently. "It was junk, and high time I was rid of it. No, I just wanted to ask you over for coffee, maybe some coffee cake, Great Grandma's recipe? We haven't sat down and caught up for a long time. I think we are overdue, don't you?"

"So that your neighbors can butt in again? I don't think so."

"Okay, I know you are busy. But if you change your mind the invitation is open." Moon was just about to hang up when Joy's voice, a soft hiss, came back over the line.

"Does Dad know that you moved? Does he know what you are up to?" The line went dead, leaving Moon wondering what, exactly, had happened. Geordie had never paid any attention to how Moon was doing after the divorce, and she wasn't sure she even knew where he was or how he was. Did he know she had moved? Why would he want to? Did he care? She doubted it. Well, she certainly wasn't going to find him and tell him. As for Joy, she would have to wait and see what happened. To prepare, and because she was hungry for it herself, she found the recipe for her grandmother's coffee cake and began to assemble the ingredients.

Across town Sue was attacking her evening chores with the organizational prowess of a born schoolteacher. She rounded up her two teenagers and set Abby to do food prep and Josh to tidying up the house, partly to get the work done and partly to separate them so as to contain the sibling rivalry. Two years apart in age and well-behaved when not together, the brother and sister were the bitterest rivals when in the same room. Sometimes Jim's calming presence was enough to dampen the emotional fires that blazed, sometimes the only answer was to separate the combatants and pray for the day when they would each be off to college or to live their own lives somewhere else. Happily, that time was only a year away as Joshua, the eldest, was a senior in high school and would be entering the state university system the following fall on an athletic scholarship. His plan was to coast through four years of college in his beloved chemistry department, accept the job waiting for him at Sherman Pharmaceuticals in their lab and continue in his comfortable bachelor lifestyle. Not exactly a slob, he was nevertheless not nearly neat enough, driven enough, caring enough, or indeed, sometimes human enough for his younger sister.

Abby was the drama queen of the family, hyper sometimes to the point of perpetual motion. She fought hard for every good grade she received, fought to keep her space clean and private, fought to belong to environmental and political clubs, fought for attention in the presence of an older brother whom she perceived as lazy, smug, entitled, uncaring, and selfish. In truth, he was none of those things merely as introverted as she was extroverted. Both Jim and Sue hoped that time apart and mega doses of maturity would smooth over the rough spots. Privately Jim doubted it but refrained from saying anything to Sue. He and his own brother had not spoken for twenty years for much the same reasons. Sue was on excellent terms with her four brothers and two sisters. She could not understand the violent clashes between Josh and Abby.

That evening the daily sibling storm had blown itself out by the time she returned home from shopping; both teens were now going ahead quietly with evening chores.

"Did you get Moon outfitted?" Jim asked as Sue tucked the casserole back in the oven to let the topping brown before serving.

"Yes, we found a nice hair style for her and a couple of outfits on sale, so she won't blow her budget. And I found a nice suit for the autumn conferences in Madison. Cranberry, your favorite color. It will look lovely with that scarf with the leaves that your mother gave me for Christmas."

"Always thinking ahead," Jim approved. "Is Moon still looking for a computer?"

"Possibly, but she can't afford it right now. She's got old wallpaper hanging down to her toes and dried paste up her nose and it's giving her strange dreams. Of course, that row with Joy didn't help any."

"I saw Joy the other day, with some man in her car. It wasn't her husband or her dad, I don't think I've ever seen him before," remarked Abby as she set the last dish on the maple dining room table.

"I don't think it would be wise to draw conclusions or discuss it until we have all the facts," Jim counseled.

"What facts?" demanded Abby. "I saw Joy, driving around town, with a man who was neither her husband nor her father. He looked to be about halfway in age between the two. And she has told me she's not happy at home. Those are the facts. Period."

"There are a number of facts missing from that scenario," Jim cautioned. "Who is he? How does she know him? Was she helping him out in some way, for some reason? Were they carpooling? There are literally hundreds of reasons for any one action. Let it go, Abby."

"Don't you think Moon should know that her daughter is running around with someone other than her husband or dad?" Abby demanded. Jim and Sue shared a look before Sue responded.

"Truthfully, sadly, now that Joy is an adult, what she does isn't Moon's concern unless Joy chooses to tell her. Your dad is right, Abby. I know you want to help but you need to leave it alone. Sometimes that's the best course of action."

"I know," said Abby sadly. "I just hate to see Joy throwing her marriage away too."

"What do you mean 'too'?"

"Like Moon did."

"Moon didn't throw hers away, Abby, that situation was different."

"Was it? Really? She didn't do anything to save it. That's what Joy said.

"Joy is entitled to her opinion. The only ones who *really* know what went on in Moon's marriage are Moon and Geordie. The rest of us need to worry about our own business. Remember what Grandma says…"

'Minding your own business is a full-time job, and more people ought to be employed in it.' Abby laughed. "She's right, I know. It's just that I like Moon, and I used to like Joy. Now I just don't know…"

"Dinner," announced Jim removing the casserole from the oven and setting it on a trivet in the middle of the table. Abby added some chilled fruit salad from the refrigerator as Sue poured coffee for herself and Jim. "Milk or juice?" she asked Abby.

"Milk." Abby got a glass tumbler from the cupboard.

"For me too," Josh agreed, coming in from the living room where he had been ordered to tidy up from his gaming session with his friends. Abby reluctantly took a second tumbler from the cupboard and set it in front of Josh's place at the table. Had it been up to her, she would have told him to get it himself, but rudeness was a groundable offense, and she had plans for the weekend. Instead, she avoided looking at him, took her place at the table and concentrated on centering herself for evening prayer before eating. Nothing more was said about Moon or her daughter, but Sue quietly wondered about Joy's latest antics.

It was the first day of kindergarten for Susan McNeely (never known as Susie, only Sue) who was as excited as a six-year-old could be. Year after year she had watched her three older brothers and one older sister collect their school bags and lunches from their mother (who didn't believe that school lunches were good for children,) and leave, not to return until nearly suppertime with wonderful stories about their friends, their activities, and the things they were learning. She had listened, quietly, taking in everything they brought to the supper table, praying for the day when it would be her turn for such adventures.

Here it was! Today was the day! Her new outfit was all set out on its hanger: dress, tights, panties, sweater, ready to be worn. She had a package of new clips to hold back her thick blonde hair, new shoes in her closet, still in their box. As she dressed, she almost felt sorry for her younger brother and sister, still waiting their turn.

As asked, she reported to her older sister, Jean, for inspection before going into the kitchen to help with the younger ones' breakfasts. Mother was cooking, Grant (the eldest of the group) was buckling baby Jane (the youngest) into her highchair, and Tom (second oldest) was settling Frank (next in line for the wonders of education) into place.

Sue took out cereal for herself and Frank, poured some into bowls, and set one, without milk, in front of her brother. A fussy eater, Frank preferred his cereal dry, but he would drink milk and/or orange juice if offered in his favorite cup. She added milk to her own cereal after moving it out of Frank's reach, lest he be tempted to eat both helpings. Trent (second middle brother, named after Grandpa) was nowhere to be found but that was not unusual. Trent was often long gone from the house by now, having inherited Grant's morning paper route when Grant had been offered a better job helping in Uncle Alfred's grocery store as a bag boy after school. Tom's paper route was an afternoon Shopper's Guide route that only came out once a week but covered four times the territory as Trent's and so paid nearly as well. Tom had his eye on a position higher up in the company in a few years so was content with his current schedule and pay. It left him more time for after-school activities like sports, music, clubs, which was also a plus.

It was obvious that Dad wasn't home yet, probably wouldn't be done at work for another hour or so because of overtime. By the time he got home for breakfast Frank would be off playing with some neighbor kids and Janie would be quietly building blocks in the playroom. Mom would be working her way through her list of morning chores; everyone else would be in school. He would fix himself a quick meal, sleep until school let out, then spend the evening playing with them, talking to them, sharing their schoolwork problems, before leaving for his overnight shift at the auto assembly plant.

Sue finished her breakfast. Baby Jane was still being fed by Mom, so Sue left Jane's bowl but put hers in the hot soapy water and washed it out. Rinse. Set in dish rack. Her schoolbag and lunch were right where Mother had said they would be. She scooped them up, handed Jean hers, ready to follow her to school. Jean was three years older than Sue, a seasoned veteran of school but not too old to mind showing her younger sister around. She would walk Sue to school, Sue would walk home on her own while Jean attended her after-school clubs. They had been practicing for weeks.

A couple blocks down the street they passed a large dark house with white shutters. A small girl was sitting quietly on the abbreviated front steps, half hidden by overgrown evergreen shrubs that looked like they might be dying. Sue shivered, but Jean called out to the girl: "Moon! Don't sit there waiting for a taxi! Come walk with us!"

"Moon?" Sue asked her sister. "What a funny name."

The girl heard. "Margaret Olive O'Brian Newsome. I hate my name. I've been 'Moon' all my life. It suits me," she said without embarrassment.

"Cool," said Sue. "I'm Susan, never Susie because I hate it, only Sue. This is Jean. There's five more of us but the rest have all gone ahead except the two littlest at home. Are you coming or staying?"

"Coming," said Moon grabbing her bag from the steps. She was dressed in jeans and a sweater, her long brunette hair neatly braided in a single plait down her back. Sue noticed that she wore canvas tennis shoes instead of leather oxfords and her jeans had embroidery around the cuffs. Sue was impressed. The stitching looked like it had been done by hand rather than machine. Moon saw her admiring it and said simply, "My grandmother did it as a 'starting school' present but I can stitch too. Want me to show you sometime?"

"Oh, yes," breathed Sue while Jean just laughed and shook her head.

"Well, now you'll have someone to walk home with, so I don't worry about you getting lost." And so, it began...

Moon wore her new outfit to work the next day. It didn't feel right to drag out one of the tired old pantsuits. New hair, new clothes, new make-up, Moon almost felt like dancing all the way to work. It felt like it had the first day of school, the first day she met Sue and Jean, the day she knew she had found a friend for life.

The scale she bought informed her that she was indeed overweight but not as badly as she had feared. Moon suspected that all the working, walking, and better eating had something to do with it.

She was done stripping the wallpaper: now she would begin the painting, something in the coffee-with-cream range. She was feeling incredibly pleased with the way things were coming along.

Because of her good mood, she avoided Lacey's desk during work. No point ruining a great day deliberately. She accepted the complements of the secretaries in the break room, knowing full well it would get back to Lacey before the end of the day; she buried herself in her work, getting ahead on the next day's paperwork in preparation for the meetings and audits on her calendar. By the time she left for home her desk was cleared, important papers locked away and she was satisfied that she had put in a full day of her best work.

There had, of course, been no word from Joy.

Moon walked home, enjoying the early evening: the hint of rain to come. She had a small steak ready to broil and potatoes left over from yesterday to go with a salad and a single-serve bottle of wine chilled and ready to be opened.

By Monday, the dining room and living room would be fresh and ready for her next project: furniture. The old chair was ready for either the attic or the dumpster and Moon had some ideas about the way she wanted her place to look. She was planning to use some of the online gift cards to buy some lace curtains for the bigger windows and to scour the Farmers Market for some potted plants to keep over the winter. After five years in her cramped, dingy apartment Moon wanted to keep furniture and accessories to a minimum. The idea of a fireplace nagged at her, but she didn't see how it could be done. Gas? Wood? Pellet? Electric? How expensive would it be to build and run? Moon didn't own a television, didn't want one; she quite liked the idea of reading on a fall or winter evening by the fire with maybe a floor lamp for extra light.

So, her bookcases, a couple of chairs, a table and maybe that fireplace with an area rug to tie it all together. Moon knew she was being old-fashioned, but it also felt like she was finally making a home, not so much the physical place but the feeling of security and belonging. She could hear the echo of Sue's voice saying, "What made you happy back then?" What do you want now?"

Home, for Moon, had always been her grandma's house, more so than her own. Other than Sue's house, it was the one place where Moon had always felt welcome, where things were the same from day to day, year to year. Once Grandma settled on something, it almost never changed. Moon never had to worry that when she got to Grandma's her favorite chair would be gone, or rooms would be changed around. All would be comfortably the same as it was the last time she was there. Moon understood that she was modeling her new home after Grandma's: do what makes you happy. Reconnecting with her beloved Grandma was fast becoming Moon's way of finding her own happiness.

Music! Grandma's home always had music either from the kitchen radio or Grandpa's old radio/phonograph in the living room. Moon decided that along with the curtains her next purchase would be two radios: one for news in the kitchen, a larger one for music in the living room. She would find one that came with a turntable for playing vinyl records and she planned to buy at least two to play on it: one symphony for listening and one mix of music she had grown up with, for dancing.

Over the next few weeks, the living room and dining room slowly took on the ambiance that Moon associated with her grandma's house. She found an oak dining room table and four matching chairs at a craft sale. Made of solid wood by a local Amish man and his two sons it was the sturdiest table Moon had found, having rejected pressed wood and MDF. She wanted something that would last the rest of her life and beyond, so she bargained and haggled until both parties were happy. The day the table was delivered and set in its place on the wool rug, (one of a pair she had found at an estate sale), was one of her happiest days since moving in. No more eating at the tiny wooden table in the kitchen. Moon had other plans for that, but first, she dragged it up to the attic, out of the way. She set one placemat and table setting on the new table, so she could face the alley when she ate and set a second placemat, for company. There were now African violets in the window, chrysanthemums had bloomed alongside the house.

Moon made her payment a day or two early each month, copying the receipts at the library: the originals went into a safe deposit box at the bank and the copies into a file in her bottom dresser drawer. Moon did not trust The Family and she wasn't going to take any chances.

There was still no word from Joy.

The right living room chairs were harder to find. Estate sales and yard sales yielded interesting pieces but nothing that said 'home' to Moon. She avoided thrift shops and department stores, wanting instead something that had first been loved by someone else and was sturdy enough to be loved by someone new. With winter coming she knew she would have to find something soon.

Two months after she moved in, Moon was awakened by a crash in the kitchen. The cupboard on the East wall that held her toaster, electric fryer along with her pots and pans had come loose from its moorings. The contents were fine, but the cabinet was not salvageable. Moon went back to bed.

The next day she contacted her 'landlords' about new cabinets.

"You knew what condition the house was when you signed the papers," she was told. "You are buying it as is. We are sure you can adjust."

'Adjust, my ***! Moon grumbled. *'Time to check the lease!* **Repair costs would be split between Moon and the estate, upgrades to be paid for by**

Moon alone. *'No 'wonder they don't want to repair it. I may wind up up-grading after all! Rats!'*

For the time being, she rearranged her cupboards, moved her china to the dining room hutch until she could decide what to do. Looking at the effect, she decided she liked it better that way even if she still wasn't thrilled about the old dishes, but it didn't solve the problem of the kitchen cabinets. *'Which ones will fall down next,'* she wondered.

There was also the worry of whether new cabinets would change the final cost of the house. She still was afraid that The Family would try to raise the price if she put in too many improvements. She would have to double-check with the realtor to be sure before she decided.

The fireplace continued to haunt her, especially on nights when she would dream of sitting in her living room by a quiet fire. *'Where did this desire come from?'* she wondered. *'We never had one when I was growing up, neither did Grandma and Grandpa. Wait, Grandma had one when she was a little girl. She used to tell me stories about popping pop-corn, and roasting sausages, warming herself on a cold day and drying her clothes on a rack in front of the fire after playing out in the snow. She and her brother used to tell spooky stories on Halloween with just the fire for light. There were a hundred stories! Oh, I had forgotten it all until I dreamed about it. Thank you, Grandma, for all those memories.'* Now she knew she absolutely must find a way to put a fireplace in the living room, for Grandma and all the stories she had shared. She made enquiries about a regular fireplace and the cost staggered her. It would also involve tearing apart several walls to install the chimney and flue. A gas unit would be much more economical and easier to install since there were already gas lines run for the stove and hot water heater. The problem was that Moon was still technically renting the property. She would have to get permission from the family if she wanted to install the gas fireplace. Moon couldn't see that happening without a lot of ar-gument. There had already been an issue with the cupboards, and she was not eager to tangle with them again.

A week before Thanksgiving, Moon found her chairs: a matched pair of deep blue brocade wing chairs with a small oval table to set between them, at an auction a couple of towns down the highway. The big draw was a selection of plants that Sue was interested in for a small greenhouse the church was building. It was an experiment in growing some simple fruits and vegetables over the winter for the soup kitchen and community dinners that the church sponsored. Sue borrowed Mr. Snow's pick-up truck and Moon blessed the man who owned it several times over when she won the chairs and table. The truck easily handled two dozen plants (tomatoes, onions, and beans), as well as the chairs and table, a set of oak plant stands, and some bedding for the homeless shelter. Moon was cheered to see her living room looking less empty even though she had been enjoying the open space. Now she had a comfy chair to sit in to listen to her favorite public radio station. She still refused to buy a television. Nor was she any closer to obtaining a laptop or tablet. Moon didn't care much about either. She happily continued to use the library computers for anything but work. As for the television, no programs appealed to her, so she just didn't bother.

After checking the language of the contract, Moon and the realtor decided that the family couldn't raise the price of the house based on any upgrades Moon made, but that it was not a wise idea to overdo it. Repairing/replacing the cupboards was a necessity. Moon thought about it for a while, then went to talk to the Amish man who had built her table. Within the month, Moon had a completely new set of solid oak kitchen cabinets that made the whole kitchen glow and pantry shelves in the small back bedroom. Moon celebrated with a new coat of pale-yellow paint on the kitchen walls, a cheery wallpaper border, grapes and leaves, up by the ceiling, a ceiling light and fan to circulate the air. The family didn't say a word.

Thanksgiving and Christmas came and went. There was still nothing from Joy. Not even a card.

The fireplace issue solved itself temporarily with clearance sales in January. Along with bedding and home furnishing sales, the department store was offering electric fireplace/space heaters. All lights and warmth from an energy-efficient LED display surrounded by a wooden mantle. It looked real enough, warmed the room, wouldn't destroy the electric bill, and the store agreed to deliver it already assembled. The day it arrived, Moon invited Sue, Jim, and the kids over to listen to old time radio programs and eat popcorn in front of her fireplace. Snow fell through the January evening, but no one paid any attention. The kids were so enthralled by the radio suspense and comedy programs that they forgot to fight until it was time to go home.

"It's so great that PBS does these old radio shows," Sue sighed. "It's nice to be 'unplugged' occasionally. Maybe we can do a sponsored Lock In with the old shows for the youth group. Might be fun.

"I love your fireplace," she added, "but I can't wait until you get a real one!"

"Me, neither" Moon agreed. "But until then this will be fine and won't upset the contract. I hope. Things are coming along slowly but I am in no hurry."

"What are you going to do with your front bedroom and the back room off the bathroom?" Sue asked as Jim separated and quieted the kids.

"Still deciding," Moon responded pushing Sue toward the car. "I have the pantry shelves there; I can always add plumbing later for a washer and dryer. Go, before the situation deteriorates even further!"

6

Bad News Coming

Moon loved walking to work, even in the snow. On days when the weather was truly terrible, she either left early or arranged for a cab the day before to be sure of getting one on time. She hated to spend the extra ten dollars each way but sometimes there was just no other way of getting to the bank safely and on time. The walking had been good for Moon. She no longer waddled when she walked or puffed up and down the stairs at work. Her old pantsuits were gone or re-purposed. Thirty pounds lighter, she was wearing skirts or nice dresses to work. The secretaries oohed and aahed over each new outfit as they had over Moon's new hairstyle, once the shock wore off, but Lacey had said very little after remarking, "Nice, but not really your *natural* color, is it?"

"Oh, that's rich, coming from the original 'bottle blonde'," Sue had laughed. "I'm sorry, that's not very kind of me but I've two full days of holding my tongue in church meetings, and if I don't say something catty, I will explode. Besides, I can't abide double standards, I never could. Mother served on committees with Lacey's mother and that woman was pure vinegar bottled to look like salad dressing!"

"What?" Moon doubled over with laughter.

"One of your grandma's sayings that just stuck in my head," Sue mumbled, red faced.

"I remember that!" Moon exclaimed. "There's so much about grandma I had forgotten that is just now coming seeping back to me! Thank you for reminding me. Now, every time I see Lacey, I'll think..."

'*WISHBONE!* remarked Moon to herself as she stepped carefully down her snowy back steps the next morning and saw Lacey's car parked in the alley. She had been looking forward to the walk to work but this could spoil the mood very quickly. '*What is she doing here?*' Moon wondered.

Lacey rolled down the passenger window of her car, a sleek-looking red coupe, and called out to Moon, "Get in! I'll give you a ride to work!"

"I can walk," responded Moon. "I have plenty of time."

"No, you don't, the police are waiting for you at the bank. They thought you'd be to work by now."

"I don't work until nine today. It's barely eight o'clock."

"Well, they don't know that do they," demanded Lacey. "Get in already!"

Moon got in.

Tommy Williams was waiting at the bank, alone, lounging in a chair in the reception area. He stood quickly as soon as Moon and Lacey walked in and indicated an empty conference room. Lacey started toward the room also but was stopped by a no-nonsense look from Tommy. He followed Moon in and closed the door.

"Have you heard from Joy lately?" he asked coming straight to the point as he perched on the conference table.

Moon sat in a chair and indicated that Tommy should do the same.

"Not since just after that dust-up in the alley shortly after I moved, "she admitted. "I called her, wanting to smooth things over, offered her coffee and cake, but she wasn't having any of it, hung up on me after asking me if Geordie knew that I moved or what I was up to, hasn't called me or stopped by since, that I know. Why do you ask?"

"She's missing. Been missing for over a month but her husband just got around to putting in a report, wanting us to find her so he can continue with the divorce."

"Did it take him this long? Why? What's Neil been doing all this time?"

"He's been out of town, out of the country in fact. And yes, we've already checked. We will be checking a lot of other things about him, meanwhile we are hoping Joy turns up on her own. We will be looking at financials to see if her credit cards have been used recently but I need you to keep trying to get in touch with her, ask around if anyone has seen her, and LET ME KNOW if you hear from her. Can you do that for me?" Tommy softened his tone, regretting his outburst. He was obviously worried about Joy, and it showed.

"Sue Branwell's daughter, Abby, saw her a few months ago with some man in her car, Abby didn't recognize him. She was all worried and told Sue about it. I didn't think much about it at the time but now it has me concerned."

"Who was driving?" Tommy had his notebook out and was scribbling quickly.

"Abby said that Joy was, but you'd better talk to her in case I don't have the story straight. Have you called her dad? She was always closer to him than she was to me."

"Not yet," Tommy admitted. "Do you know where he is these days? Have you kept in touch?"

"No," Moon said shortly, and Tommy looked up from his notebook, surprised.

"It was that bad?" he asked softly. Moon nodded.

"Ask Joy's husband." Moon suggested. "He should know where Geordie is."

Tommy made another note on his pad. "Okay, Sue and Abby, Geordie, any other of her friends that you can think of?"

Moon shook her head sadly. "I don't know Joy's friends anymore. She didn't have much time for me the last few years, except when she was afraid that I was going to have to move in with her. I think she blames me for the marriage breaking up, you know. Like I should have done something more, or even something!"

"You did the best you could, at the time," responded Tommy. "We all watched the whole thing implode and we hurt for you and for Joy, but we felt powerless to help either of you. I imagine you felt powerless too. The thing is to find Joy now and make sure she is safe." He put his notepad in his pocket as he stood to go. Moon stood too, wanting to give him a hug, remembering the boy who had raided her cookie jar at her daughter's urging, but put off by the uniform and authority.

"You have my business card, call me if anything new turns up, or you hear from her." He was professional now, Officer Williams, back on the job.

Moon escorted him from the conference room before returning to her own desk. For a long time, she sat there with her head in her hands wondering how it had all gone so wrong with Joy. Should she try to contact Geordie? Or let the police question him about Joy's friends. Who were her friends, and who was the young man in her car that day? Would Neil know? Should she call him? There was no friendliness between them, it might open a hornet's nest of angry accusations and recriminations on both parts, which would get them no closer to finding Joy.

'Do nothing for the moment, let the police handle it—and pray!' she decided as she prepared for her first client. That much she could do.

Moon didn't have to worry about calling Geordie after all. She had no sooner finished her evening dishes a few days later than the phone rang, Private Caller on the I.D. that she had finally talked herself into buying, *'Technology!'* For a scared moment she let the phone ring, refusing to answer it. Finally, shaking, thinking it might be the police with news about Joy or more questions, she picked up the receiver, "Hello?"

"Margaret? It's Geordie. Can...we talk? About Joy? Did you know she's missing? Have you heard from her?"

"I heard, from Tommy Williams," Moon sat down heavily in a chair by the phone. "Do you remember him? He was part of the group

Joy hung around with in junior high and high school—he's a police officer now."

"I remember him. The cookie thief," Geordie almost laughed, then caught himself. "Have you seen her recently? She used to call me every week, then once a month, then…nothing. I know she and 'what's his name' were having issues," Geordie growled. "Never should have married him!"

"You and I have no right to give advice on the subject of marriage-we made enough of a hash of our own," Moon admonished gently. Geordie coughed but didn't agree or disagree.

"Where the hell are you these days?" he demanded. "I went by the apartments a while back, but they were all empty except for a couple of squatters. Thought you might be among them. I didn't want to go to the bank, not with Lacey still working there…"

"How do you know she still works at the bank?" Moon asked curiously, avoiding the question of where she lived. She wasn't sure she wanted Geordie poking around her nice home, not until she knew how things were going with him.

"Her son, Geoff, told me. I see him now and then at Fitz's Bar."

'I wonder if Lacey knows about that?' Moon mused to herself. Aloud she offered, "Why don't we meet at the diner for coffee, we can talk about it and see if there is something, we can do to help Joy."

"Don't want me to see where you live?" asked Geordie shrewdly. "Shacked up with some guy you don't want me to meet? Afraid I'll spoil it for you? Or maybe you're living out of your car—no, you can't because YOU SOLD IT," he yelled.

Moon sat for a moment in shocked silence. *'Why does he care? More to the point, why do I let him get to me this way,'* she thought. Then she pulled herself together. "Meet me at one o'clock tomorrow at the diner if you want to talk," she offered. "Good night, Geordie."

Moon hung up, thought about leaving the phone off the hook, but decided against it in case Joy called. She settled herself in her favorite chair to read and listen to the evening classics as her dad had always done after supper, but she found she couldn't concentrate. The phone kept ringing until well after midnight and the I.D. always said, "Private Caller".

"You hung up on me!" Geordie accused as he slid into the booth across from her. He was a tall man, clean shaven, middle aged, with gray at the temples of his dark brown hair. Once neatly cut and styled, it was now collar-length giving him a rakish look. He still wore the horn-rimmed glasses he had always favored; his blue jeans were clean and mended at the knee. Moon noted the recycled army shirt and high-top sneakers and thought, *'he really hasn't grown up at all, but then again, neither have I. We are still the "kids" we were back when we were dating.'*

"I said good-bye first," She reminded him as she stirred the chicken soup the waitress brought.

"You said coffee," Geordie said petulantly. Moon poured him a cup of coffee from the pot on the table and set the sugar and creamer in front of him. "And what have you done to yourself?"

Again, she ignored him, silently gritting her teeth. It was getting harder and harder not to lash out at him.

"It's my lunch hour," she said quietly, ignoring the second remark. "Have you heard from Joy?"

"No. I would like to rattle the cage of that husband of hers. I am sure he's behind this!"

"You may be right, but let the police handle it. Just because Neil called in the 'missing person's report' doesn't mean he is in the clear. When did they file for divorce?"

"Divorce? Who said they filed for divorce!" Geordie demanded.

"Officer Williams said that's why Neil is looking for her, so they can finalize the divorce," Moon was surprised. "You didn't know? Well, okay, neither did I. Strange, isn't it?" She finished her soup and set her bowl to the side.

"Boyfriend joining us?" Geordie asked snidely as he ordered a cheeseburger and fries. "Is that why you're all spiffed up?" His eyes took in her dark green sweater, simple strand of pearls, tweed skirt, and dark green suede boots, resting his gaze on her shoulder length page boy haircut and freshened color. "Make-up too? He must be worth impressing. Someone from the bank? You are going after money?"

Moon ignored the overture. "Joy did say a while back that the relations weren't good between them. I'm going to have Tommy check on that divorce-see if they really filed. It might be a lead, but from what I remember, the respondent doesn't have to be present for the divorce to be finalized, only the initiator of the case."

Geordie looked surprised but again, she ignored it. No point in baiting him if she wanted to walk out of this unscathed. She signaled the waitress for her check and began gathering her purse and coat. To her surprise, Geordie took the check before she could pick it up.

"On me, for a change," he said sheepishly. "I was way out of line just now, and you didn't hit back. I would have deserved it. You do look genuinely nice today-you've changed Margaret."

Now it was her turn to be surprised. He rarely used her given name since he had learned of it decades ago except for their wedding vows, and even then, he had half-jokingly offered to substitute "Moon" for her full name. The minister had not been amused.

"Thank you. It was 'nice' seeing you again, Geordie, and thank you for lunch. Let me know if you hear from Joy, please?" Moon gathered up her things and left the restaurant before the good feelings could deteriorate. She realized later that leaving Geordie with the lunch check had been a mistake. Officer Williams could find no record of a divorce filing, Neil was also missing, and Geordie had left without paying for either of their meals.

"He did WHAT?" Sue was astonished at Geordie's nerve. "I knew he had changed from the man you married, but I didn't think he would stoop to theft! How did you find out?"

Sue and Moon were having coffee and very stale Christmas cookies (Abby's first efforts on her own) in Sue's kitchen, Moon still avoiding her phone which had been ringing a lot lately with calls from "Private Caller". Moon refused to answer them. She contemplated getting an answering machine so she wouldn't have to be bothered.

"The diner called me at work the next day and I paid the checks over the phone. I don't know about Geordie anymore. Something is wrong, but I don't want to get caught up in it. It's like he is now where I was a few years ago. He even accused me of "shacking up" with someone, of having a rich boyfriend, and he seems angry that I wasn't homeless and living in my car. He yelled at me for selling it. I never liked that car anyway. he 'granted' it to me in the divorce, so I would have a vehicle, that's probably why he's angry: I have rejected his 'largess'. Did you know he hangs out at Fitz's with Lacey's son? That's what he claims."

"I wonder if she knows about that?" Sue mused. "She would raise the roof if she found her 'precious baby' frequenting a dive like Fitz's."

"I wondered the same thing. Geordie says that's how he knew that Lacey works at the bank with me. And I expect that's how he found out I sold my car. Good thing no one told him where I live now, there would be no end of trouble from him."

"How do you know that no one told him or that he hasn't found out."

"Because he asked, no, demanded to know where I was staying. He went to the old apartment but couldn't find me so he kind of freaked out. I guess Joy didn't tell him where I moved. She doesn't keep in touch with him the way she used to."

"This is a small town and people love to talk about other people's business. Someone is going to tell him eventually," Sue warned. "Better be prepared."

How?' Moon wondered. *'Should I let Tommy Williams know?'* She sipped her coffee in silence. Finally, she asked the question she had been wanting to ask Abby. "Any idea who the man was with Joy in the car that day?"

"I forgot to tell you! They found him, two days ago, at a gas station. Abby saw him filling up his car—a different one, not Joy's, and called Officer Williams right away on her cell phone. He's an ex-con, no warrants out for him now, I guess his car was in the shop, so he begged for a ride from Joy to see his probation officer in Columbus because he knew she was going that way. He said she dropped him off and left, headed west out of town. He hasn't seen or heard from her since. Tommy checked out the story with the P. O. and I guess the guy was telling the truth. Small lead that she was heading west but not much to go on. Tommy said there are bulletins out for the car and Joy, but no one has called anything in yet."

"Wonder why he didn't tell me?" Moon looked hurt.

"Because it was a dead end of sorts," Sue comforted. "I only heard about it because Abby saw the man, called Tommy, and told me later."

"So, nothing important enough to move this along. Where would she be going? Why would Neil claim filing for a divorce that doesn't exist? Where is Neil now?" Moon wasn't about to be lulled into a sense of security. "And what part is Geordie playing in all this? I wonder if he only met me at the diner to score a free meal and some information! You know, I love living alone but sometimes I wonder if it is the safest thing for me, with all this going on."

"You may have a point," Sue conceded. "But I wouldn't want you to jump into anything like taking in a roommate. Not yet anyway. Why don't you sign up for some self-defense classes first, and maybe think about getting a dog as a companion. They don't pay rent, but they don't steal your silver, either." Sue laughed.

"Hmmm," Moon responded, remembering the cat who had hated her. "No promises on that front. I can't see taking on an animal right now. My place is clean and neat, and I would like to keep it that way, thank you. And what would I do with a dog when I go to work? They HOWL when left alone! No, I don't think my neighbors would appreciate that! It's not a good idea, not for me, not yet."

Sue said nothing, knowing that the seed had been planted. Moon would keep coming back to the idea until she decided it had been her idea the whole time and go down to the pound. She would want to rescue a homeless dog, perhaps a beagle like the one she had loved as a teenager. Moon had hated to part with that dog when she married Geordie, but she wouldn't have been able to keep it. Geordie was adamant: no animals. Her cat had been an act of rebellion that had backfired; Moon was not a 'cat person' and the cat had figured that out early in the relationship. At that point it had become a cold war between two unhappy housemates. A dog, on the other hand, would fit Moon's personality perfectly.

"But I will look into the self-defense classes. Maybe Tommy knows where some are offered. Better yet, come with me! We can take the class together; it will be fun, and you can keep me from quitting halfway through."

"That's not a bad idea," Sue mused. "You find the classes and I will come along." She gathered up the plates and mugs, setting them in the sink. "Abby can wash these later. Come on, I'll give you a ride home."

"I can walk, it's not that far and it's a nice evening."

Sue sighed. "Have it your way. When are you going to buy a bicycle? Call me when you get home, so I know you're ok."

"Will do. I'll be fine." Moon ignored the bicycle question.

"I'd feel better if you were walking a dog home!" Sue muttered as Moon stepped off the porch.

"I heard that," laughed Moon. But she was extra vigilant all the way back to her house.

7

Richard and Another Cat

Spring took its time showing up that year, but eventually green sprouts began to show up around the house. Moon watched them eagerly, anticipating the flowers to come. She hadn't paid much attention to the plants next to the house when she signed the contracts, being more concerned about a place to live before being evicted, but she had noticed chrysanthemums on the north, thought she remembered some peony plants on the east side beyond the kitchen door, as well as the grape arbors outside the bathroom window. She was thrilled to find tulips, crocus, and hyacinth on the west by the porch. She would be careful of the bulbs if and when she planted her hydrangeas. There were also irises on the south side of the house and hostas cuddled in away from the peonies in the shade along the border with the next property to the east of her. It was a good start.

Geordie stopped trying to call her, probably embarrassed about ditching the check, at least she hoped he was. There was only occasional word from Officer Williams. No one had reported seeing either Neil or Joy, so the case remained open and cold until one or both had been sighted.

Moon and Sue completed their first round of self-defense classes: Sue signed the youth group up for lessons and Moon continued to advanced classes, adding Tai Chi to the list. Her weight was now nearly down to her high school size: she looked and felt thirty-something rather than fifty. Soon she would be updating and altering her closet yet again. A bicycle was finally on her list of planned purchases for that summer; something with a wire basket for carrying packages. And a garden hat. Yes, a garden hat.

Men were starting to notice Moon, at work, at church, and in the community. One of the tellers at the bank, Richard Lemanski, a widower who had worked there for a couple years after retiring from his previous career in sales asked her out for coffee, then for dinner. She enjoyed Richard's company. She whispered to Sue that Saturday as they selected their weekly books from the library, that she hoped he would ask her out again. He was intelligent with a college degree in business, a home of his own, two grown sons, three grandchildren, and a cat that he adored.

"But then again, nobody's perfect, right?" Moon mused.

Sue just laughed. "I thought for sure the cat would be a deal-breaker. What kind is it?"

"Siamese. And if I don't have to live with it, I can stand it. I may have to get a dog after all, just to even the score!"

"Oh, my," Sue choked. "You are serious about this guy! What kind of dog are we talking, here?"

"Hmmmm. I don't know," mused Moon. "Something not too large, not too small. I wonder what they have at the pound. I think you might have had a good idea after all. The self-defense classes are great, and I feel safer because of them, but I see how happy Richard is with his cat. You are also right: I do miss my beagle puppy. Maybe as the weather warms up and I want to take it for walks. We'll see...."

Sue said nothing; Moon was particularly good at talking herself into (and out of) things. Better not to push. Moon could be very stubborn. She had been stubborn about marrying Geordie, stubborn about not seeing her marriage disintegrate, stubborn about not caring about herself or anyone else after the final explosion. And now Moon was being stubborn about putting her life back together. She had come a long way in the past year. Patience!

"So, if he already has a college degree, why is he starting out all over again as a lowly teller? What's going on with that?" Sue artfully changed the subject.

"Oh, didn't I tell you," Moon considered a book, a mystery by an unknown author, put it back, then changed her mind, adding it to her basket. "He is only part time as a teller now, just to help out when we are shorthanded. He is middle management, working his way through the ranks of the bank upper echelon, by his own choice. He wants a Vice President position, but he wants to understand all levels of the organization first. Very thorough, I suppose..." her voice trailed off as she considered choosing a second book by the same author.

"I, well, it sounds a bit over-the-top if you ask me. Seems like he would already understand all this, with a degree in business," mused Sue.

"Um," Moon wasn't listening. Maybe she was still thinking about that puppy. The friends made their final selections and parted at the parking lot, but Sue remained uneasy. On a whim, she dug her cell phone out of her bag to leave a voice message for Officer Williams, a hint to check out this 'Richard Lemanski'.

Moon was indeed thinking about a puppy: the little beagle mix she had raised as a teenager. Chowder, he was called, after the first food he had stolen from the counter. Mother had left a bowl of corn chowder unattended on the kitchen counter. The resourceful starving puppy had climbed from the floor to the chair to the table to the counter to avail himself of a good meal. Mother was first scandalized, then amused at the planning that went into the raid. The incident later became a favorite family story, told often at parties. Chowder. Moon remembered her wedding day, saying a last goodbye to her most faithful friend, knowing that his life would be happier staying with her parents, even if he didn't understand it. Geordie was rabidly anti-pet. Joy had not been allowed even a bird or a fish as a companion. Would things have been different if she had been allowed to have her dog? No way to tell but Moon wondered. As she left her shoes on the rack by the door before putting her library books on the bookshelf reserved for them and thinking about the hot dish she was planning for dinner, she caught herself looking around for Chowder, certain she heard his nails clicking on the hardwood floors. Did her rent-to-own lease say anything about pets? Maybe she should check after supper.

Happy with the way her home was progressing, she turned on the wooden RCA radio on her kitchen counter, threw on a pink flowered apron over her new embroidered shirt and jeans (she had done the embroidery herself and was pleased with the result), ready to begin putting together the spaghetti casserole that had been her father's favorite. Mother had used canned spaghetti when Moon was little, but she preferred to cook the pasta fresh before combining it with ground beef, marinara sauce and fresh peas. It took longer but Moon liked the result better and there would be more than enough to freeze for a meal when she was too tired or too busy to cook. She was just ready to drain the pasta when she heard a voice at the back door: "Is there extra spaghetti or are you putting it all in that awful hot dish?"

Geordie stood on the back porch, laughing at her through the locked screen.

"Geordie. What timing! What do you want?"

"Dinner. And an apology."

Moon turned off the heat under the spaghetti, leaving the sauce on low to heat up before adding it to the mix.

"I'm not sure I owe you either," she ventured, wishing she had invested in a cell phone. She doubted she could reach her landline and dial 911 before it was too late.

"You misunderstand me, I owe YOU an apology, a lot of them, and I really was hoping for dinner. I always liked your spaghetti. Especially the kind you made with the bacon and all the fresh vegetables."

"Irish spaghetti," Moon remembered that it had been Joy's favorite as well. "Have you heard from Joy?" she enquired.

"I have," Geordie held up an envelope. "Let me in, call Officer Williams, and I will share all the news I have. For the small price of a plate of spaghetti. Deal"

"Why don't you call Tommy?"

"No phone now. Let me in and I will explain everything."

Moon reached for the phone, keeping an eye on Geordie. When the call connected, the dispatcher promised to send Officer Williams over immediately. Moon set the receiver down but not securely in the cradle. Just in case. She flipped the hook on the back-door screen as she switched on the porch light. In the distance the evening church bells formed a counterpoint melody with the whistle of the late-afternoon freight train coming into the city limits. She paused a moment to listen before turning back to dinner preparations. Meanwhile Geordie had taken off his jacket, making himself at home on a kitchen chair.

"What happened to the table?" he asked.

"Storage," she replied, declining to say where. She drained the pasta, setting some aside to give to Geordie before mixing the rest with sauce, meat, and peas. She added some sauce to Geordie's spaghetti, beckoning him to move to the dining room for the meal. She set out salt and grated cheese before returning to the kitchen to dish up her own meal. Through the screen door she saw Tommy Williams' squad car pull up in the alley. Silently she set the phone securely in its place disconnecting the call.

"What would you like to drink?" she called to Geordie. "I have milk, wine, water, and I can make coffee."

"Better do the coffee," Geordie replied. "The police just pulled up." Moon flipped the switch on the coffee maker as Tommy knocked on the back door. "Join us?" She indicated the casserole: Tommy declined.

"I'll wait for the coffee, and a cookie, if you have any," he grinned.

Moon carried her plate to the dining room, gestured Tommy to sit as she took her usual place.

"There's enough for seconds for you if you want," she told Geordie. I made extra to freeze for later."

"Down to business," he announced handing the envelope to Officer Williams. "This came in the mail yesterday. I didn't get it in until tonight, came right here to tell Moon."

'And check out the house, score a free meal, as well as anything else you can get!' Moon thought sourly. She kept her eyes on her plate to avoid saying something she would later regret, probably while she was sitting in a holding cell, awaiting arraignment on disorderly conduct charges!

Officer Williams read the letter through two- or three-times making notes as he did so, the coffee maker in the kitchen bubbled and sighed as it expelled the fragrant brew, Moon ate in silence paying careful attention to each bite, Geordie eyed the neat rooms visible from his seat at the table, taking in every visible inch of the little bungalow. Moon desperately wished she had bought a dog.

Finally, Tommy passed the letter to Moon.

"Have you seen this?"

"Not yet. Geordie brought it by tonight, just before I called you.

"Read it," he urged. As Moon read, he turned his attention to Geordie. Insert letter from Joy.

"You said this was delivered yesterday?" he accused. "It's dated last week. Is this the first you have heard from Joy since she was reported missing?"

"She, uh, doesn't keep in touch the way she used to. I guess she didn't feel especially welcome around my girlfriend, then she took up with Neil, married him."

"What do you mean, 'she didn't feel especially welcome around' your girlfriend?" Moon looked up sharply from Joy's letter.

Geordie looked a bit sheepish as he cleaned up the last of the sauce from his plate. "Wonderful, as always, Moon."

"Thank you. Don't change the subject: what do you mean, 'she didn't feel especially welcome around' your girlfriend?" she repeated, laying down the note paper.

"Later." Tommy brought the subject back. "Is that Joy's handwriting? It doesn't look the way I remember it."

"I think so," Geordie responded, pushing back his chair. "Is there more?" Moon nodded, collected his plate for seconds.

"I recognize certain letters that are particular to Joy's way of writing: The way the tail of the 'M' in 'Mother' dips down below the line, the way the 'L' in 'Love' loops around, the break between some of the letters that should be joined but aren't. That's Joy. Grandma had similar penmanship," she answered from the kitchen. "But I don't understand the letter. Is she alright or not? Did she leave on her own? What is she running away from? When is she coming back? Most importantly, WHERE IS SHE?"

In the kitchen Moon put her head in her hands and sobbed in sheer frustration.

"I can't answer that right now," said Tommy softly as she returned to the table with more spaghetti, a plate of cookies to go with the coffee. "All I read in that letter is that she's fine, she doesn't want you to worry about her. I don't know if she was forced to write the letter, under some kind of threat, or exactly where she is but I will trace that postmark and see if I can locate her. Has either of you heard from Neil?" Both shook their heads. "Okay then he will remain a 'person of interest' until we know more. May I?" He held out his hand for the letter.

Tommy glared at Geordie. "Now, can I trust you to behave yourself? I need to get back on patrol, I don't want to get a call from dispatch to break up an altercation here. I heard all about the scene at the Downtown Diner. You owe Moon an apology for that. She paid the bill you ditched the next day, otherwise they would have pressed charges."

Geordie turned red around the ears. "I, uh, I meant to treat her to lunch, but I found I left my wallet at home. When I went home to get it, well there were some problems, so I forgot and didn't remember for a couple of days."

"Bullshit." Tommy pushed his chair back to the table. "This is me, remember? I watched how you treated Moon years ago and you are still disrespecting a lady who doesn't deserve it. Knock it off, or you will have me to deal with. Understand? No more. And if I hear you have been mistreating Joy in any way or if Neil has, I will deal with that issue as well. Am I making myself clear?"

Geordie started to say something, thought better of it, nodded in agreement. Moon sat silent, drinking her coffee.

"My advice," Tommy said kindly, "is finish your dinner, say 'Thank you' and be on your way. She's doing okay now, Geordie. She's getting her life back, whether you and Joy approve or not. Joy gave her a terrible time when she moved here last spring. I suspect now that it had more to do with Joy's problems than with concern for her mother, but Moon handled it fine and she's doing okay. Leave her alone unless you can be a positive influence in her life! Now, you have a good night, sir." Tommy touched his cap. After hugging Moon who had begun packing up leftovers for freezing and running dishwater, he climbed into his squad car, answering the squawking radio that was calling him to another location. He hoped Geordie would take his advice, that he wouldn't have to come back here again tonight to take him or Moon to jail.

Moon hoped so too. Watching Officer Williams pull away down the alley, she was left with misgivings about being left alone with Geordie.

"Once again, that was really good, Moon," Geordie was standing in the open door with his empty plate. "Thank you. I'd uh better get going, let you get on with you evening chores."

Moon nodded. "You are welcome. And thank you for bringing the letter over. I just hope she really is okay." She took his empty plate, added it to the dishes in the soapy water.

"Want me to dry?" Geordie asked softly. Moon shook her head.

"I have it under control," Moon smiled. "But I appreciate the offer anyway."

"It's the least I can do after pulling that stunt in the diner. I *am* sorry about that."

"Let's make a deal, we start over. From the beginning. Leave the baggage behind and go back to the way we used to be, as friends." She held out a sudsy hand for him to shake.

Geordie shook his head. "I would like to, but I need to be in a better place mentally, Moon. Give me some time, please. I've got a lot to work out first. You seem to be doing better, I admire that, but I'm not there yet. I thought I was, I thought I had a handle on all of it, but now it feels like I'm grabbing at nothing. I saw you the other day and I really resented the fact that you seemed to be doing better, that you hadn't completely collapsed without me, even after five years. It was a real mean thing to think, it made me mad at you and mad at myself for feeling that way. I want to be friends again, someday, but I'm not ready yet. Does that make sense?"

Moon eyed him critically. She remembered the Geordie she had fallen in love with so long ago and how it had hurt to lose that. His illness had taken a lot away from him, he wasn't at all the man she had loved and married. Neither was she the same. She felt like she had been through the fat and come out of the fire, newly minted into something better than she had been before. The years hadn't refined Geordie, they had weakened him. He was right. He would need more time.

"I will be here when you are ready," she told him. "I forgive you, but that doesn't mean I will put up with anymore abuse. I meant what I said, I want to start over and be friends, for both of us and for Joy. We have put her through enough, not meaning to, but we did. It's time to stop this. Have a good night, Geordie." She walked him to the door, locked it behind him. *'I really think I am going to get a dog.'*

Moon's father wasn't much of a 'pet person'. He didn't like cats at all, nor had his father before him. Michael Newsome was a busy man, a professional man, an accountant who had no time for the stray animals that always seemed to follow his wife and daughter home. He actively discouraged the cats that came calling, chasing them away with a broom. He meant them no harm; he just didn't want them to ruin his wife's flower beds.

Mr. Newsome was more tolerant of the occasional dog, but still leery of bites, fleas, as well as general dog mess. He encouraged the dogs to move along to their 'real' homes rather than to continue their stay with his family by quietly calling animal control to return the dogs to their owners.

The exception was a tricolor beagle puppy that Moon brought home from high school one day. It was the last of the litter, unclaimed, and the boy who brought it to school had been told to dispose of it. Period. 'Don't bring it home.'

Moon couldn't bear to see the little pup mistreated, abandoned or murdered so she talked the boy into giving it to her with the idea that her mother would help her save it.

Mother's help had not been necessary: the pup had taken care of the problem all by himself. After finishing a meal of puppy kibbles, it had wandered into Mr. Newsome's living room, climbed onto his lap while he was reading his evening paper, and fallen asleep. When Mother and Moon tried to remove the pup, so Father could finish his evening paper in peace, Mr. Newsome declared the puppy 'paper trained' and shooed them away before they could wake it. After the raid on the counter, 'Chowder' became the puppy's name. Moon watched as her father grew as attached to the puppy as she was, and although she missed it terribly when she moved out, she knew it would be better off remaining with Lynn and Michael Newsome. The pup did indeed live a long and comfortable life, passing away at the old age of seventeen, next to Michael Newsome's empty recliner where it had spent so many happy evenings.

Moon put the leftovers in the small chest freezer she had talked herself into buying, even though she was wary of overspending. She still had not bought a tablet or laptop, preferring to save money and use the library computer. Moon refused to put anything personal on the computer at work. She had often noticed Lacey sending e-mails to family and friends from her workstation during breaks: it made Moon shudder.

She washed the remaining dishes in the sink, reveling in the feel of the hot soapy water on her hands. Tenderly she dried each chipped, cracked plate and cup. She still hadn't been able to bring herself to purchase new dishware. Pots and pans, yes, but not plates or flatware. If the cabinets in the kitchen hadn't fallen off the wall and had to be replaced, or if the family had chipped in on the new ones, maybe she would have, but that hadn't happened. She still had some of the gift cards attached to the playing cards. Maybe if a sale came up in the future, if she found a pattern she really liked, she would replace the old china and silver. In the meantime, she carefully placed each dish in the glass front hutch of the dining room, wiped down the table, setting out clean placemats and a fresh place setting for breakfast the next morning. She watered the plants in the window, turning them to make certain each side caught the early morning sun, tidied the parlor (she had stopped calling it a 'living room' shortly after the fireplace had been delivered), dusting each surface with a soft rag. She went over the carpets in the dining room and parlor with a carpet sweeper, too uneasy about the letter from Joy and Geordie's visit to be soothed by music. Before she turned in for the night, she called Sue.

"Well, he knows where I live now."

Monday morning would mean seeing Richard at work. Moon took the time to look especially nice without being too obvious about it. She no longer wore pantsuits except on Fridays, choosing instead a navy-blue linen dress with a light blue cropped sweater that she had knitted over the winter and navy flats that she kept in the bottom drawer of her desk at work. The snow had melted enough, and the sidewalks were clear, so she wore her white trainers and a new light blue spring coat she had picked up on clearance. She tied a blue and white nylon scarf that had belonged to her mother over her hair before she set out to walk the eight blocks to the bank. She remembered how she used to stop every morning for coffee and donuts on her way to work. Now she carried a small thermos of coffee from her own pot in her tote bag, along with her library book or latest needlework project. Busy hands kept her from eating too many treats in the break room. Moon was still on the lookout for a sewing machine at a reasonable price—she really missed hers, but Geordie had given it to Joy. Lord knew where it was now. She feared buying one from the thrift stores, who knew what problems they had, but maybe a refurbished one from the vacuum repair shop downtown behind the diner was an option.

It was a pleasant walk: the buds were just starting on some of the hardier trees, south facing lawns were showing the tips of early crocus and hyacinth. Moon used the time to think about seeing Richard that day, maybe having lunch with him (she hoped), her first appointments of the day, the fund raiser at church, anything to not think about Geordie's visit. She hadn't seen or heard from him since Saturday's dinner, but she had tried Joy's cell phone again and left a message for her to call back. She had an uncomfortable feeling about the letter, about the whole visit that she could not explain or shake. Moon thought about talking to Tommy Williams again, alone. Maybe he could put her fears to rest.

She arrived exactly on time, Lacey was just pulling into the parking lot behind the bank with two of the other secretaries, John Miller, the bank president, was unlocking the side door, Richard was not there yet.

Moon waved to the secretaries and Lacey as she hung her coat, scarf folded neatly in the pocket, on a hanger behind her desk. She took a Fiesta ware mug from her top right drawer, poured herself a cup of steaming coffee while she went over the paperwork for the first of her appointments. It was a loan application for a New Home loan: a young couple moving up from an apartment into a place of their own. Moon hoped that they had all their documents ready when they came in later that morning. She really wanted to help them qualify for the money to buy the house they had set their hearts on. It was a newer ranch-style on the east side of town. There was a small subdivision being built there that was attracting a lot of young couples. Moon remembered that it had been an outdoor drive-in theater when she, Geordie, and Sue had all been in high school. Geordie had driven over from the next town to take both girls and Sue's two younger siblings to a movie there on summer weekend nights. Geordie had never minded having the youngsters along. They were well-behaved and making out during the movie had never appealed to either Moon or Geordie. Even the dark drive-in was too public for that sort of thing, though other couples did. Moon and Geordie preferred more privacy. Now the huge screen, concession stand, parking lot and speakers were all cleared away, four homes were built, and more were planned. They were selling quickly: the young couple would be lucky to get one of the proposed homes due to be ready by Thanksgiving. Ground had already been broken for two of them. She made a few notes on pad, paperclipped the sheet to the application, set it aside to go on to the next.

Richard arrived at work around ten o'clock. Moon was with a client, so she didn't catch a glimpse of him until her break. She took her knitting and coffee to the break room, bought a cereal bar for a midmorning snack, settling in to listen to the gossip, Richard didn't join them. Instead, he was closeted with John Miller until lunch, leading to rampant speculation. Was he being fired? Transferred? Promoted? Demoted? Moon had plenty of thoughts on the subject but offered no comment.

Lunch was a treat: soup and half a sandwich at the Diner. Moon didn't even bother with her coat, regretted it, told herself that it was good for her circulation to jog through the cool spring weather. At least it wasn't raining.

The afternoon went by the same way: clients, break, gossip, until it was time for Moon to leave for the day. She packed up her tote bag, buttoned up her coat with one hand while pulling her scarf out of her pocket with the other. It was then that she discovered the note tucked into the folds of the scarf. "I WILL CALL YOU LATER, RICHARD."

'Interesting,' thought Moon. *'He must have put it in my pocket when I was at the Diner.' A watery sun shone* as she walked through town. *'Wouldn't it be nice to walk a dog on a day like this? And wouldn't it be a pain in the middle of a snowstorm!'* she laughed. Still, it seemed as though Chowder's shadow followed her all the way home.

Richard called that evening, but Moon was out behind the house checking out the grape arbor and daydreaming of home-made jelly.

Officer Williams also called so Moon was finally able to voice her suspicions about the letter and Geordie's visit. Tommy was quiet for several beats after Moon finished.

"I didn't want to say anything, I didn't want to worry you. We have been keeping an eye on your house for about a week now. Your neighbors reported a man walking around your house when you weren't home or late at night. We talked to the family that owns the place, but it isn't any of them. Most of them are out of the area until the next probate hearing in June and now they are concerned as well. I don't want them to find a reason to break the contract with you, so I promised them we would look into it. We haven't caught anyone, but Geordie is certainly a person of interest. Please be careful. Call me immediately if anything seems out of the ordinary, or if you don't feel safe. Maybe get a cell phone, yes, I know you don't have one. But you should, for your own safety."

`"I will think about it," Moon promised, but she shuddered at the extra expense. Maybe one of the cheap, disposable ones that only had a limited number of minutes, but what if she ran out of minutes just when she needed it in an emergency. This was a problem. She might be able to afford it if she gave up her landline, but she wasn't sure she wanted to do that. "I *will* think about it, Tommy. I promise. In the meantime, let me know if anything turns up about Neil or Joy."

"I will. And I suggest you give Geordie a wide berth for now. Until I find out what's going on. Something is not quite right, but I can't put my finger on it."

"Have you talked to his girlfriend? There were planning on getting married a while back."

"See, that also doesn't make sense, because they broke up some time ago and he's not with her or anyone else, as far as we know. He still works for the paper but only part time and the address he gave as his home is actually hers. He hasn't lived there for over a year now. And, by the way, he sold his BMW—some fellow in Columbus owns it now."

Moon caught her breath. What was going on here? Joy missing, Geordie on the outs with Victoria, the woman he had left Moon for, his beloved car sold, and someone was evidently watching her house, other than the police.

"Relax, we've got this," Tommy reassured her. "Just go about your usual routine, avoid Geordie, call us if you notice anything out of the ordinary, and we will have your back." Moon hung up the phone wishing again that she had bought a dog or advertised for a room-mate.

Grandma had a flower garden in the back of the house: roses, lilies, pop-pies, pansies, marigolds geraniums, petunias, peonies, hostas, coleus, lily-of-the-valley. Moon helped weed until Grandma discovered mulch—she loved the mix of scents. There had been an old stone bench under the birch tree where Mama and Grandma sat with their knitting (the porch swing was Moon's territory). Beyond the flower garden were Grandma's grape arbors and berry patches: gooseberries, raspberries, blackberries, strawberries. Once upon a time Grandma had cultivated a larger garden with bean poles, radishes, tomatoes, lettuces and carrots. She even had a few pumpkins and some Indian corn for autumn decoration. As she got older, the garden got smaller until it was just the flowers, berry bushes, and sometimes a few toma-toes by the back porch. She said she could get all the produce she needed from the farmers' stalls on the square, often bartering cleaning help or needlework for vegetables to can. Fresh all summer, canned in the winter.

Moon craved the garden of her childhood, almost as much as she wanted the fireplace. There was far less yard at her new place, and not all of it was sunny enough for vegetables, still she had managed some tomatoes, peas, spinach, and flowers the summer before There were already grape arbors be-hind the house; berry patches could wait until next year.

Moon put her thoughts about Joy and Geordie out of her mind to concentrate on her home, her job, her tai chi classes. She convinced herself that the best way to handle things was to let Officer Williams do his job without interference from her. She and Sue were busily planning to expand the small garden in a sunny spot of the side yard: lettuce *and* tomatoes this year, more in the years to come. Moon was also making careful note of the flowers already in residence and dreaming of adding more. Only early spring flowers seemed to be growing in front of the porch, so Moon went to a plant show and bought five hydrangea plants. It would take them awhile to settle in, but the blooms someday would be worth the wait.

Moon contacted the family and received written permission to re-paint the outside of the bungalow, as long as she stayed with the same white color. Moon had no problem with that, but she set up a spe-cial account at the bank that would be used to put maintenance-free siding and better insulation on the house as soon as the rent-to-own agreement was up so the house was completely hers.

Meanwhile the front bedroom remained empty; there was nothing she really wanted to put there, and she liked the empty feel of the room. Her notebook had a dozen suggestions for the possible use of the space (sunroom for plants, spare bedroom for guests, reading room or library/sewing room among others) but nothing really pulled at her, so she left it alone until she could find exactly the right use.

She still took her clothes to the laundromat, often on a Thursday evening when the place was less busy. The walk was neither as far nor as difficult as she had first feared. Though she longed for her own machines, the laundry-room/pantry remained mostly a dream: the shelves holding canned and bottled goods kept Moon supplied for meals, but she held off on running the plumbing and extra electric for a washer and dryer. It would not do to upset the family with too many changes. She did get estimates from some plumbers and filed them away with her rent receipts for the day she decided to go ahead with the project. She also kept a garment rack there for old pantsuits she loved but could no longer wear, planning for the day she could buy a good sewing machine to alter them. The high school sometimes upgraded their home economics machines and sold the used ones. Moon had hopes.

So, the wishlist in her notebook grew: new dishes, plants and a small garden shed, siding, shutters, a "real" fireplace, plumbing for washer and dryer, new stove and refrigerator, sewing machine, coat hooks in the front hall, ceiling lights/fans for the dining room and living room, bookcases, bicycle, 'and a raise in salary to pay for it all,' she thought ruefully.

Richard hadn't been seen in the bank since Monday, the day Moon found the note in the pocket of her coat. Rumors flew but of course no one knew anything for certain. Even Lacey, usually a reliable source of information, insisted that she had no clue about his where-abouts. He hadn't tried to call Moon again, nor had he answered her return call. Truly he had vanished into the spring rainstorms that buffeted Jefferson. Moon dodged raindrops, (she almost regretted not having a car), and hoped that Richard and Joy were ok wherever they were. Following Officer Williams advice, she upgraded the locks on the house, installed motion sensor lights on the back door to match the ones on the front and added her address to a neighborhood watch list, only to find it was already there, courtesy of the altercation with

Joy over the trash left behind in the old apartment. *'Got to love the Crawfords,'* Moon thought.

Work on the demolition of her old apartment building was nearly done. Now there were a number of differing opinions among the secretaries about what was to replace it since the original plan had been abandoned. Finally, their curiosity was satisfied by Lacey who had handled the bank's part in the finances.

"They are putting in an office complex with two small penthouses for clients' use, FAR out of your price range," she remarked to Moon over coffee in the break room. "Although the way you are throwing away money on new clothes, fancy dye jobs, and a house you can't afford perhaps you are better set than we think you are—or is someone else footing the bill? It all came on VERY SUDDENLY a year ago."

Everyone sat in shocked silence while Moon seethed. Lacey had a reputation for snarky comments, but she had never gone so far as to be outright mean before. Her comments echoed Joy's vitriol and Geordie's rudeness. Where was all this coming from? Jealousy?

'Pure vinegar bottled to look like salad dressing!' The phrase suddenly popped into Moon's head, and she almost laughed.

"Oh, Lacey," she said gently. "You mustn't listen to the gossip your son brings home from hanging out with Geordie at Fritz's Bar. Try watching reality T.V instead like everybody else does. Mercy, is that the time?" She poured her cold coffee down the drain, rinsed her cup before returning to her desk. She didn't know whether to laugh or cry, so she chose to laugh. She could just imagine what Sue would say! "WISHBONE!" She put it out of her mind the rest of the afternoon until she checked her interbank memos at the end of the day to find one, unsigned, that simply read 'Liars are not welcome here or anywhere else. Be careful!" 'Then why is Lacey still working here?' she wondered.

8

Lacey Escalates

"Happy Birthday!" Sue, Jim, and Abby trilled as Sue brought out a small cake that Abby had baked and decorated. Josh eyed the dessert distrustfully but didn't say anything. He had been forced to sample enough of Abby's experiments to be wary, although lately her creations had been what he considered to be 'passible'.

Moon was surprised and delighted. Sue had promised not to fuss when she invited Moon to dinner on her birthday because 'no one should have to cook on their birthday.' Moon agreed and rode over after work on her new bicycle, her birthday present to herself, laughing all the while about her 'fat women riding around on bicycles' comment to Sue a year ago. She had a basket for carrying things, a light and reflectors for night riding even though she had little reason to ride after dark. Sue was delighted. She at once began pestering Jim about buying bicycles for themselves, which caused Josh and Abby to flee the room in disgust. The idea of OLD people riding bicycles!?!

Sue had fixed a pork roast with baked apple slices, new potatoes cooked with the roast, green bean casserole (Moon's childhood favorite) to go with Abby's cake.

"If I keep eating like this, I will be back to living in Muumuus except that I threw them all out!" Moon sighed, refusing a second piece of cake that was surprisingly good. Josh looked astonished. Abby merely glowed.

"I'll send a piece with you—you can have it with your lonely supper tomorrow night," Sue offered. "Do you remember your birthday last year?"

"How could I forget? Short of my divorce it was the worst day of my life! I don't remember celebrating at all: I only remember finding out that I was being evicted from that dump I was living in. I even took off work early and binged on ice cream at home, I was so upset. Everyone else could see it coming except me: even the cat had a plan to leave!

"It made friends with my neighbor and her cat—-now it's living in splendor out in the country. I'm glad for the cat, but good riddance! And I remember going out to lunch with you the next day: you gave me the push to start moving on finally, and I thank you. You made me think, really think, about what I wanted to do with my life."

"Well, you've come a long way in the past year," Jim said. "Sue and I are proud of what you've done with your little cottage."

"You should see her wish list notebook!" Sue exclaimed, "Which brings me to your present. Now, don't scold me, I found it at an estate sale, still in its box, never used. The mother bought it for her daughter who had already bought her own, so it sat in the closet—and now it's yours," Sue gestured to Josh who brought in a large box from the front hall closet. The picture on the carton showed a newish portable Singer sewing machine.

"You and your estate sales!" Moon exclaimed.

"Well, it beats furnishing your hovel with castoffs from the Salvation Army and Goodwill!" Sue laughed.

"Touché," declared Moon, hugging her. "Now I get to figure out how I am going to get it home on my new bicycle!"

"Nonsense," Jim glanced at Sue. "We can drop it off tomorrow anytime you wish. Or Sunday, after service if that is more convenient. And now I will leave you ladies, I have a sermon to work on."

Moon collected her extra piece of cake, took one last grateful look at the sewing machine, before steadying her bicycle while she hugged

Sue. "Why do I get the feeling that you would have come up with a washer and dryer if you could have managed it?"

"Well, there was a set available for sale, but it was gone before I had a chance to put in a bid," Sue admitted.

"Don't you dare!" Moon exclaimed. "The sewing machine is lovely, but a lot of the rest will have to wait until I own the place. I can't incur a lot of expense or it may cause the family to try to raise the purchase price. I only have four more years, then I can do as I please. I hope."

"I'll bring the machine over tomorrow afternoon. Do you know where you are going to set it up?" Sue asked.

"In the laundry room/pantry for now. I may bring the old kitchen table and chair down from the attic to sew on."

"I will help you. The two of us can wrestle it down in no time."

"I accept! Now I am out of here before I wind up riding in the dark! By the way, I found a birthday card from Richard in the mail before I rode over. They transferred him to another branch out of state. His cat hates the new place. Picky little animals, aren't they? I really must think about getting a dog. I think the people across the alley would keep an eye on it while I am at work, if I asked nicely."

"Are you serious?" Sue called out but Moon only waved as she rode away.

Moon could barely wait to haul the table downstairs to the pantry, but she remembered what a tussle it had been to get it up to the attic in the first place, so she contented herself with bringing down the old kitchen chair and measuring to figure out where to put the table. The pantry shelves took up two walls, the garment rack sat against the third, leaving one wall for the someday washer and dryer. Outlets were scarce but if she put the table in the exact center of the room and faced the back wall, she could access the outlet above the bottom shelf and use the table for counter space now, for folding laundry later. It seemed like the perfect solution.

As Moon was leaving for church the next morning (walking, not riding), Ellen Crawford, the neighbor across the alley hurried up to her.

"We just thought you ought to know, Paul saw someone on your porch yesterday when you were out. A man, tall, wearing a hooded jacket, and it looked like he was trying your doors to see if they were unlocked. We called the police right away, they drove by, but the man was gone by then. He wasn't anyone we recognized, that's why we were concerned. He left right away—but we still thought you should know."

Moon was stunned. Officer Williams hadn't called her, probably because they hadn't found the man—had it been Geordie?

"If I bought a dog, would you be willing to look it on it during the day while I'm at work, maybe let it out for a break? I wouldn't want the dog to be alone all day."

"Depending on the dog, I suppose so. Not if it's big or mean or anything. I wouldn't want to risk getting bit, you know?"

"No, nothing like that, I don't have anything specific in mind, but my friends have been after me to get a dog for company, for protection. Maybe they're right, I'm not sure. I will let you know." Moon hurried off, already late for service. She would have to sneak in the back before the offering and pretend that she had been there all the time, not that it would fool either Sue or Jim. Sue would want a full report and would probably urge Moon to get a dog that would be left alone all day. Moon worried about the dog she didn't have.

Back home, in comfortable jeans and her chambray shirt, Moon helped Sue move the table, tried out the sewing machine before storing it neatly on the bottom shelf of the pantry section where the shelves were a bit wider with slightly higher gap between them. Afterward they took advantage of the nice weather to have cake and coffee on the porch swing, while Moon recounted Mrs. Crawford's news.

"It might have been, Geordie, but I don't think so. They didn't find the guy, so we don't know but Tommy, said they have had other reports about some man watching my house—it's been going on for a while. They told me to avoid Geordie, so I didn't call him, even though I wanted to. I mean, I try not to let it bother me, the police are watching out for me, and the family has been told. Who knows, it might even be one of them! I don't know...." her voice trailed off as she sipped her coffee.

Sue got up and walked to her car, returning with a copy of the Sunday paper. She opened it to the For-Sale classifieds: Pets.

"There are some German Shepherd puppies for sale," she noted.

"Too big for me," denied Moon, "and they need to be well-trained. The neighbor won't watch the dog while I'm at work if it's too aggressive: I asked."

"Chihuahua?" Sue inquired.

"Too small. I would step on it," shuddered Moon. "And it would remind me of that wretched cat, but they do make good watchdogs, I hear. Any beagles for sale? Even an adult?"

Sue shook her head. "Nothing here about beagles. Horses, cats," (Moon winced), "okay, I hear you! Not many dogs. The Humane Society Pet of the Week is a nice-looking black Labrador."

"That might do—a bit big for me though, like the shepherd, I would be more comfortable with something a little smaller, but I can stop in and talk to them tomorrow."

"I'll give you a ride after work," Sue offered. "It's 'way out by the county line and I need to get away for a bit. The kids will be home all day tomorrow, some sort of in-service that was supposed to be last week but got moved forward to Monday, and I will need a break, so you will be doing me a favor!"

"And make sure I don't wimp out, right?"

"Well......"

"No, I will at least go and see. I could call my Amish carpenter too. Maybe he knows someone with a litter ready for new homes. Or wait!

What about an attack parrot? I hear if you teach them to talk, they make good watch pets!"

"Now you are being ridiculous," Sue exclaimed. "Watch parrot indeed!" She handed Moon the paper and stood up to go.

"They are better at being left home alone," Moon said, not moving from her seat.

"Yes, well, see you tomorrow. Are you biking or walking to work?"

"They are predicting more rain, so I believe I will walk. Easier to handle an umbrella," Moon laughed.

"Then I will call for you at the bank at four?"

"Better call the Humane Society first to see what their hours are."

"Good thinking. Call me when you know."

The Labrador was already spoken for, they told her. They had a Staffordshire terrier pair, brother and sister, which might make good watch dogs, an elderly basset hound with health issues that had been dumped there because the owners couldn't afford the medical bills, a dozen cats (Moon shuddered), and a little stray dachshund mix that was on hold pending contact with the owner. Moon asked about the basset because she felt bad about the sick dog abandoned so callously, but all was well, they said, a rescue was contacted and would take the hound, treat its medical issues, and find it a home. No worries, the dog would have golden years after all. Moon was relieved.

She left her name, address, phone number so they could send her an application. 'Things take time,' she reminded herself as she walked to work in the light rain.

Lacey was avoiding her, which suited Moon fine for the moment, but which she realized couldn't continue indefinitely if they expected to work together. With an eye to a better salary, she had applied for the post of chief loan officer that would be opening sometime that summer. That would put her in charge of reviewing all loan applications as well as managing the workload of the two assistants the bank usually carried. It would also make her Lacey's immediate boss. Moon decided that with her experience she had a good chance, and if not, then maybe there would be other opportunities.

The Humane Society no longer necessary for the moment, they went for a drive anyway, out of town, just to get away. "I wish I had a convertible," Moon dreamed. "Pipe dream. I really don't want one, maybe just drive one someday."

"You could rent one for a few days, as a treat or a reward. Do you still have your license?" Sue suggested. "Wouldn't that give Lacey something to talk about?" They both laughed at the idea of a seething Lacey.

"Of course, I keep the license for identification," Moon rolled down the window and let the light rain spatter her face. "That's actually a good idea. It wouldn't cost much just to drive it around town for a couple of days, just for fun, and you are right, it certainly would give Lacey something to gossip about. Did I tell you; she still isn't speaking to me? I shouldn't have lost control like that, but she just pushed one too many buttons, so I told her about her son hanging out with Geordie. I imagine there was quite the explosion when she got home!"

"No, you shouldn't have done that," Sue agreed quietly. "I imagine what you said hurt her deeply more than it shocked her. She probably knew it all along, but she doesn't have any more control over her son than you have over Joy. I think Sherle is the only one he listens to these days."

Moon looked surprised. "What do you mean, 'hurt her'?

Sue shook her head. "Leave it alone, Moon, or apologize to her. That's the only way things will smooth over."

"I see," Moon said softly. "I... didn't mean to... it was thoughtless of me, just to get a little dig back at her. When she inferred that I was nearly prostituting myself, I just lost it, but that's no excuse. I heard enough of that ***t from Geordie when he met me in the diner that day for lunch, remember, the day he skipped out on the bill? I thought it was just sour grapes because I finally came out of my funk, was doing good things with my life. He always told me that I was nothing without him, it was part of his control agenda; you know how he hates to be proven wrong.

"But to hear that come out of Lacey's mouth in front of the other secretaries, Sue, I think that was the tipping point! Somebody sent me an e-mail through the company server later that day, accusing me of being a liar. Maybe I was, maybe she didn't hear it courtesy of Geordie. Maybe she really _is_ that dirty-minded." Moon stopped to reflect. "I just never thought she'd sink that low on her own. Her comments were always snarky, but this truly felt like character assassination! I wonder what triggered it?"

"Now you may be getting somewhere," Sue remarked enigmatically. "Talk to her, gently. Buy her a cup of coffee or bring a piece of your grandma's coffee cake. Apologize. Try to mend the fences before this hurts both of you!"

Moon said nothing. After a stop at a roadside flower stall for some strawberry plants and honey, they turned toward home, pleased, for the most part, with their brief escape.

Moon planned to talk to Lacey first thing at work the next day, but her desk sat empty all day. The secretaries speculated, no one knew anything for certain, so Moon decided not to waste time worrying. Instead, she put in her application at the shelter, concentrated on her own clients: new loan papers were piling up fast. She stopped by personnel to enquire about her job application, learned that no decision would be made until interviews were held in the coming weeks.

The little black doxie was still on hold as a stray. Moon felt like she was on hold as well. She bought paint for the exterior of her house and collected names of possible painters, feeling the job might be better left to the professionals. She planted strawberries and called electricians for estimates on her laundry room. She rode her bike, talked to Mr. Yoder about building four glass-front (lawyers) bookcases to go with the ones from Grandma, made new cushions for her porch swing out of old pantsuits that she cut apart and resewed in a simple nine-patch pattern, carefully saving any embroidery, happily curling up among the cushions, drinking iced tea and reading mysteries and romance books from the library.

No one came to claim the dachshund. The Labrador left for a farm, the basset moved to a rescue foster family who found they couldn't part with him and filed adoption papers, the bonded terrier twins found a home with an engaged couple, other animals (including a parrot) came and went, but the little black doxie languished in a cage alone. She was available for adoption but had developed kennel cough, the shelter could not release her until she was healthy. Moon visited the puppy several times after work, fell in love, and happily contributed to the medical bills. She was a quiet little dog as a rule: shy, lonely, a little frightened, but she seemed to be comfortable sitting on Moon's lap when she came to visit and check out other dogs that had been surrendered. By mid-July she was healthy again, ready to be released. Moon bought a small indoor kennel for the puppy's new home, filled it with bedding and toys, bought dishes and dog food, a leash, a harness and a dog license. She arranged for the little dog to be spayed, microchipped, rechecked for heart worm or other parasites with medication to keep her free of them, and updated her vaccinations. With a clean bill of health 'Pansy' (the Humane Society's name for her) was finally ready to be 'sprung from puppy jail,' as Moon reported to Sue. Moon rented a red Chevy convertible for a week from the local car dealer in celebration, and, as she had predicted, it set off a storm of speculation in the breakroom.

Lacey was particularly vocal. "She buys a house, dyes her hair, now she's running around in a convertible. Talk about a mid-life crisis! Where is she getting the money? Who IS the mystery man who is footing her bills, I ask you? Why haven't we seen him, let alone met him?"

"Maybe because he doesn't exist," Moon laughed. "And who gave her the right to 'parent' me? Does she have final say over my decisions? I don't think so! She's upset because she can't access my account records at the bank: she doesn't have the clearance!"

She was determined not to let Lacey get under her skin. Lacey had so far resisted Moon's attempts to apologize or lay the issue to rest. After one bout of verbal sparring Moon again threw caution out the door.

"Lacey, you may not know it, but my little house is a rent-to-own, the new hair style was Sue's idea as part of a house-warming gift, and the convertible was rented from Crosstown Motors for the week as a treat. You don't see me driving it now, do you? I've always wanted to drive one, but I can't afford/don't really need a car right now, so I rented it. Returned it. It was fun, and now I can cross that off my Bucket List!"

"Bravo for you," one of the secretaries cried. "I'm proud of you. You've come a long way in the last year! I sometimes wish I were as brave as you!"

"Oh, yes, bravo for you," Lacey spit. "You have an answer for everything, but I would bet my Buick that if someone did some digging, they'd come up with a lot that you not only aren't telling, but don't want anyone to know. Like why the police are watching your 'rented' house!" With that parting shot she snatched up her coffee and sandwich and left the breakroom. "Dig away," whispered Moon.

Lacey was closeted with the bank's vice president the rest of that afternoon leaving Moon to wonder what childish nonsense Lacey was up to this time. By closing time, she decided that she had had enough: outburst aside, it was past time to end this. She caught up with Lacey in the parking lot as Lacey was unlocking her Buick.

"Okay, no audience, just you and me," Moon began. "We've had our issues over the years, you and I. Geordie was always a contention between us..."

"I have NO idea what you are talking about, and I need to get home and get supper started," Lacey interrupted.

"It can wait, or you can pick up take-out." Moon leaned against the driver's side door so Lacey couldn't open it. "All of a sudden I seem to have done something to make you mad and you have been absolutely cruel in return. That set off a chain reaction and here we are. I was way out of line with that remark about Fritz's Bar, I admit it and I'm sorry for it. It was mean of me, and it was uncalled for. I have been trying to apologize since I said it, but I can't seem to reach you without escalating the situation. Now, I'm done with the fighting, I want a truce even if it's a cold one."

"Where did you get such an awful lie anyway? You KNOW my family doesn't frequent such places!" Lacey exploded. "And why would you say that to me in front of the girls we work with?"

"From an admittedly unreliable source: Geordie. He stopped by a few months ago to talk about Joy, dropped quite a few tidbits about my personal business that he would have no way of knowing, and when I asked him, he said he heard it from Geoff, from your son, down at Fritz's. He indicated that they were hanging out there quite often, although now that I think about it, I should not have believed him, much less thrown it in your face. He met me for lunch the next day at the Diner, picked up the check, and 'forgot' to pay it. I had to settle the bill when they called me about it. Why on earth would I be so stupid as to trust anything he says!"

"So now you blame Geordie?" Lacey cried. "You can't take any responsibility for your own actions; you can't see that you are being plain mean-spirited?"

"Lacey" whispered Moon as she caught sight of two of the secretaries leaving by the side door. "You asked where I heard it, I told you the truth, and I've apologized for saying it in the first place. What's going on here, that we can't even talk this out?"

"Please get out of my way." Lacey was crying, oblivious to the scene she was causing. Moon backed away, giving her access to the car door. Lacey jerked the door open, barely missing Moon, and howled "I wish you happiness in your new job. Looks like once again you got exactly what you wanted. You always do!" With that parting comment she put the car in reverse and roared back onto the street before screeching away.

'*What was that all about?*' Moon wondered. '*What new job? What have I done now?*'

9

No Answers

"Well at least <u>you</u> are happy to see me," Moon greeted a crazed dachshund who was alternating between jumping up to greet Moon and auditioning for the Daytona 500. On one pass, Moon grabbed Pansy by the harness so she could clip the leash into place. It was now her habit to take a walk with the dog as soon as she got home after work. Ellen Crawford came by once in the morning, once in the afternoon to take Pansy out so there were no messes in the house and Moon left her plenty of fresh water. Pansy had proved herself very adaptable to Moon's schedule as long as she could have her dinner in the evening when Moon ate. Moon hoped that Pansy's presence would deter rodents as well as burglars, although she wasn't too sure about Pansy as a guard dog, but her very presence was more comforting than the cat had ever been. At night, curled at her feet, needing to touch Moon even in her sleep, the little dog showed her in every way how grateful she was to have a home.

Together they explored the neighborhood on foot and, surprisingly, on Moon's bicycle. Pansy seemed to enjoy riding in the basket on the back of the bicycle, taking in the sights and sniffing new smells. She was friendly but cautious when Moon stopped to talk to people, happy just to be with Moon wherever she went.

Moon was sleeping, once again dreaming of Grandma's house: she could hear her mother and grandmother consulting each other over plans for supper, hear her father exclaiming as he read the evening paper, hear Chowder barking at a squirrel in the yard. She moved restlessly in her sleep. Chowder's barking would upset her father or the neighbors. Chowder needed to quiet down, she should distract him with a toy, she should......

Moon sat bolt upright in bed. There was no sign of Pansy curled at her feet, and the sound of barking was still ringing in her ears. There it was again! Not Chowder's bark, but Pansy's, coming from the living room.

Moon scooped up her robe from the foot of her bed, just in time to see a shadow vanish from her porch window. Pansy was frantically jumping at the window, barking, snarling, desperate to get at whoever had been on her porch. Carefully Moon crept toward the window, avoiding moonlight and streetlight flooding into her living room. She peeked out through the crack between the curtains and the window frame to see a tall man standing in her front yard, staring at her house, apparently talking on a cell phone. Moon drew back from the window, crept into the kitchen, called the police.

Once again, the man was gone by the time the squad car arrived, but thanks to the streetlight Moon was able to give them a little better description of the man than they had before.

"He was tall, thin, wore glasses, jeans, and a dark hoodie. He had work boots on, his hands were bare, at least the one holding the cell phone was. I couldn't tell you if he was clean shaven, but I didn't see a beard. What I want to know is why my front light didn't go on. I specifically put in a motion detector for just this reason! Hush, Pansy, you've done your job!" Moon cradled the excited dog, wishing she had a way to settle the animal.

"I can answer that question," the senior officer responded pointing to the front porch light. "Somebody cut the wire here, probably during the day while you were gone. An electrician can fix that so it can't be cut again. Call somebody tomorrow."

"And we have a footprint," called the second officer, softly. He was photographing an indentation in the rain-softened front yard, taking measurements, writing notes. "It's too soft for a plaster casting, but it is good enough to compare if we catch someone," he declared.

"I guess that's all for tonight. I don't think you'll see him again, if you do this little pumpkin will let you know. Good girl!" He offered Pansy a dog treat from his pocket ("It pays to keep some handy on the beat!") reached out to rub her ears and Pansy quieted.

"Well," said Moon. "I guess it was a good day for both of us when I brought you home! I think we need to find you a reward for all your hard work!"

Lights were on in the Crawford's across the alley: Moon could see Paul Crawford standing in his kitchen doorway, obviously worried about her. The second officer finished his notes and walked across the alley to reassure the Crawfords that all was well. Moon thanked the senior officer for coming before taking an exhausted dog back into the house.

"No point going back to bed now," Moon told her as she put a pot of coffee on. "Might as well get a shower, get dressed, get busy. We have enough time for a nice breakfast, maybe a breakfast burrit...really?" Moon laughed as she spotted Pansy fast asleep on her dog bed, in the crate in the corner of the kitchen. "Sleep little one. You earned it."

Moon tiptoed out of the kitchen, made the bed, showered, dressed in a toast-colored linen suit with a simple necklace made of tiny, polished river stones, and her favorite walking shoes. She pulled some Canadian bacon and some shredded pepper jack cheese from the refrigerator, heated up a soft taco shell on the stove while she quickly chopped some onion, tomato, lettuce, and the meat. She added a dollop of chunky salsa, rolled the mix in the soft shell, taking care to turn up the bottom before sealing the mini burrito.

After breakfast she fixed herself a peanut butter sandwich for lunch, packed with a small to-go container of her favorite vegetable soup, filled her thermos with the left-over coffee, before giving the kitchen a quick wipe down. She dusted the dining and living rooms, ran the carpet sweeper rather than the vacuum so as not to wake Pansy. She had enough time to call the electrician and leave a message before leaving for work on her bike an hour early. She planned to spend the extra time doing some window shopping for some things on her wish list. Her new bookcases would be delivered sometime later in August, the painter would be starting on the exterior next week (she must remember to introduce him to Pansy) so those things were on track, but the library was having a book sale that weekend and she was eager to see if any of her favorite authors were offered. It would be nice to get the books she already owned out of boxes in the front bedroom and add to her collection. Maybe some juicy mysteries would be good to set aside for the long winter months ahead. Moon spent a lovely hour walking around town, making notes, jotting down ideas in her notebook.

As she strolled past the realtor's office, the agent spotted her through the large front window, left her desk hurriedly and called to Moon from the doorway. Moon returned to the realtor's, her head buzzing with questions.

"I just wanted to give you a head's up," the agent whispered, "I think there may be trouble with your little house. A member of the family was in the other day asking about the contract, someone who wasn't a part of the original arrangement, and they didn't look very happy. As far as I know that contract is iron-clad but that doesn't mean they won't try something. You've paid your rent, on time, every month. Done nothing to violate the contract. I don't think they can do anything, but I wanted to warn you. I think someone in the family has their eye on that house for one of their kids, and they aren't happy that you got in there first. Just be warned."

"Thank you. I'll contact one of the bank's lawyers to look it over—second opinion. Just in case."

Moon hurried back to the bank to check the in-house directory for the name of the lawyers the bank employed in its real estate transactions. To her surprise, one of the names on the list was the law firm that had drawn up her contract. Interesting. If anyone would know if and how to break it, they would. Moon wrote herself a note to call them and added another lawyer to the list as a safeguard.

In the meantime, she had clients to see, paperwork to fill out, and a memo on her desk inviting her to a meeting with personnel that afternoon. She looked for Lacey during her break that morning, but her desk was unoccupied, and no one had seen her. 'Figures' thought Moon.

She still refused to use her work phone for personal calls so the lawyers would have to wait until after work. *'Eventually I may have to buy a cell phone,'* she thought, still hoping to postpone it if she could.

The afternoon meeting went very quickly: Moon was indeed promoted to head loan officer beginning in September, and she learned that Lacey had requested a transfer to another branch of the bank. Not surprisingly, it was the same one that had taken on Richard. *'Hmmm,'* thought Moon. *'I don't believe in coincidences.'* The new position came with an actual office, Moon would be moving up in the world. She discovered from the office gossip that Lacey had also applied for the head loan officer position, had accepted the transfer instead. *'No wonder she was so angry with me. Well, she was flirting with Richard before he left, I hope she likes cats better than I do! I wonder if that had anything to do with her transfer?'* she thought as she began boxing up her personal items from her desk. She decided she wouldn't move any sensitive files from their locked cabinet until she took possession of her new desk. They would be safer that way, locked in the desk she was still using.

Moon hurried home to take Pansy for her walk as soon as she had placed calls to the lawyers, requesting return calls to her desk at the bank. She would break her rule long enough to set up meetings with the law firms and schedule her clients to accommodate them. She needed to know her house was safe from repossession. After a year of living in the little bungalow, she knew she couldn't give it up, not without a fight. Perhaps she should talk to the bank about a loan and not wait until the contract expired. She needed to know what her options were. *'One year down, only four to go.'*

She also hesitantly placed a call to Officer Williams, hoping for news of Joy. It had been nearly a year and Moon was more worried than she would admit except to Sue.

As she was putting a small chicken and dumpling casserole in the oven to bake, she reached the dispatcher who promised to contact Tommy for her as he was off duty. He returned her call within the hour, admitted that she had caught him having supper with his parents, "But if you put on the coffee, I will bring enough of Mom's infamous peach crumble to share, if that's okay with you? Then I can meet the crime-fighting dachshund."

"Oh, did you hear? Well, I look forward to it. Your mother's baking is legendary!" Moon laughed.

Pansy barked to let Moon know that she intended to be included in the dessert so when Tommy arrived Moon dug out some ice cream made especially for dogs and dished up a small scoop for the pup. Just enough for a treat, not enough to encourage fatty puppy.

"My mother used to feed our beagle a piece of buttered toast every morning for breakfast, Dad didn't know, and he wondered why the little dog was getting so fat. I won't do that to you. I want you to have a long, healthy life." Pansy barked, approving of Moon's plan.

"I want to know!" Moon remarked to Tommy as she carried a tray of coffee and cobbler to the dining room table, "I want to know what is happening with your search for Joy. I want to know everything you've done, everything you've heard, everything you are planning to do to find her. What happened with that letter? Was it really from her? Is she okay? Tommy," she said firmly, "talk to me! tell me something!"

"I wish I could," Tommy savored his coffee. "The letter seems to be Joy's handwriting. I compared it to some notes she passed me in class...."

"Wait, you kept the notes she passed you in class?" Moon was surprised.

Tommy blushed. "Yeah, I don't know why, but I did. Now I'm glad I did because I had something to compare the letter to, in case it was a forgery. I don't think it is, but it looks like she was upset when she wrote it. I have been trying to track the origin through the post office, but not much luck, I'm afraid. We are still looking for Neil as well, for either of their cars, anything."

"What about the man that Abby saw with Joy?"

"Probably a dead end. She was just helping him out. His probation officer confirmed it. Wherever she is, her car is probably in a garage, and she doesn't want to be found. Moon, Joy is a grown woman. If she doesn't want to come home, she doesn't have to. What I find more concerning are Neil's reasons for wanting to find her, reasons that turned out to be lies, and where he is hiding out. Something about this whole thing is just rotten!"

Moon slapped his hand lightly as she caught him trying to feed a piece of piecrust to Pansy. He started, looked guilty, the piecrust went back on his plate. "Don't push it, Tommy. I may overlook purloined cookies, but I won't have you teaching my dog bad habits!" Pansy sighed and took herself back to her kennel. She knew that tone, Moon would not be swayed.

"Moon, I'm sorry. I just don't have anything to tell you, other than that we are still looking. At least I am. I won't rest until I know she is safe, I promise. I am still not sure that Geordie isn't mixed up in this somewhere. I hope not, I really do," Tommy stood to leave, "but something is off about him too. I will figure it out. You know I will!"

Moon hugged him and walked him to the front door. "I have no doubt that you will get to the bottom of this. So, don't worry about me. I have my guardian angel watching out for me." In her crate Pansy snored.

Moon gathered the plates, rinsed them, but set them aside to wash with the morning dishes. She did a quick tour of the house, locking doors and windows, turning on nightlights in the kitchen and parlor, before changing for bed. She would be relieved when the electrician fixed the motion detector. He promised to come before the week was out. She wondered if Pansy would continue to sleep in her crate: by the time Moon climbed into bed, the little dog was in her usual spot against the footboard, snuggled down in the afghan Moon kept for cold feet.

Moon herself lay awake until long past midnight, watching the stars through her bedroom window, listening to the train whistle in the distance and Pansy's deep breathing at her feet. *'Who was that man? Where was Joy? What, if anything, was the connection?'*

10

So Little Joy

Flashes of light and color, bangs that sounded like gunshots, Pansy cowered in her crate, shaking and crying. Unable to calm her, Moon sat on her front porch swing alone, watching the show above the trees. The Fire Department always put on a grand show at the fairgrounds south of town, in combination with the annual county 4H exhibits and death-defying rides. Moon and Geordie had gone every year when they were dating, Sue usually took the Youth Group on an outing in exchange for their help with the church's food stand.

Margret, Sue, Lacey, Jenny and Mike Hildebrandt: it shouldn't take five people to run a food stand but these five had a system down that made for a smooth-running operation. With Lacey on the cash register, Sue and Moon waiting tables, Jenny doing some food preparation, and her brother Mike bussing and washing in between bouts of hawking the food stand's delights, they always managed the maximum amount of business with a minimum amount of fuss. They loved doing it: loved the crowds, the excitement, the familiar faces woven in with strangers, the challenge of meeting each order with improved time and service. The tips were pretty good too, although by common consent they didn't keep them. Instead, they collected them in a locked box, separate from the cash drawer and turned them over to their minister on the last day of the fair. It was his usual policy to take part in the tip money and treat the workers to rides and a show, before donating the rest to the Sunday school fund. The church used the money to buy Bibles for the youngest readers, materials for all classes, scholarships for church camp/

retreats, and goodies for a picnic at the end of the year. All the shifts con-
tributed, as well as the other fundraisers throughout the year. There were
other treats too for the youth group at different times of the church calendar:
haunted houses and scavenger hunts in the fall, ice skating parties around
Christmas, the "I Can't Wait for Spring" musical revue that the kids put on
right before Lent, but the 4th of July Food Stand was a favorite: it was THE
place to be during the fair, so all their friends used it as a hangout, bought
food, traded gossip, formed new romantic attachments.

So, today she sat on her porch, watching the display from a safe distance, eating popcorn, and enjoying the evening. Earlier she had worked at the food stand with a couple of the kids that had helped her move (a trip down memory lane!) to give Sue and Jim a break and to buy a couple of meals for herself to enjoy later. Mr. Snow and the Men's Fellowship were on duty at the stand now: always an active time when the fireworks were going up. Sue and Jim were off making plans for their annual vacation starting in a week: they usually went out East to visit Jim's parents: this would be one last family outing before Josh left for college—which Abby was doing her best to get out of participating. Sue would have let her stay with friends, but Jim was adamant.

"What doesn't kill us makes us stronger. We are going as a family. No. More. Arguing." Josh and Abby both knew they might be able to convince Mom, but when Dad made up his mind there was no changing it outside an emergency.

The fireworks ended so Moon went back into the house to try to coax Pansy out and calm her. No more bangs. No more bright flashes. She wondered if she should ask the vet about some calming medicine or some trick of the trade to soothe the poor dog. Chowder never minded the fireworks—he didn't pay them any more attention than a thunderstorm.

Pansy seemed a little more high-strung. The explosions confused and frightened her—perhaps that was how she came to be a stray? Moon lured the trembling dog out of her crate with her favorite tidbit and cuddled her until she stopped shaking. Moon found a concert on the radio, turned on the fireplace (lights without heat) to listen in the dark. She talked to Pansy about possible vacation plans that would include dogs. It might be nice to get away from all the drama for a while, but could she leave the house unattended? Moon decided to avoid thinking about it at all for the time being. If nothing else, she could rent a car and do some day trips with Pansy, visit some near-by hiking trails or historic spots. The Crawfords across the alley would keep an eagle eye on the house during the day, just as they did now. Paul was on disability and Ellen worked from home: she would miss walking Pansy twice a day as the two were now comfortable friends, but Moon could bring them back treats from her travels to compensate. She could call about the car as soon as the lawyers assured her that her lease was solid!

Well, not so fast.

"It's unlikely that they could break the contract," the lawyer looked up from her paperwork without smiling, "but since this particular potential inheritor was not part of the initial agreement, they could very well try to have it voided; if they happen to have a 'friend' on the bench or a VERY good lawyer, they might actually be successful. You should prepare for it to go either way. Have they filed a challenge to the contract in court yet?"

It was the day after the fireworks, Moon was meeting with the bank's attorney for a consultation: the news was not exactly what she was hoping for.

"I...I don't think so. I haven't gotten any notice, just an alert from the realtor that found the house for me."

"Have you done any improvements to the house? Are they documented?" the lawyer pulled out a legal pad and began making notes.

"I've stripped off the old wallpaper in the dining room, repainted the main rooms, and had new kitchen cabinets built when the old ones fell off the wall in the middle of the night. I've also done a bit of landscaping around the house: a few new flowers and plants. I have receipts for everything I've done, as well as the realtor has documentation concerning the kitchen cabinets. When they came down, we contacted the family about sharing the cost of new cabinets. They declined, said it was my problem, and I paid for the cabinets myself. I can put you in touch with the carpenter, if you need to talk to him..." Moon's voice trailed off. She was having trouble breathing. *'Where will we go now, Pansy and me? I won't give her up, but where can I go and still keep her? Was Joy right? Was this a huge mistake that is going to cost me everything I have?'* she thought.

This time the lawyer did look up from her notes, smiling reassuringly at Moon. "First, let's see what is going to happen, if they chose to file, if a judge will even consider hearing the case. Most judges don't have time to mess around with contracts that the majority of the parties have agreed to and signed, especially a year down the line if there have been no violations. Even if this fellow does file, it may get tossed out before it can get going and you have nothing to worry about. Legally you are on pretty solid ground, but I think it pays to be prepared for anything. Talk to your bank about getting a loan to buy the house right now instead of waiting another four years. As a back-up plan. We don't want to see you lose your home because someone decides to be a jerk. I will be talking to the realtor, and to your carpenter. Leave his name and contact information with my secretary and let me do some investigating."

"What will this cost?" Moon wanted to know.

"Nothing for this consultation—and a small fee for a couple hours work, nothing beyond that if nothing comes of it except big talk. I have some contacts that might have some information, but we'll see. In any case, I think we can handle this for you fairly reasonably—you are one of the more senior employees at Tri State Bank and we are on retainer with them so...."

Moon left the lawyer's office feeling only slightly better than when she went in. In the old days she would have taken herself to the Dairy Queen for the biggest sundae they could build with massive amounts of chocolate. Today definitely called for a chocolate binge—Moon considered her options, considered the new skirt and blouse set she had sewn up over the weekend with its white background against tiny blue flowers and green leaves embroidered on the hem as well as on the short sleeves, and decided that a small nonfat mocha latte would serve just as well. She could offset it at supper with some fresh vegetables and fruit instead of the pasta salad she had chilling in the fridge.

The latte was wonderful—all the better, thought Moon, since she hadn't had one for almost a year. She remembered ruefully when a grande vanilla latte was an "every morning" routine to wash down the donut she always bought for breakfast as she rushed to work. Now the lattes were a rare treat that Moon savored on special occasions. She nursed this one, making it last as long as possible as she sat on a bench by the bus stop, watching the shoppers come, go, and return with purchases. Moon returned to her desk feeling a little better, but more determined than ever to hold on to her home. She sent a memo to the bank president's secretary requesting a meeting before pulling up a copy of the application needed from anyone wanting a loan. Time to be prepared...

It wasn't the alarm that woke her, but the train whistle, long and low, crossing the streets a quarter of a mile away. She lay quietly in the dark, knowing it was too early to be up and about, knowing that she probably wouldn't be able to go back to sleep. The little doxie snored on, oblivious to the train, to Moon's wakefulness. She stirred briefly, snuggled deeper into the afghan, returned to her dreams. Moon lay for a while, listening to the train, the early birdsongs, the occasional car on the quiet street. Several blocks away the garbage truck was already on its rounds. No hurry, Moon's garbage bin was already sitting on the curb, waiting to be emptied. Moon stretched lazily, enjoying the peace, the beginnings of light that highlighted the next-door neighbor's house just beyond the arbor.

The train moved on, heading southward with its freight, probably pulp or logs from the paper mill north of town. The shadows shortened, the clock hands crept forward, Moon eased herself out of bed so as not to disturb the sleeping pup. No use: as soon as her feet hit the floor Pansy was awake, alert, ready to get an early start on whatever adventure Moon had in mind, even if it was only breakfast!

She waited patiently as Moon pulled on jeans and a sweatshirt, quivered when Moon's feet found her sandals, bounded off the bed to make sure Moon knew where the leash was hanging. Moon ruefully remembered the days of tripping over the malcontented cat in her haste to get to the bathroom herself; less weight on her bladder had solved that problem. Now it was Pansy first, then Moon's turn for toilet and shower while Pansy ate her breakfast. If there was time (there almost always was), they might do a short walk before Moon left for work. Time with Pansy had become the highlight of her morning, replacing the joys of lattes and donuts.

The phone was ringing when they returned from their walk-unknown caller-Moon had an odd feeling about it so she answered it though usually she would have let it go straight to voicemail.

"Mom?" The voice was soft; so soft Moon almost missed the words. "Mom? Do you have to work today?"

It sounded like Joy, scared and confused, but definitely Joy.

"Yes," she replied cautiously, thinking that if there were going to be trouble, better downtown where the police could get there faster—and where there were more witnesses. "Joy? Do you want to meet me at the bank?"

"Yes," she heard before the line went dead. She felt a chill run from her neck down, better alert Ellen and Officer Williams. Would Pansy be ok alone today? Probably. She always locked the doors and Ellen had the spare key. Moon stopped there on her bike before going on to work early so she could leave a message in person at the police station.

"Goodness, you lead an exciting life!" Ellen Crawford exclaimed.

"Not by choice," Moon replied. "I'd rather have things dull, thank you. But until I know that Joy is safe, well, my peace and quiet comes second."

"I understand completely. Paul and I never had children of our own. Oh, I don't regret it," Ellen added quickly, "We were happy just with each other...and then his accident at work, well he was enough for me to take care of you see, and it's all worked out well, but goodness you lead an exciting life!" she repeated with a laugh. "I will keep a special eye on the house today for you. If you think it wise, I will even bring the pup over to keep Paul out of trouble. He's gotten so fond of that little dog, we may have to rescue one of our own—but only if Pansy approves," she added.

"Thank you," Moon said, sincerely. "I don't know what I would do without good neighbors like you two. I just hope that things get boring around here eventually!" With that she rode off to work in a soft rose "Friday" pantsuit tied at the ankle so it wouldn't get caught in the gears. She still thought of herself as a *'fat lady pedaling herself around town,'* but now she didn't let it bother her. She enjoyed the ride to and from town on her bicycle, regretting only that it wasn't suitable for the winter. Moon still thought about getting another car, but she really didn't want to be trapped in the financial nightmare that a vehicle could bring. Her life was much simpler now, she was determined to keep it that way, especially if she needed the money to keep her house!

Her next stop was the police station to report contact with Joy. Officer Williams wasn't in yet, but the desk sergeant promised to give him the message and send him by both the house and the bank. Moon should call if anything else occurred. Nothing to do now but wait.

Moon blessed the training she would need for her new position, due to start in a couple of weeks. It kept her busy, kept her mind off the odd early morning phone call, kept her focused on the job of learning new skills, rules, and practices. There was a lot to take in; it completely occupied her until her lunch break, so no need to hover over the vending machines. She had forgotten to take her lunch out of the fridge that morning. The diner was the best choice, especially since her lunch times would now be a little longer with the promotion. Moon slid into her favorite booth, thinking longingly of the BLT salad still chilling in the fridge, she was almost ready to order soup and half a sandwich when a voice behind her whispered, "I thought you might be here. Can you spare an extra lunch, or do I have to wash dishes?"

Moon looked around quickly as Joy slid into the bench seat opposite her and buried herself back in its farthest corner. She pushed the menu over to her daughter as she waved the waitress away: "Give us just another minute or so."

"How hungry are you?" she enquired as Joy poured over the lunch specials.

Joy looked up, ready to snap a retort, but her face crumpled in on itself the way it did when she was a child. "I haven't eaten in a while so, starving!" she gulped back a sob. Moon pretended not to notice.

"Have the chicken dinner special," she suggested. "It will be here the quickest. You always liked the chicken here." Matter-of-factly she signaled the waitress so they could place their orders, the waitress refilled Moon's coffee without being asked as she provided a cup for Joy.

There were a thousand questions Moon wanted to ask; she didn't. Instead, she waited in silence, knowing that saying anything to Joy, even in kindness, especially in kindness, would often cause her to either bolt or explode. Joy would tell her in her own time. Instead, Moon reached into her tote bag for the book she was reading and in doing so opened a call to Officer Williams. He would hear their conversation, know where to find them, know how to approach Joy.

"Isn't that one of the books I gave you for your birthday a hundred years ago?" Joy smiled through teary eyes. She seemed to appreciate the absence of what she often called 'the 3rd degree'.

"It is," admitted Moon. "I finished the first three in the series, realized I already had the fourth, so I didn't need to check it out of the library last week. I popped it into my bag last night, getting ready for today. It makes it easier for me in the morning if I set most of it up the night before: not so confusing and rushed. Of course, this morning I grabbed my tote, forgot my lunch still in the fridge, so you see, it isn't fool proof. Kind of a work in progress." Moon laughed. "But if I had remembered to take my lunch, I would have missed sharing this with you, so I guess maybe forgetfulness isn't such a bad thing all the time?"

The waitress brought their orders with more fresh coffee. "You don't use sugar or milk?" Joy asked curiously. She, too, remembered her mother's fondness for flavored sugary coffees.

"Not so much, anymore," Moon admitted, stirring her soup. "I still like my lattes and cappuccinos, but they are more of a special treat now, rather than an everyday staple. How is your chicken?"

"As good as I remembered," Joy said with her mouth full, turned red around the ears, then laughed, nearly spraying mashed potatoes. Moon handed her a napkin, finished her own chicken salad half-sandwich.

They ate in silence until Joy scooped up the last bite of her dinner. Her eyes were on Moon half the time, on the front door of the diner the rest of the time, so she didn't see Tommy slip in through the kitchen and seat himself behind her in the next booth. Moon did. She shut off her phone while retrieving a handkerchief from her tote to polish her glasses. If Joy recognized the handkerchief, she didn't comment on it.

"Full? Or would you like some dessert?" she asked. "I have about fifteen minutes before I have to be back at work, but you could stay and eat in leisure."

"No! I mean, no, thank you. I'll leave when you do, if that's ok. What do I owe you for the meal?" Joy asked, suspiciously.

"Nothing. I offered you coffee and cake on a Saturday, but you couldn't join me, so we do this instead," Moon said quietly. "And when you are ready, you can tell me what else I can do to help you. Don't!" she quietly cut off Joy's protests. "I won't judge, but you need help. That's still my job, like it or not. Now, we can argue, or you can tell me what I can do." Moon waited. Joy struggled with opposing inclinations. On one hand fear made her want to lash out, but the girl was obviously tired of fighting.

"I think I need a place to stay. A safe place. I don't know how long. And I don't want cops involved, that will make it worse."

"The first I can do, easily. I have an extra bedroom that is unused at the moment. The second, well, it may be too late for that."

"What do you mean?" Joy looked terrified. She slid across the bench as though ready to bold out the door.

"Neil called the police weeks ago, reported you as a missing person, they have been looking for you all summer. We were so afraid for your safety…"

"Neil called? When? Why? How could he? He's known where I was the whole time, he…" her voice trailed off as Tommy pulled up a chair. "What have you done?" she accused Moon.

"What we told her to do. Let us know when she heard from you, that you were safe. Moon, go to work. Joy and I have a few things to talk about, then I hope we will close this case so I will drop her off at your place. In time for supper."

Joy glared at them both. "And if I won't go?" she demanded.

"Joy, whatever you want, whatever you need, I will be there for you," Moon assured her. She packed up her tote bag, paid the bill on the way out, praying that Tommy would be able to talk some sense into Joy.

Back at the bank she was dimly aware of a commotion in the breakroom, but her mind was still on Joy as she tried to shift into work-mode. She had training scheduled for that afternoon and clients to see. It was necessary to keep her mind occupied, Moon knew she had done all she could for the moment. Now it was up to Officer Williams and her daughter.

As she was leaving for the day, she heard still more commotion coming from the breakroom. Now it was time to investigate!

The usual goodies were set out on the counter and a fresh pot of coffee enticed her. She ignored the bakery offerings, poured herself some from the pot into her favorite cup and inquired, "What's the celebration all about?"

"You just missed her!" "Well of course you're going to the wedding with the rest of us—I mean it's high time!" "They've been seeing each other since they both worked here…" their voices *trailed off, leaving Moon more confused than ever.*

"Who just left? Who's getting married?"

"Lacey," replied the Alice, the head teller. "She was just here to show us the ring and leave a group invitation. She and Richard Lemanski, you know, the guy who worked here as a teller for a while before he was promoted up to management level, were dating, and she followed him to his new job. Now they are getting married in September! Isn't it wonderful? I just love a good romance," Alice sighed happily.

Moon was speechless, but not for long. "I hope she likes Siamese cats," was all she could manage. So, Richard had also been seeing Lacey. Well, well, no wonder she hadn't heard from him. *'Who won that round!'* she wondered. *I'll be too busy with the new promotion to go—should I send a gift, maybe just a card? I'll ask Sue when she gets back from vacation.'* Moon packed her tote for the ride home, confirmed her appointment with the vice president in charge of loans for the coming week to discuss her options. Best to prepare for every challenge they might issue. Moon felt chilled riding home although it was a nice afternoon. What would she find waiting for her at home? How much longer would it be her home? Where would she and Pansy go (she would not abandon the loyal little dog, not like her former family had. Moon still wondered why no one had come looking for her). To distract herself, she paid special attention to her route through town.

Jefferson was not a big town. It had its share of bars, gas stations, churches, as well as a comfortably sized central business district. From the bank she rode west for a couple of blocks to avoid the major traffic through town, as well as to pass the public library. Every Saturday morning Moon stopped there to return the books she borrowed, examine the latest arrivals, check out some new material. Sometimes they were audio books that she could listen to as she sewed or did her morning chores. Sometimes they were hardbound books that she could read on break at work instead of raiding the candy machine.

She crossed the railroad tracks behind the library, tracks that curved out of town to the northeast, it carried the freight train whose whistle woke her in the morning. Once there had been passenger service to the town with a bustling train station just west of the library. Now it was only freight on a train twice a day that didn't stop. The station had become a restaurant, then a scouting headquarters. Now it was a series of artists shops where Moon and Sue loved to browse. Her Amish carpenter kept a showroom there; Moon often visited to complement him on his work and dream about furniture she would love to have but couldn't afford. Someday.

By the time she had crossed the tracks she had left the business district behind for single family homes with well-groomed front lawns and small backyards. The church that Jim and Sue served was nestled among these neighborhoods, it was a bit of a hike for Moon but certainly not out of walking distance. Even winter wasn't bad. Most of the families on the north side of town were particular about keeping the sidewalks clear of snow and ice.

To the south of the business district the neighborhoods were a little bit rougher. Moon's former apartment building, now leveled and rebuilt, had been in that section of town, the city council was hard at work to 'gentrify' the area, but the bars and one 'nightclub' type establishment were located on the southern edge of town. It wasn't really a skid row, but it was not an area you wanted to wander around in late at night. Moon was so grateful she had found her little bungalow when she did, before she was reduced to looking for a flat down by Fitz's. She would have been running into Geordie far more often if she had moved there! Then Joy would really have had something to complain about.

Thinking about Joy brought her back to reality as she was locking her bicycle in the garage/shed just east of her back porch. She wouldn't want to keep a car there, Moon mused, the building was in too much disrepair. It probably should be torn down and rebuilt before it fell down. In the meantime, it was useful for bicycle and garden equipment storage.

There was no car parked by her house, no one sitting on the porch waiting for her to come home, only Pansy who knew exactly the moment Moon set foot on the property. She would be waiting by the back door, possibly with her leash in her mouth, ready for the 'before supper walk' that always gave them a chance to reconnect after a long day apart. Moon wondered for the hundredth time why she had resisted getting a dog. *It must have been bad holdover from the cat,* she thought.

Back from their walk, Pansy polished off the last of her own meal as Moon set the table: two places, just in case. There was no sign of Joy, but Moon was not one to give up hope easily. If and when Joy showed up Moon decided she would behave as though nothing unusual was happening, that it would probably be less stressful for Joy if she didn't make a fuss. She dished up her own supper, the forgotten salad, eating alone at the table overlooking the alley. Pansy lounged in her open crate; Moon knew she would be up and ready at the mention of a late evening walk.

She was nearly finished with her dinner when she heard a knock at the back door.

"No bark," she remarked as Pansy roused and began to woof. It wasn't Joy at the door, but Officer Williams.

"I won't come in,' he demurred," I just wanted to let you know not to wait up for Joy. We are holding her for 'observation' since she threatened a police officer down at the station. She may be on something that's causing these mood swings, anyway she's staying put for 36 hours until we are sure she's not a danger to herself or you, or anyone else!"

"Of course," Moon agreed. "Let me know if you need anything. We should let Geordie know at some point; don't you think?"

Tommy hesitated. "Let me deal with Geordie. That way he can't blame you for not telling him yourself. If he shows up here, call me, just like you did with Joy. Okay?"

"Yes, Okay. For five years I barely had a single word from either of them. Now that my life is going well again, POW, every time I turn around! Makes me almost miss my old apartment and homicidal cat," Moon laughed. Pansy looked up expectantly at the word "cat".

"Not your play-buddy, sweetie," Moon assured her. "There's a cat that lives on our favorite walk. They like to converse through the fence!" she explained.

"Ah," said Tommy. "Opposites attract?"

"Something like that. So, you are holding her for 36 hours? Then what?"

"At least that, and beyond that it's up to Joy. She's not being terribly cooperative right now."

Moon sighed. "I guess I can't expect it to go smoothly all at once. Thanks for stopping by anyway, Tommy. I won't look for her tonight."

Tommy looked as though he was about to say something else, thought better of it. He touched the brim of his hat and stepped into the night, leaving Moon to her quiet evening. There was more to this business with Joy, but Tommy wasn't certain yet how deep it would go, how much Joy was mixed up in, and how much to tell Moon. It would all come out eventually, but he hoped he could do some damage control before that happened.

11

How Deep Does This Go?

The bank was more than happy to help Moon to secure her little home against a possible lawsuit. The fact that she had already been making a year of steady payments, on time, with receipts, worked in her favor, as did her long association/job history with the bank itself. They even recommended that she switch now to outright ownership with an excellent mortgage rate instead of continuing with the rent-to-own agreement. Moon wasn't sure she could legally do that since she had signed a contract for five years, but if they were ready to try to break the contract, well, so was she! Moon left the meeting feeling much surer of herself. The lawyers had promised to let her know if any motions were filed. Now it was a waiting game. Moon went back to work.

Across town, Officer Williams had his hands full with Joy's detainment. She was loud, she was belligerent, she was upsetting nearly everyone at the station. Tommy spent the morning ignoring her screamed threats while he followed some anonymous information which he had been given the evening before. By noon he had enough answers to his inquiries to venture back to the holding cells.

"Pipe down and I will put you someplace a little nicer, maybe get you a burger from the Diner. Keep squalling like this and your next stop won't be nearly as comfortable as where you are now!" he advised her. "I have a good idea about what's really going on here, I may even be able to help, but you've <u>got</u> to meet me halfway."

"Why should I believe you when you're the reason I'm SITTING IN A DAMN JAIL!!!" she screamed. "You lied to Mom; you lied to me! NOW LET ME OUT!"

Tommy stared at her until she stopped yelling, then pulled up a small stool to sit outside the bars.

"Are you done?" he asked, just as he had years ago when occasionally her temper had gotten the best of her. He had been on the other end of her angry outbursts far too often to be swayed by them.

"No!" she snarled and turned her back on him.

"Good. Just making sure. You are in here, not because of me or your mother, but because of your own actions, Neil's, and possibly Geordie's. I haven't gotten to the bottom of that yet, but I will. I suspect he's involved with at least some of Neil's shenanigans, maybe even deeper than you are. Now, are you willing to work with me and let me help you get out of this mess or are you going to keep making a nuisance of yourself until they move you out to County, because Joy, I promise you, that is your next stop, and you won't be home by Tuesday!"

"Liar!" Joy said with her back still toward him. "You are lying to me again. Cops can lie and get away with it—you're a liar."

"Think what you like," Tommy said quietly. "When you're ready to work with me, I'll be here, with the proof." He stood up to replace the stool. "Your call. Transport to County will be here by suppertime so, think carefully." By the time he was back at his desk, Joy was screaming again.

"How much longer is she going to go on?" his sergeant demanded.

"She will calm down shortly, I expect," Tommy replied without looking up from his paperwork.

"Did you request a transport to County?"

"No. But she doesn't know that. If she doesn't settle down within the hour, I *will* make the request, and she can chill out in the general population out there. I don't think it will be necessary, though. She knows exactly how deep she is in this; she wants out or she wouldn't have come for lunch at the Diner yesterday. She knows me—we went to school together, and she knows I'm her best chance right now." Tommy looked up, cocked his head. "Hear that?"

"I don't hear anything," the sergeant replied.

"Exactly. She's done screaming, she's probably crying. She won't want me to see her that way, so I'll wait until she's cried herself out. Then I will go talk to her again. In the meantime, I have a few calls to make, I'll be back shortly. Page me if she starts up again, but I doubt that she will. Also, if Neil or Geordie try to get in to talk to her I want to know immediately! I don't want either of them anywhere near her."

"What about the mother? Is she mixed up in all this?"

"Joy's mom is working with me at the moment. She won't contact Joy until I give the 'go ahead', and no, she isn't mixed up in this. I know the lady well. She's nowhere near any of this."

"If you're sure..." the sergeant said doubtfully.

"I'm sure." Tommy was out the door before his sergeant could say anything more. His next stop was Fitz's Bar, a store-front bar on the south edge of town, to see if anyone knew where Geordie could be found.

Fitz's was empty of clientele when Tommy opened the door half an hour later. He had parked down the block a bit to keep the curiosity at a minimum. He wasn't looking for trouble, he didn't expect to find any, but he was hoping to find some answers.

Fitz himself was in the kitchen area of the bar setting up the grill for the minimal lunch crowd he served. Most of his patrons merely wanted a beer and chips or a ham sandwich from the cooler behind the bar, but Fritz's ancient grill also provided some of the best burgers in town, when it could be coaxed into life. It looked like today would be a good day: the grill was grumbling but it wasn't smoking and spitting sparks, so Fritz was running on positive vibes that all would be well, at least through the lunch rush. His grandfather had built the bar in the 1920's, his father had worked it before and after Gramps passed away. Fritz, now an old man in his own right, began his career bussing tables and washing dishes for Gramps and Pop. Alone for the last twenty years, he fought hard to keep it up and running. "Up" was maybe a misnomer. The building leaned and creaked, threatening to collapse in every spate of bad weather. So did Fritz. He couldn't afford to fix it up or remodel, had no children to pass it along to, so he was just trying to make it last long enough to see him safely through this lifetime. It was likely to be a photo finish.

Tommy leaned on the old walnut bar and called out to Fritz as he puttered with the grill, "Two with everything if you can get it to behave!"

"Humph," Fritz replied, banging on one of the grates. "You're out of your jurisdiction, ain't you? Isn't your beat on the other side of town? Or are you slumming, Tommy Williams?"

"Ah, you caught me!" Tommy sang out. "Actually, I'm hoping to get on the good side of a certain young lady, and I happen to know she always fancied your cooking. So, two with everything, if you please—to go."

Fritz stuck his head out through the swinging door and stared at Tommy. "You. Got a girlfriend? The world is coming to an end! I thought you'd never look at another girl after that 'Joy What's Her Name" ditched you back in high school. Out of your league, she was, boy."

"You could be right, there. What can I say—first love."

"Humph. You didn't come all the way down here for a burger for some girl. What else you want?"

"A Coke. And some information. I'm looking for Geordie Carpenter. I know he comes here fairly often. Know where I can find him now?"

"What's in it for me!"

"An invitation to the wedding if the burger does the trick?" Tommy offered.

"How about a cruiser past here a couple of times on a Friday and Saturday night? They don't come down this way much, we could use a little support before things start getting rough, catch my drift? Then maybe it wouldn't get to the point where they're talking about shutting me down because of all the rough stuff."

"I think something could be arranged, if the information you have is good. So, where can I find him?"

"Upstairs on my couch, sleeping off last night's 'supper', that's where he is. He's got no place else to go so I let him sleep on the couch, until his girlfriend calms down. She kicked him out a while ago—he's been talking like he's going back to his ex-wife, but I don't believe it. She'd be a fool to take him back. He's better off with his girlfriend, in my opinion."

"Ah, your opinion, yes. For the record, I don't think there's any chance that his ex-wife will take him back, but stranger things have happened. If you point the way, I will deal with Geordie while you fix those burgers. Deal?"

Fritz gestured toward the stairs at the back of the kitchen, "Be my guest, He grunted as he continued banging on the old grill.

Tommy moved quietly up the stairs to Fritz's apartment. It was neat, clean, well-lit, well-kept except for the snoring lump in the middle of the sofa. Tommy shook Geordie's shoulder a few times before getting a response.

"Fritz, I said just let me sleep until this afternoon, then I'll be on my way!" he muttered. Geordie rolled over, forgetting how narrow the couch was, only to wind up on the floor.

"Now are you awake?" Tommy asked, "Or do I have to throw a glass of cold water in your face? After all, that's how you used to wake us up when we crashed in your living room after a party. By the way, I assume you didn't tell Moon about that little incident?"

"No point," Geordie muttered. "I handled it. What do you want?"

"To buy you lunch and ask you some questions. Somewhere else. You are bad for business if you stay here."

Geordie grunted. "Better be somewhere else. No telling if the grill is working today..."

A string of expletives from down below followed by "That's better" and more banging cut him off.

"I think Fritz has things under control. Let's go find out, shall we?" Tommy motioned toward the door behind him.

Geordie struggled to his feet and staggered toward the bathroom door. He was back within a few minutes, slicked up a bit, ready to meet the world.

"Fritz! Make that three to go!" Tommy called down the stairs.

"Got them here," came the reply. "That'll be $12, please."

"Highway robbery," muttered Geordie, as Tommy fished the money out of his wallet.

"I charged you some extra for the couch," growled Fritz.

"And happy we are to pay it," observed Tommy as he herded Geordie out the door, bag of lunches in hand.

"So where are we going to eat this? And who gets the extra burger?" Geordie wanted to know.

"We can eat back at the station. I want to take the extra sandwich to someone waiting there. As a matter of fact, I could use your help in exchange for the free meal. How about it? Feel like helping me out?"

"If you think I would be of help, of course I'll try. What do I have to do?"

"I will let you know when I'm ready. First, we eat."

Tommy pulled into the station parking lot, into his assigned space, and gestured for Geordie to follow him.

"We can sit in one of the conference rooms. More comfortable than the break room with everyone staring at us. Pop or coffee? Or we have juice in the vending machine."

"Yuck. Hate cop coffee. Coke please, cold, not lukewarm."

"Coming right up. Have a seat," Tommy ushered Geordie into one of the conference offices at the left of the desk, closed the door and gestured to his sergeant that the room was occupied. No interruptions, please. He took the third burger to a quieter Joy but didn't tell her that Geordie was there. "If you need me, I will be in a room down the hall with a client. Ask nicely and they will come get me. Okay?" He left without waiting for an answer. Joy would work this out by herself in good time. Right now, she had nothing but time.

Instead, he joined Geordie in the conference room which often doubled as an informal interrogation room. Over burgers the questions began: Did Geordie know anything about Neil's business dealings? Was Joy involved in them? How deeply? Did he know if Joy was using drugs? Was Geordie involved with Neil in "business"? Was he conducting business out of Fritz's bar? Did Fritz know or was he a party to it? How did he obtain the 'merchandise'? Could he name his supplier? How far was he willing to go to help Joy?

The list went on. At first Geordie was angry that Tommy would accuse him of dealing drugs and claimed to know nothing about Neil's backroom dealings. But when Tommy let it 'accidentally' slip that Joy was in the holding cell eating the third burger, Geordie began to tell a different story.

Slowly the tale of Neil's hold over Joy and ultimately over Geordie came out: names, dates, places, people, all started to make sense to Tommy. The man watching Moon's home, thinking that she was involved because of Joy and because of her job at the bank, the stranger Abby had seen riding in Joy's car with her, Neil's panic-driven search for Joy when she disappeared, Geordie's connections down at Fritz's—he even 'suggested' that Lacey's son might be involved which caused Tommy to raise his eyebrows in surprise. It looked like this was going to be a whole lot bigger than he first believed. Already his mind was working on how to set up an investigation to figure out just how deep this went and how to bring it down. It was imperative that Joy and Geordie be kept safe until he could bring Neil in for questioning and break this organization apart! And who could he trust to spearhead this investigation? It would have to be one of the senior detectives, Tommy was only a beat officer, so he wasn't high enough up in the department. Perhaps bring someone in from the state level?

There might already be something in the works. Time to loop in his sergeant....

Geordie finished his burger and soda; he sat at the conference table with his head in his hands. He was scared. He was in this thing too deeply and he was even more afraid for his daughter. How far could he trust Tommy to help Joy, even if it were too late for her dad? How had he let it get this far? It was only supposed to be some quick money to help pay his medical bills, maybe buy back his BMW, and now it had spiraled way out of control. When he lifted his head, his eyes were teary.

Tommy was unmoved. "Geordie, you got yourself in this on your own—you taught us when we were kids that actions have consequences. I will do what I can, but both you and Joy are going to have to help. I will do what I can to keep you safe, but you are both in something dangerous, and deep! Now, I'm going to leave you here, you don't leave this room until I get back! I am going to bring my sergeant in so we can go over the whole thing again, you are going to write out a signed statement for me, and my boss will decide what the next step will be."

On his way out, Tommy beckoned to one of his fellow officers. "Marty, there's a man in the conference room that the sergeant is going to want to talk to ASAP. I'm going to get him, make sure the guy doesn't leave the room. He may try a con, but he is not to leave the room for any reason until I get back with Sarge. Not for any reason. Okay?"

Marty looked skeptical. "Is he dangerous?" he asked.

"Slippery and more than a little desperate," was Tommy's response. "Go in and sit with him. Talk to him. Just don't let him leave the room. Not even to use the bathroom. I'll walk him there when Sarge says it's okay, not until."

"Got it," Marty assured him.

"And no one else comes in, until I get back!"

Tommy took off at a fast walk as Marty headed into the conference room.

"I'm Officer Martin Dane. Can I get you anything while we wait for Tommy? Coffee? Another soda?"

"I'm fine, for now," Geordie answered. "Could I make a phone call, do you think?"

Marty considered the request. "Sure, sure, as soon as Tommy comes back. You'll want to wait for him before you make any decisions."

"It's just that I want to call my daughter. She will worry about me, I didn't make it home last night; crashed on a friend's couch, you know how it is, and she'll think I got into an accident or something."

"She lives with you?" Marty enquired.

"No, but we're close, you know. I won't tell her where I am, don't want to worry her too much, I just want to check in, so she knows I'm ok."

"What's her name? Maybe I can call her for you when Tommy gets back."

"Joy Harrison Howard. I have her cell number here, but if she doesn't recognize the person calling, she probably won't pick up."

"That's not a problem, I can let her know in person. She's sitting in our holding cell in back, has been here since yesterday, in fact. Quite a little spitfire, your girl!" Marty's grin died with the look on Geordie's face.

"You've had my girl locked up since yesterday and didn't see fit to tell me or her mother?" Geordie's voice rose to a shout. "Because if my ex-wife knew, she'd have Joy out of that cage IN A HEARTBEAT."

"Geordie! Calm down! Moon knows where Joy is and is helping us!" Tommy stepped into the room followed by the sergeant. Marty beat a hasty retreat, knowing he would be called to account for his lapse later.

"What Joy doesn't know is that you are here, yet. So, let's take this one step at a time and MAYBE we can get everybody home safe and sound." Tommy pulled up chairs for himself and his sergeant and faced Geordie squarely.

"Whatever happens, Joy isn't going home with you. I'm sending her over to stay with Moon, or she will remain in custody until I think it's safe for her. I don't trust Neil farther than I can throw him, he's put you in danger, and worse, he's put Joy and by extension Moon in danger as well. None of you are safe until he's behind bars for a long time and his racket's broken up. He's a conduit at the very least and possibly the brains behind the drugs and other trafficking that you were telling me about earlier. If you don't care about your own safety, or Moon's, then think about Joy, because Neil will either try to take her down with him or sacrifice all three of you to save himself. I. Will. Not. Allow. Him. To. Continue. Hurting. Joy. Or. Moon. Am I clear?"

Geordie hung his head, but Tommy could tell that it wasn't out of shame or contrition. Geordie was buying time, trying to decide how best to get himself out of his predicament.

"It's not good, Geordie," Tommy said softly. "It's done. The best you can do is to tell me how to find Neil. Now."

"How much does Moon know?" Geordie asked, still stalling.

"Very little. Enough to keep her in the loop about where Joy is but not enough to put her in more danger than she already is. Someone has been watching her house, trying on the doors etc. Her dog chased an intruder away not long ago, so I've had a squad car add her block to his route to make sure it doesn't continue, but this is all down to Neil and you, and your dealings down at Fritz's. How involved is he in all this?"

"How do you think he keeps that sink hole in operation?" Geordie asked, surprised. "The trade Neil sends through that bar accounts for more than half his business. If you close it down, he'll lose the bar, everything. 'They' might even take out their frustration on him personally. You go after Neil, and you are going to open up a hornet's nest in this town that's going to cost a lot of important people a lot more than just money. Be very careful, gentlemen. You don't know anywhere near the whole story."

Tommy and the sergeant exchanged looks. "We have reason to hang on to Joy for the time being but no reason to keep Geordie, and if we try or turn him loose, we tip our hand," Tommy mused. "It's your call, sarge, but I think we need to tread carefully."

"Stay here with him while I make a few calls. It's going to be a long night."

"Do you mind if I bring Joy in as well? Get her out of the holding cell before she starts a ruckus again?"

"Done! My ears are still ringing from the last time," the sergeant exclaimed. "Marty! Bring this gentleman's daughter to the conference room."

"No, I'll get her. She knows me, she'll give Marty a hard time and wind up right back in holding or on her way to County—which might still be an option if she doesn't cooperate." Tommy was out the door and back within minutes with a suspicious Joy in tow.

"Sit down across from your dad, relax, and behave yourselves, both of you," Tommy ordered as the sergeant and Marty went back to their work. "I don't need to remind you that you've gotten yourselves in over your heads, so if you want to clean this up, you'd better start talking to me. I'm going to record our conversation so there is no debate later over what was said. Consider your answers carefully. Very carefully. And understand that I am going to double-check everything you tell me, so don't even think about lying to me. Now, a question for either one of you: where can I find Neil?"

"I don't know," growled Joy. Tommy stared her down until she changed her tone. "I swear, I don't know. I left while he was out, no clue where, I have no idea if he's been back to our place."

"Where were you staying?" Tommy produced a notebook and pen, jotted down the address Joy gave him then turned to Geordie.

"Anything to add?"

"He's due to be down at Fritz's later tonight to meet a buyer. Lacey Burnham's son, Geoff, is supposed to be there too. He's bringing in the contact. Some friend or relation or other. Lacey knows him too, but I don't think she knows what he actually does for a living. She sure doesn't know about her boy. She'd throw a tantrum, haul that boy out of there, make one hell of a scene. She's already pissed that Moon told her about her boy hanging out down there. Swore a blue streak until her new boyfriend calmed her down, told her it must have been a mistake, the boy had been with him the whole time. Lacey's still sore about it. She's been trying every way she can think of to get back at Moon—being passed over for the promotion at the bank was the last straw for her! But now she's engaged to her new boyfriend, she doesn't have as much time as before to worry about Moon or pay attention to what her son's been getting up to down at Fritz's," Geordie laughed. Joy turned her face away.

"It wasn't so long ago she was pulling out all the stops and making a play for you—telling you how bad Mom let herself go and how she could help you get your live back on track after "what's her name," oh, yeah, *Vicki* ditched you. You laughed in her face; told her she was no better than she was in high school. Neil was there—he came home laughing so hard he was almost crying. Said you dropped her flat!"

"Yeah, so we aren't exactly best friends," Geordie mumbled. "I don't seem to have much luck with the ladies these days. The ones I want can't stand me, and I can't stand the ones that want me."

"Cry me a river!" laughed Joy and Geordie grinned too.

"So, Geoff Burnham is in this as well? What about his girlfriend, Sherle, the one that bought Moon's old car? And you don't think Lacey is involved or knows what's going on? What about the new boyfriend? How deep is he in this?"

"Couldn't tell you," Geordie said thoughtfully. "Haven't met him yet. I only see the kid and sometimes Sherle, the girl he hangs around with. That's how I knew your mom sold her car," he told Joy. "Sherle bought it—she drives them to Fitz's in it, so his new one doesn't get stolen or partsed out. I saw that beater I gave Moon in the divorce down at the bar and just about lost it. I knew she had been having a rough time; I got really scared when I thought she might be hanging around with Fritz. Then when I found out I was wrong, well, it just made me that much madder at her that she was finally moving on and I still felt stuck."

"She's a pretty awesome lady, your ex-wife," Tommy muttered as he scribbled notes. "Not many could pull themselves back the way she has. She was smart to keep her job. Having spent those years at the bank has helped her find that little house of hers. Speaking of which," he glared at Joy. "You have a choice, and I want you to think about it carefully. Neil is going to come looking for you. Do you want me to set you somewhere safe until we bring him in, or do you want to calm his fears and make it look like 'business as usual' by going to stay with your mom? Moon will take you in and I already have people watching her place since the break-in attempts."

"Wait! What?" Geordie stared at Tommy as Joy began to rev up for a screaming session.

"WHAT DO YOU MEAN BREAK-IN ATTEMPTS?" she yelled. "Was she hurt? Was anything taken? Did they catch who did it? WHAT ARE YOU DOING ABOUT IT?"

Geordie half rose from his chair, but Tommy was quicker off the mark.

"Joy! Easy! They were only attempts, nothing was taken, and Moon wasn't hurt at all. The first was while she was at work, the second time her dog ran the guy off before he could get in. Brave little doxie she has there. Your mom is fine, for the time being. And it might be the best thing if you stayed with her. That way I can keep an eye on both of you at once. And the longer you stay in our custody the jumpier Neil is going to get. I need him calmed down and back to 'business as usual' as soon as possible. If he gets skittish it could blow this whole thing—then nobody is safe. Do you understand?"

Joy nodded. "Are you going to call her, or should I?"

Tommy considered. "I will call and give her a heads-up, then you call and finalize the details, just as if you were visiting for a while. Sound good?"

"What about me?" Geordie demanded. "Do you want me there as well, because you know Moon won't put up with that. Not at all. Not…after the last time, the diner…."

"The diner?" Joy enquired.

"I…met your mom for lunch, told her I'd pay the bill, and I…forgot to leave the money when I left."

"No, you deliberately dumped the check," corrected Tommy. "They called Moon the next day and she paid it. Geordie, I would suggest you start straightening out your life by being honest. You wanted to make Moon look bad, to punish her, and it backfired. Too bad. No sympathy here or from Joy." He glanced in her direction as she shook her head 'no'.

"So, I will get to you later. First, I want to make sure Joy is safe. If I have to, I can hold you on a charge of vagrancy and Neil won't get too suspicious. Joy, what's it going to be?"

"I hate getting Mom involved in this, and I have aa LOT of apologizing to do. Do you think she'll even let me stay once she knows the whole story?"

"In a heartbeat. I imagine Moon will insist upon it," Tommy smiled. He dialed a number on his cell and put the call on 'speaker' as it was ringing. "Shh!" he indicated Geordie. "I don't want Moon to know about you---yet."

Geordie covered his mouth with his hand to indicate that he understood.

"Tommy? Officer Williams? Any word about Joy?" Moon's voice over the phone was concerned but deliberately calm.

"Yes, she's here, she's fine. She wants to talk to you."

Moon was silent for a moment. "Okay. Put her on."

"Mom? It's me. I…I owe you an apology…I…want to come home. Can I, may I come home?"

Again, there was silence on the line, a murmur of voices in the background. Then Moon was back on the line. "Yes, you may come home, but Joy, there will be some ground rules. It...won't be quite like it was before. I won't have your verbal abuse! You will have to be polite to me, to the neighbors too. Can you do that?"

Joy swallowed hard. "I will try. I..."

"Okay, I will come by for you whenever Officer Williams says I may. Please put him back on."

"I'm still here. Joy, do you still have your car?"

"No, Neil took it. I'm walking these days," she laughed hollowly.

"So am I, or on my bicycle. I biked to work today so I can bike over to the station if I need to."

"No, that's okay," Tommy replied. "I will borrow an unmarked and bring her to the bank in a bit. Can we use a conference room there? We need to talk a bit before you all go home for the day."

"I have no more clients so yes come any time and we can chat in the back conference room. I'll have coffee ready, and I think there is some cake in the break room. I'll check on it."

"We will be there in half an hour," Tommy advised her, ending the call. "Get your stuff together," he told Joy, "We are leaving as soon as I clock out. "Geordie, stay here for now, be cool, I will get you some dinner, bring you back a book from the library if you like, whatever, but stay here until we are ready to go to Fritz's tonight."

"Tonight? Already?" Geordie looked panicked.

"The sooner we wrap this up, the sooner you, Joy, and Moon are safe. We are going over tonight.

Tommy left the two of them in the conference room while he signed out one of the unmarked cars, then returned for Joy.

"Dad wants a mystery novel or true crime if you can find him one," Joy indicated her father who was sitting with his head on his arms on the table.

Tommy took her by the hand. "No problem. Bob always has some in his locker. I'll borrow one that he's done reading and make sure

Geordie gets dinner." He beckoned to another police officer, whispered something, without letting go of Joy, and led the way out to the car.

"Nice ride," Joy remarked, and Tommy thought he could hear a sarcastic edge to her voice. He decided to ignore it as they buckled their seatbelts.

"Not nearly as nice as the limo we all rented on Prom night, remember? It threw a rod on the way home from post prom supper, we had to walk five miles in our "finery", and we all got in after curfew! If the limo company hadn't backed up our stories, we'd probably all still be grounded!" He was thrilled to hear Joy laugh.

"You and Markie Jones, Bryan Murphy and Liz Compton (did you know they are married?), me and Teddy Walsh. You, Bryan and Teddy all were in maroon tuxes, I had a dress Mom made especially for me as a surprise, she copied it right out of Seventeen Magazine, I felt so grown up until the limo broke down."

"We got those tuxes on special 'cause nobody else wanted that color and we were too broke to rent anything better. You were the best dressed girl at the prom. You should have been queen," he added softly.

"Pipe dreams, Mom calls them," Joy shook her head. "I was lucky to be on the court, but you are right about that dress. It was spectacular!"

"Do you still have it?" Tommy asked her.

"Somewhere, packed away where Neil can't find it and sell it. Nothing is safe around him. What's mine is his, I guess." Joy hunched down in her seat.

"You might want to call a "war council", sit down with Moon and figure out your next steps, once we get Neil and his band of Merry Whatevers under wraps," Tommy suggested. "I'll be around too. If you need any help, that is."

"I…appreciate that," Joy said. "I…I'm scared, Tommy, I can't see how this is going to work out. I have a bad feeling about this."

Tommy pulled into the parking lot behind the bank. "I won't lie to you, it's not going to be an easy fix, but this has gone on far too long and it's getting worse. A lot of innocent people are going to be hurt if this doesn't stop now, and I can't look the other way, even for you and Geordie. You all mean the world to me, always have, and the best way I can show you that is to help you both out of this mess, but I can't protect you from all legal consequences if Neil involved you too deeply. All I can do is to keep it from getting any worse for you. Understand? Good. Let's go talk to your mom!"

Moon met them at the back door of the bank and escorted them into a nearby conference room. Once the door was closed, she gestured to the chairs, then held out her arms to Joy, asking for a hug. Joy didn't think twice.

"I'm. So. Sorry." Her voice was muffled by Moon's shoulder while Tommy discretely took out his notepad and began examining his jottings. When Moon and Joy sat, he began.

It took nearly half an hour to catch Moon up on all the particulars of Tommy's investigation, as well as his ongoing operation.

"What about Geordie?" Moon wanted to know.

"I will continue to keep Geordie under wraps for now—you concentrate on keeping Joy out of trouble. She will be staying with you for the near future, away from Neil, and we will be watching the house more closely. We want him to think she just went home to her Mother. I suspect, although I can't prove it yet, that the fellow who has been hanging around your place upsetting Pansy is either one of Neil's "business partners" or somebody wanting a cut of the profits. Either way, they linked Joy to Neil, and you to Joy. Did you get the motion sensor repaired?"

"Yes," Moon assured him. "All taken care of, and I haven't seen anyone around there since, although Pansy notices something different once in a while. She hears better than I do," she laughed.

"Okay, I will leave you two ladies to settle in, call me if you see anything, or need anything." Tommy stood and looked at Joy. "I'm counting on you. Behave. Lay low. Help your mother, okay? I will check back with you in a day or so—I'll keep you updated as we have more information." He let himself out of the conference room, out the back door to the unmarked squad car.

Begin Again

"First things first," Moon looked at Joy. "You need a place to sleep. I have one bed and some semi-comfortable chairs. We need to get you a bed to sleep on at least. I'm done for the day, let's see what we can find. Okay?"

Joy nodded wordlessly and followed Moon out to her desk. Moon collected her things, signed out with the secretary, and escorted Joy out the back door. "We don't need everybody knowing our business quite yet. They are all still gossiping about Lacey getting married. That should hold them long enough for you to get settled. I wish Sue was home—this is a perfect opportunity for a 'war council' but they are on vacation until tomorrow so... let's start with the new Rent-to Own place. I hear they have some nice things. What do you say?"

"Why are you doing this?" Joy wanted to know. "You would be well within your rights to tell me to 'take a hike' after the way I behaved when that apartment house kicked you all out."

Moon considered as they wheeled her bicycle down the street. "Yes, I would be, but what would that gain? Family comes first. I've always taught you that. And, I suspect your attitude had more to do with your own life coming apart at the seams that it did with me leaving garbage behind. Twin or full size, do you think?" she asked as they stopped in front of the rental store.

"Whatever you think best," Joy agreed.

"Then let's see what they have and how soon it can be delivered."

The fates must have been smiling on Moon and Joy that day: they found a twin bed and dresser set for very little down, delivery set for the next day. Included were mattress, box spring bedframe with an oak headboard and a large matching dresser. Joy also found a chair that matched the set, so she had someplace to sit or set out her clothes.

"You mean the clothes I don't have," Joy remarked after they left the store. "Everything I own is back with Neil—he won't let me have my stuff unless I come back home. Could...we stop by the Thrift Shop so I can get a couple pairs of jeans and some shirts? I don't want to lay a huge burden on your pocketbook, but I really can't wear these clothes one more day—it's already been three!"

"Joy, whatever you need, within reason, we will get you. You will need bedding also. I suggest Johnson's Department store: they always have sales and clearance. I have a sewing machine so if we find some nice pattern, I can run you up a couple of summer dresses—the way I used to "back when". How does that sound?"

Joy nodded wordlessly and followed Moon down the street. Johnson's Department store was an imposing building close to the center of town—Moon preferred shopping there to the discount superstore one town over. Johnson's Department Store was closer, and familiar. She had been shopping there all her life and knew every department. She locked her bike to the rack outside and within minutes she and Joy had found the bargain bins with a treasure trove of clothes that fit Joy nicely. They selected jeans, tops, undergarments, pajamas, socks and sandals.

"What do you say we give those sneakers of yours a decent burial at home?" Moon asked gently, not knowing if the ratty shoes had some special significance.

"They are Neil's. I say burn 'em," Joy shrugged. "I stole them from his closet since he locked up all my clothes."

"He. Did. What?" Moon was shocked but tried not to show it in the store.

"He didn't want me leaving...again," Joy said matter-of-factly. "I'll tell you everything later. Over dinner? Or will that spoil your appetite?"

"We will find a time to talk," Moon promised as they pointed their shopping cart toward the bedding section.

Joy chose pastel pink sheets, a rose-pink blanket, and a traditional white bedspread that was the only item not on sale. When Joy was occupied elsewhere, Moon slipped a set of pink flowered sheets that Joy had been admiring into the cart, just to have a back-up set for wash days. Moon's mother had been adamant that sheets wore better if they were rotated. She would think about flannel sheets like the ones she had for her bed for winter, if Joy stayed that long. Moon was hoping that Joy would stay for a while, that they could bury some of the past pain. One thing at a time. Today was a day for basic necessities. Enough to get through the next few weeks, then they would see.

The bill was hefty, over two hundred dollars, but not exorbitant for everything they had bought. Now came the fun of getting everything home.

"If Sue were home, we could call her to come rescue us," Moon laughed as she wrote the check and filled in the amount in her checkbook register.

"Do you mean Sue Branwell? Rev. Branwell's wife?" the clerk asked. "I thought you might because I see you in here together often enough! My husband's brother goes to that church. They must be home from vacation—she was just in here this noon."

"May I use your phone?" Moon asked, indicating the phone by the cash register. "My cell phone ran out of charge earlier," she explained to Joy as the clerk dialed the number and handed the receiver to Moon.

Joy checked her phone. "My battery died too, I didn't think to charge it at the station."

"No problem. Sue, it's Moon...are you okay?"

Sue sounded as though she had been crying, but quickly pulled herself together when she heard Moon's voice.

"Of course, you know I am! What's up?"

"Do you have your car available? Can you come rescue us? We have been shopping and we got a bit carried away," Moon laughed.

"Define carried away," Sue was intrigued.

"Bedding and clothes and half the store—on sale, so don't have a seizure. I have lots to tell you, but not on the phone."

"More bedding for your room? I thought you were set—or have you started hoarding?" Sue laughed.

"Linens for a bed for the spare bedroom," Moon confirmed.

"Oh, good, you finally decided how to use it!" Sue exclaimed. "Did you buy a bed too?"

"At the Rent-to-Own. They are delivering it tomorrow; we can make do for tonight."

"We?"

"Joy is with me. She can take my room tonight and..." Moon had the oddest feeling she was talking to dead air. "Sue? Sue?" She looked at Joy who just shrugged.

Moments later Sue was back on the phone. "Mr. Snow is here finishing up the church lawn and flower border. He will meet you out front of Johnson's, pick up your stuff from the Rental place and your other goodies and give you a lift home. He has to kill some time until his wife is done with her committee meeting here anyway so he's glad to do it, but you will owe him coffee. From the Latte Wagon across the street. Grande, nonfat, double pump vanilla with two sugars, and a chocolate chip cookie. Otherwise, he says you will both walk behind the truck!"

"Perish the thought!" Moon exclaimed. "Mr. Snow to the rescue again! Well, tell him he's got a deal, and many, many thanks!"

Moon and Joy collected their packages and walked across the street where Moon ordered the treats for Mr. Snow and small iced coffees for herself and Joy.

It didn't take long before the big blue pick-up was parked in front of the department store and Moon's bike was being secured in the back. The packages joined it, and they were off to the Rent-To-

Own. No problem about putting the bed, dresser and chair into the truck, the store manager promised that it wouldn't upset their delivery schedule, and Joy would have her bed that night.

At that point it was well past the hour when Moon would usually get home to walk Pansy so they put Moon in the cab of the truck, Joy hid among the packages in the back so passers-by wouldn't see her, and they were home in no time.

The first order of business, as Joy and Mr. Snow unloaded the truck, was for Moon to take Pansy out for her bathroom break. She didn't even stop to change her clothes knowing that the little pup had been waiting patiently to do her 'business' for longer than usual.

The furniture was set in the spare bedroom, Joy began assembling the bed, while Moon took the hot dish out of the freezer to defrost a bit before cooking. She noted that she had salad veggies to go with the lasagna she had chosen as well as some vanilla ice cream in the freezer for dessert. While the meal was in the oven, she checked on Joy's progress and changed her own clothes, finding a denim skirt and yellow top with cap sleeves, and a pair of comfy canvas slip-ons. Afterward she called to thank Sue again, but no one answered. She left a message on their machine, knowing Sue would call her later.

By then Joy was in the shower so Moon set the table, fed Pansy who was desperately curious about Joy and also desperately trying not to show it. "Get used to her," Moon admonished. "She may be here for a while."

"Who are you talking to?" Dressed in a pair of her new jeans, embroidered peasant shirt, and sandals, with a towel wrapped around her freshly washed hair, Joy looked and sounded like a different person, as she sat down at the dining room table.

"Welcome to my home," Moon responded. "We will have lots to talk about in the coming days, but first, this is Pansy, my companion and friend. She is a rescue from the pound. She is as much a member of this household as I am. Be advised."

Joy and Pansy sized each other up, cautiously. Pansy inched toward Joy who didn't move, letting the little dog come on her own terms. "A big improvement over that mercenary cat, if you ask me," she remarked quietly, as Pansy sniffed her hands and feet.

"Glad you think so. I don't know why I waited so long to add a dog to my family—I guess I was waiting for Pansy."

"Why a dog?" Joy wanted to know. "And why this one?'

"We had a rescued beagle when I was growing up, Chowder, Dad said we couldn't keep him but wound up falling in love with the dog. They were constant companions until the day the dog died of old age. Why Pansy? She was a stray, and no one came to claim her. She had health issues that I helped her get over—I guess she needed me. It felt really good to be needed."

Moon finished setting the table with the salad veggies and went to take the lasagna out of the oven "What shall we have to drink?" she asked. "I can put on a pot of coffee, if you like or there are some diet cokes in the fridge. After supper we will make out a list and I will call the grocers to update my order."

Joy was now stroking Pansy's long brown ears and the little dog was sighing in ecstasy. "Your order?"

"They deliver my groceries on a regular schedule –it's very reasonable and almost a necessity in the winter, so I don't have to lug food home. It keeps me independent—I really don't miss that old car, or the extra expense. As for days like today, I get by with a little help..."

"The soda is fine—or just water. Either one. I still drink milk sometimes with my food," Joy admitted.

"Is 1%, okay?" Moon asked.

"That's great. Now, enough!" Joy took her hand away from Pansy's ears. "I need to wash my hands again! Crazy dog!" she laughed as she went back to the bathroom.

"Thank you," Moon smiled at the little dachshund as she wandered back into her crate and curled up on her pillow. "You made her feel welcome, and I appreciate it. But remember, you are <u>my</u> dog!"

Moon set out milk for Joy and a diet soda for herself along with the lasagna. Joy returned with her hair still in the towel.

"Do you still braid hair?" she asked as Moon dished up salad and hot dish. "Could you do something with this after supper?"

"I can try. Maybe out on the porch after dishes are done. How is your bed coming along?"

"All assembled, mattress protector and pad are on. Trying to decide which set of sheets, but I will get it done before bedtime. Most of my clothes are in the drawers—There's hardly any closet for that room—and we forgot to buy hangers."

"I knew we were missing something," Moon said thoughtfully. "I have a few extras by my sewing machine and we can pick up more to-morrow. Goodness! Is someone at the door?"

Someone was pounding and calling Joy's name. She went white and looked to Moon for help. "Neil!"

"Shoot! Go into the kitchen, call 911, give them this address and leave the line open! I'll answer the door. Go!"

Joy jumped up and ran for the kitchen as the pounding began again. Pansy barked and growled, not liking the interruption at all. In the background Moon could hear Joy talking to the 911 dispatcher. Help would be here soon.

"Just a minute!" she called out as she scooped up Pansy and shut her in her crate. The little dog would be safer there. "I'm just getting the pup under control. There!" she said as she opened the front door to reveal an irate Neil.

"Where is she!" he demanded.

"In her crate," said Moon calmly, deliberately misunderstanding.

"Not the damn dog!" roared Neil. "MY WIFE!"

"Oh." Moon was acting much calmer than she felt. Neil had never been one of her favorite people and now he was terrifying.

"She went to get something from the fridge..."

"I'm here! What do you want?" Joy was standing behind Moon with an apple in her hand. "I felt like having some fruit for dessert. Why?" she demanded.

"Get your things, it's time to go home," Neil demanded though not as loudly as before.

"Supper's on the table, Neil, we have plenty. Come join us." Moon turned her back to Neil and motioned Joy to sit down. As she set another chair for an astonished Neil she whispered, "Phone off the hook?"

"Yes," replied Joy. "left it the way you wanted it. Neil, my mother offered you dinner and it's better than you will get anywhere else. I'm not cooking tonight, I am eating here, catching up with my mom. Sit or go home. I haven't seen Mom in months and right now I need to make sure she's okay." She glared at Neil standing in the doorway. "What's it going to be?"

"You don't give the orders here..." began Neil, but Moon cut him off.

"No, I do!" She set another place setting by the chair. "Soda or water? Joy has the last of the milk."

Neil glared at them. "Neither! She's coming home. With me. Now!"

"Why?" Joy was stalling for time as Moon sat down and began to eat her salad.

"Because you are my wife, and you don't belong here." Neil advanced as if to grab Joy who stared him down. "I am eating dinner. If you touch me, I will scream, and I can tell you from past experience that if anyone is causing trouble over here the neighbors will call the cops. They called them on me when I caused a scene last summer and they will do it again! Your choice, but I am staying for a bit. I'll come home later."

"Where'd you get the fancy duds?" Neil pointed to her clothes. "Woman, if you took any of my money for that crap..."

"Your money?" shrieked Joy as a squad car pulled up in front of the house. "I EARNED that money; I had a good job until you made me quit so you can GO TO HELL! I didn't take any of the damn money, but if I did, so what. IT'S MY MONEY!!"

At that point the screen door behind Neil opened and Tommy Williams put a hand on Neil's shoulder.

"This will all get solved down at the station, Neil. We've been looking for you. Nice of you to drop in!"

It all happened too fast for Moon to realize what she was seeing. Neil swung around, fist balled, ready to take Tommy out, but the officer was ready for him. As Neil whipped around, Tommy threw him off balance through the open screen door where another officer waited to help Neil up and into hand cuffs.

"Are you ladies ok?" Tommy asked with exaggerated courtesy. Moon and Joy nodded. "Then we won't trouble you any further. You have a good evening now!" Tommy paused as Neil was led out to the curb loudly protesting his innocence and the police brutality with which he was being treated. "Thank the 911 operator and hand up the phone, please. I'll be in touch."

With that he followed his senior officer out to the curb and Joy closed the door with a resounding thump. "Well, we knew he's come looking for me, we didn't think it would be so soon. 'Johhny on the spot,' isn't he?" She deliberately changed the subject. "What did you say you had planned for dessert, because this apple will do me okay."

"Ice cream. Vanilla. We can have some later, before bed." Moon dished up some lasagna, then rushed out of the room. From the kitchen Joy heard a muffled "Thank you so much. Everything's fine" the click of the receiver, followed by the click of the crate latch and Pansy bounded into the room, ready to throw Neil out herself. Moon resumed her seat at the table: "Do not give her scraps, please," as Joy quickly put the morsel of beef back on her plate. Pansy glared at both of them. "I have special 'doggie ice cream' that she can have as a treat when we eat ours. Don't worry. She's not mistreated," Moon laughed.

Supper progressed comfortably. Ellen stopped by from across the alley to see that they were all okay and to meet Joy. She gave no hint that she recognized Joy from the earlier altercation, instead asked Moon if she would still be needed to check on Pansy during the day.

"I haven't thought that far ahead," Moon admitted. "I really hadn't thought past dinner dishes. I'll stop by in the morning and let you know. How's Paul's back?"

"Bothering him as usual. Some days are worse than others, you know?" remarked Ellen offhandedly. "He's out for a walk to stretch his muscles so I'd best get back. See you tomorrow. Nice to meet you, Joy."

"I thought sure she'd tell me off for last year and for tonight," Joy mused.

"They aren't that way," Moon assured her as she began washing the dishes. "Grab a towel."

"Do I HAVE to?" Joy was laughing. It was an old routine for them.

After the food had been put away, dishes dried and put in the dining room hutch, Moon suggested they sit on the porch and fix Joy's hair before a walk with Pansy.

"There are some beautiful gardens around here that I want your opinion on for this place," Moon remarked.

Joy's dark brown hair was longer than Moon remembered it, and it looked like Joy hadn't bothered with it for quite some time. It was easily waist length, but the ends were split and frizzy.

"Would you like me to trim a little—even it out? Or would you rather have someone more professional cut it?" Moon asked as she brushed the tangles out of Joy's hair. "I could cut it straight across here," she indicated a spot at the middle of Joy's back, "and there would still be plenty to braid. What do you think? Maybe not so hot in the summer."

"Yeah, go ahead. I don't mess with it much anymore." Joy didn't sound particularly interested.

'How odd,' thought Moon. 'She used to be so fussy about her hair.' She took scissors and evenly cut about a foot of dry frizzy hair off, leaving clean shining ends. When she had finished detangling the rest, she evened the bottom out, braided it down Joy's back and secured it with a rubber band. Joy had been silent all through the operation, sitting on the porch step absently stroking Pansy.

"I'm surprised," she mused when Moon finished. "She makes no attempt to run off—even after that squirrel." Pansy pricked up her ears at the mention of her nemesis but chose to be petted instead.

"She's a homebody, like me," Moon replied. "She prefers here to anywhere else. She's safe here."

"Um," said Joy. "With Neil in custody, do I stay here or go home?"

Moon was taken aback. "I don't think you should go anywhere until Tommy says it's okay. If you have things to pick up there, he could take you to get them. But just because they have Neil in custody doesn't account for the others he's mixed up with, and I think Tommy, Officer Williams, would rather you stay safely here. Don't you think? For the time being?"

"I didn't think about the rest of Neil's crew, but I should go get the cash I stashed at home. Unless he found it already. I had a good job; I was a physical therapy aide, and I was thinking about going to get my own license. They make good money, and the work was fun. Neil made me quit—didn't want me away from the house or hanging around other people. He's...different than he was when we were dating. He's controlling everything, and really paranoid about it."

"Tell Tommy tomorrow and you can go get your things if he says it's okay."

"It's just the money. I don't want anything else—maybe my alarm clock and great Grandma's silver tray. I hid it or he would have pawned it like he did the rest of our wedding gifts." She said it matter-of-factly but it broke Moon's heart.

"Whatever you need, Joy. Are you still thinking about going back to school? Do they have classes for that at the tech?"

"Yeah. They do. I don't know. When Neil gets out, he'll put the smack down on any plans like that so, well, we'll see. I better finish making my bed. Did you say you have hangers? And what about to-morrow? Do I stay here or what?"

"Yes, I have hangers. I don't know about tomorrow. I have vacation coming up, I can arrange the time off soon, but I have clients tomorrow and some training for my promotion."

"Promotion?" Joy sat up straighter. "What promotion?"

"Head loan officer, starting in September. Office and everything!" Moon laughed. "Oh, Joy, we have so much to catch up on, you better plan on staying a week at least. It will take that long and maybe longer to tell you everything! And this promotion couldn't have come at a better time. I have a rent-to-own agreement for this house and the family that I am buying it from want to break the contract and take back the house." She hastily reassured Joy before she could respond.

"One of the family members who wasn't included in the initial probate of the estate wants the house for one of their kids, I guess. But I talked to the lawyer who drew up the contract and I talked to the bank. I've made my payments on time, paid for the repairs to the place out of my own pocket (I have receipts) and I can get a loan to buy the place outright if they start any trouble. My lawyer doesn't think they have a good case for breaking the contract and he will let me know if they try, so I think we have it covered. In any event, in four years I can shift to a mortgage, and they will be out of the picture."

"You like this place that much?" Joy wanted to know.

"Honey, this is more 'home' to me than any place I have lived in since things started going south with your dad. This place reminds me of your great grandma, and I won't give it up without a fight."

"You've changed," Joy said slowly, pulling her knees up to her chin and wrapping her arms around them. "You were already changing last year when you called me tell me you were moving. It scared me, because you were drifting downhill the last years with Dad and then more so after the divorce. I didn't recognize you as my mother anymore, you had changed so much. I was afraid you had gone off the deep side of the pool when I heard they evicted everyone—not that your apartment was any great shakes, not like this place. But you've really changed, outside and inside. You remind me of Grandma, she was so strong. She'd be proud of you and ashamed of me. And she'd be right. If you go in to work tomorrow, could I go hang out with Aunt Sue and Abby? I don't want to be alone here, even with Pansy for company. Not yet anyway."

"I'll call her while you finish making your bed," Moon offered. "But first, a walk for Pansy and then her ice cream. She deserves it, don't you think?"

There was a message from Sue on the machine when they returned: "War Council?"

12

Sue's Dilemma

Sue offered to come by for Joy in the morning before Moon left for work and to meet them for lunch "someplace other than the diner, please!" she begged.

"How about if I rearrange my schedule, take off early, and we go for a picnic? We can stop by for Pansy, take her out with us, maybe do some antiquing? I want to move up my vacation if I can, to spend more time around the house and with Joy."

"You read my mind and Abby will be thrilled! I will see you before work. I will even drop you off, so you don't have to mess with the bike. And I want to see the new furniture, if you don't mind!"

Moon handed the hangers to Joy, before taking her own shower and setting out her clothes for work: a simple navy dress with three quarter sleeves and a navy and white polka dotted scarf.

Joy was curious. "I don't remember that dress."

"I made it a month or so ago, I've only worn it once. I have the pattern if you would like something similar."

Joy shook her head. "Maybe later. What I have is fine. For now." She was dressed in her new pajamas and pink robe; her feet were bare.

"Which sheets did you choose?" Moon wanted to know.

"The flowered," Joy answered as she wandered back to her room. "Do we have any more of Grandma's wool yarn?" she called.

"No, I'm sorry." Moon turned down her bed and turned off the light. This was Pansy's cue to assume her spot at the foot of the bed.

"Would you like to pick up some yarn, to do some knitting? Maybe some slippers?"

"Yeah. I think so. Maybe do an afghan this winter. It's been a long time..." Joy's voice drifted off and her light too was extinguished.

Sue was impressed with their purchases and with the way Joy had arranged her room so she could sit and watch out the window at the front street beyond the porch. Moon had chosen simple white curtains and blinds for the windows, so they worked well with Joy's choice of bedding. The room itself had pale green wallpaper that Moon hadn't felt the need to strip and redo. If Joy stayed, she could perhaps repaper or paint later. In the meantime, the room had an air of softness and youth that particularly suited her.

What was up with her anyway? No screaming fits, no accusations, no temper tantrums. This was a different Joy than the daughter Moon had raised, the 'Daddy's girl' who found fault with anything and every-thing. Something was out of place. Moon was grateful for the peace and quiet, but she wondered when the next phase would begin, what it would look like. What was driving this change? Moon opted for pa-tience. Joy would tell her in her own good time. Or she wouldn't.

Neil was behind bars for the moment, the investigation was stalled, so Tommy was willing to take Joy to get her clock, tray and money before Neil was released, if indeed he was. There were some possible charges pending on a warrant from another state that Joy claimed she knew nothing about, but it was still better to get her things quickly. Joy packed up the filthy shoes she had been wearing to return to the apartment. "They're Neil's. I don't want to be accused of stealing," she said tonelessly. Tommy promised that he would come by after work to pick her up. In the meantime, she would spend the day with Sue and Abby, Ellen and Paul would watch the house, walk Pansy, life would look like normal.

Except for Sue, who was struggling with issues of her own.

How will I tell her? How can I tell Moon that Jim is accepting a call to a new church, to a new congregation, a new town, a whole different state? I've lived here almost all my life! I can't just pack up and go—leave everything and everyone that brings comfort and joy into my life behind. I wanted to grow old in this town, with my family nearby. If I leave, I'll never get to come back, not to what this is now. It will all be different. It will have moved on and I will be stuck in the memories of what I had, what I lost. I can't do it.

Jim is so happy with the new call. How can I take that away from him? This is what I agreed to when I married a minister. I knew we wouldn't stay one place forever. How can I selfishly deny him a new start just because I can't bear to leave? Josh won't care, or will he? He'll be in college come fall, Abby in two years. Abby! She'll leave all her friends behind, friends she's had for a lifetime. She'll have to start all over too! So hard when one is in the middle of high school. Everything she has worked for, gone with a moving van. Will she see this as a betrayal or an adventure. I just wish we had more time!

Sue usually hummed or sang this week's hymns as she washed her dishes, made the beds, shifted the laundry from hamper to washer to dryer to basket to beds. There was always music on the radio when she cleaned so she could work in the rhythm. Abby thought it curious that the house had been so silent since they had come home early from vacation. Jim explained that they were returning early because of church business but he hadn't left his office since they walked through the door except to eat dinner with the family and turn in very late at night. Abby knew it was late because her dad always went to bed after the news at ten. Lately it was after midnight. She heard him come up the stairs even though she was supposed to be sleeping but was really listening to an audio book through her headphones. Why was he up so late?

She was grateful that Joy was there that day, helping her and Sue with some summer cleaning projects. Joy seemed different too. Not as brash and sassy as she had been the past couple years, more subdued, someone who startled easily. Sue said "Be nice to her. She's going through a rough patch right now." Abby said she wished Joy would talk to her, like they used to. They used to be almost-best friends in spite of their age difference. It was all different now, ever since Joy married Neil, and Abby didn't know how to start the conversation that would lead them back to the friendship that they had before. "Give her time," Sue advised.

Together they were sorting out old clothes in the attic, trying to decide what to keep, what to donate, what to throw away. There were trunks and boxes crammed full of clothes from who knew where. Abby had never seen most of them, but Sue seemed to recognize every item.

"I wore this to prom!" she exclaimed of a dress that looked like moths had also tried it on for size.

"Did you go with Dad?" Abby wanted to know.

"No, I didn't meet your dad until I was in college. I went with another 'Jim'—Jim Hatfield. He died on patrol with his Army unit a couple of years later." Sue folded up the gown and shoved it back into the box. "There's no saving it, but I can't bear to throw it away, not with all the memories that go with it." She looked like she was going to cry.

"You have other clothes in these boxes, all with memories attached to them," Joy was thinking out loud. "And most of them are in pretty bad shape, except those in those trunks over there."

"My grandparents' things and some that belonged to Jim's uncle—he was a stage actor, later a professor of theater at a college out East. That's where Jim and Abby get their talent from," Sue said ruefully.

"Why not come sit down with Mom, cut them in pieces and sew memory quilts. Use the material to tell your life story, to pass it on to Abby and Josh. It's the way women used to keep the family stories alive when they couldn't read or write."

"Better yet, talk to the quilting club at church," added Abby, "There must be other families that have old clothes they've kept for the memories. Set up a fundraiser with the club to work with one or two families at a time, do up the memory quilts. The money they raise could go into the Honor and Memorial Fund at church, so the stories and the memories won't be forgotten, by the families, the church or the community at large. If there is extra material left over, it could be made into blankets for the shelter or for the women's community."

"I'll talk to your father, but that idea may just have 'legs,' as we used to say in the theater. The quilters meet this weekend, the H&M team meets next week. In the meantime, I can't stay up here, it's too…hot. Break!"

Sue and the girls trooped downstairs to find iced drinks in the kitchen, and Sue determined to have some words with Jim before the day was out. If they moved, it would all be part of the story of the Branwell family, but she had never been anything less than honest with Jim. Now was not the time to change.

They took their picnic out into the country, to an old quarry that had been repurposed as a swimming hole/camp area with tables and grills for picnics. There was a country store a few miles down the road that sold snacks, drinks, and sometimes hosted estate/antique sales. Nothing was happening today, so the area was nearly deserted. Only a couple of teenaged boys daring each other to jump off the rocks into the quarry. Abby knew them from school, considered them not worth her attention. Finally, sensing a possibly unwelcome audience for their shenanigans, they climbed into their car and went to find some other fun.

Joy was wearing the same jeans she had put on last night but a different shirt. It was men's style, vertical striped, blue, white, and green. She had rolled up the sleeves and tied the tail of the shirt in a knot at her waist. Once again, her hair was braided down her back and she wore the sandals bought the day before. There was a nervous energy about her that she seemed to be trying hard to control. Moon and Sue exchanged worried glances, waiting for the bomb to explode, but Joy seemed to be working overtime to keep her temper.

Only Abby seemed willing to challenge her.

"Waiting for someone to offer you a lighted match?" she asked. "You look like you could blow up any second and take all of us with you. Want to talk?"

"No," said Joy shortly. "Leave it Abby. You wouldn't understand."

"I understand more than you think I do. Who was the guy in the car with you?"

"What?" exploded Joy. When they all stared at her, she quickly spun a story. "Ouch! There's something sharp in this shirt. I think I missed a pin. Abby, come help me check this sleeve!" She pulled Abby out of the shade, and they headed toward the quarry where the sun was brighter.

"How the hell do you know about Ted?" Joy demanded when they were out of earshot of Sue and Moon.

"I saw you driving around town with him. I was curious because he wasn't your dad and he wasn't Neil, so why was he running around with you?"

"Oh, god, who else knows? Who did you tell?" Joy was so frightened that her teeth were chattering.

"I told Mom and Dad." Abby flopped down on the grass and stared up at Joy. "I...didn't understand why you would be with that guy. They told Tommy—Officer Williams because Neil asked him to find you. Tommy said you were just giving the guy a ride to visit his P.O. because his car broke down or something. His P.O. confirmed it and they all dropped it. We still didn't know where you were. Where were you?"

"Hiding!" Joy snapped. "And they didn't drop it. It got back to Neil and now Ted's on the run so Neil can't beat the never-mind-what out of him. Oh, this just gets better and better!" she groaned. "I've screwed up my life, I've screwed up Dad's, I've screwed up Ted's, and I bet I will screw up this..." she stopped abruptly.

"Never mind." She dropped down next to Abby, picked up a pebble from the grass and flicked it into the quarry. It fell for some time before it splashed in the water. "Ted was trying to help me, and I was trying to help him. Neil had a choke hold on Ted, forcing him to do all sorts of stuff, and Ted couldn't take it anymore. Neither could I. Well, Neil's locked up for now and I will fill Tommy in when he comes to take me to get my stuff and give Neil back his crummy shoes. I should have known this was all going to go bad. But I really thought…for a minute…well, it seemed like a good idea at the time."

"Joy, how can I help?" Abby reached out and put her hand on Joy's.

"You can't. Not right now. Later. Yeah, later I will probably need your help. We'll see how it plays out. Okay. Just, don't say anything about anything I tell you. Okay. It might get us all in a world of hurt. And I don't want you in too deep. Please? I'll be at Mom's for a little while, but I can't stay there too long. I don't want her to be hurt, she's worked so hard to build her life back up—I don't want to bring it crashing down for her, so I can't stay, but I don't know. I just don't know. Sometimes I just want to scream!" Joy let out a piercing scream then stopped suddenly as Abby stared at her.

Abby jumped to her feet with a vibrating war whoop of her own and pulled Joy up also. "You want to scream, LET'S SCREAM!"

The two ran off along the quarry wall, screaming as loud as they could, until their race brought them back close to the picnic spot.

"Feel better?" Abby asked.

"Yes, some. My side hurts," answered Joy.

"You're welcome," bowed Abby. "Now, let's EAT!!"

Sitting under a tree a little way from the picnic table, watching the girls dish up, Sue didn't mention the move to Moon as they caught up on the family's attempts to repossess Moon's home.

"It's a cousin of the deceased, some guy who isn't even part of the estate probate. He remembers the house from 'way back when and wants it for one of his kids, probably to get him out of the house and out from under foot. But he's carrying on like it's a sentimental wrench, he should have been consulted, he won't stand for this travesty, blah, blah, blah. He's filed a motion in court to have the contract broken, to have me evicted and to force me to pay restitution for the 'damage I've done to the property'! My lawyer says it's nothing more than a nuisance suit—that he probably doesn't really want the house at all but that this is his entry point into the negotiations for the rest of the estate. He thinks the judge will either hear it in a bench proceeding or toss it out completely. If he hears it, if will be up to this cousin to prove his case because the contract is solid, and the rest of the family don't want to be bothered with the house since they are getting their money for it and not having to pay out anything. My lawyer is going to file a motion to have it dismissed. Then there's the deal with Neil, and Joy coming back home—thank you so much for sending Mr. Snow. It was good to have her in her own bed last night. Of course, she came with just the clothes she was wearing but there are a lot of sales going on, so we got some nice things very reasonably. Sue? Are you okay?"

"What? No, I'm fine-so many things on my mind after coming home from vacation, cutting things a bit short and all. I'm listening! The family is causing an upheaval about you house, Joy is home for the time being and you bought a lot of stuff for her on sale."

"Well, yes, that's the Cliff Notes version, I guess," Moon smiled and rubbed Pansy's exposed tummy. "Now, tell me about the "Memory Quilt brainstorm that Joy and Abby were going on about in the car."

Hesitantly Sue explained the idea behind the quilts and how it had blossomed from an 'attic cleaning party' to the memories attached to the decaying fabrics to a possible fundraising opportunity. "When those two put their heads together, there's no end to what they might come up with," she finished. "I remember Joy in the youth group, how creative she was. She always had such great suggestions."

"She told me she was working as a physical therapy aide, making a decent paycheck, until Neil made her quit. She was even thinking about going back to school and getting her license. I guess this has kind of scuttled that dream," Moon said wistfully. "Still, it is different having her home. I just hope I don't have to deal with Geordie or Neil. I'm not up to it, frankly. At least Pansy likes her. Joy sends the poor little dog into LaLa Land every time she rubs Pansy's ears, doesn't she, baby?"

"It doesn't have to, you know?" Sue looked thoughtful.

"Send Pansy into LaLa Land? I don't see how it can be avoided. Pansy begs, and Joy delivers," Moon laughed.

"What?" Sue looked puzzled for a moment. "Oh, no, I meant her dream doesn't have to be scuttled. There is a program at the tech, and the church has a scholarship agreement that would help with her books and tuition. There are also part-time openings all the time for aides, as soon as Tommy says it's safe for her to do that. I'll let Abby bring up the subject, slowly. It will seem less meddlesome coming from her."

"You conniver!" Moon exclaimed.

"Experienced mother of teenagers," countered Sue.

"How is Josh? All set for college?" Moon enquired.

"And then some. Jim will take him up the last week of August and get him settled in, while I get the 'Drama Queen' ready for her junior year. Right now, he is still staying with his grandparents, he didn't want to come back right away so it is quieter—a taste of what the coming year will be, I guess." Again, Sue drifted off in thought and Moon had the distinct feeling that there was a lot being left unsaid.

"How are you feeling—kicking the first one out of the nest, so to speak?" Moon asked gently.

Sue didn't answer right away. At first Moon thought she was going to change the subject.

"Mixed feelings, I guess," Sue finally admitted, still not looking directly at Moon. She seemed to be gazing inward, sorting out her feelings into priorities.

"On one hand I am incredibly proud of him. It doesn't look like it to everyone else, but I can see how hard he works, not just on his accomplishments but to make it look effortless, like it all comes easy for him. It doesn't, you know. Oh, far easier than it does for Abby, but she always makes such a production of everything, makes it look like it's harder for her than it really is. With Joshua away at college I hope that neither of them will have to pretend so much, they can each relax and be more themselves.

"I will miss Josh terribly, but I won't miss the tension between the two, the outright hostility at times. I know Jim will be glad to retire his role as a peacemaker of those two. And Abby's dramatics will be more than enough to keep us awake at night.

"Two more years, and she will be out on her own too. Then it will be just me and Jim..." Her voice trailed off, again she seemed lost in thought. Moon waited.

"Moon..." Sue began, then stopped.

"What can I do to help?" Moon asked gently.

"Nothing. I'm fine!" Sue declared. "It's just, no matter how well you think you are ready for this, I guess you really aren't. So, we muddle through it and figure it out as we go. Right?"

"Or block it out for five years!" Moon laughed. "Allow me to be an example of what <u>not</u> to do."

"Absolutely!" Sue agreed. "And that said, I think we'd better be heading home. We've been lazy enough for one day. If you like, I will make a couple calls and get some information for Joy and I need to talk to the Quilters about Abby's fundraising idea. That's going to take a bit of organizing but the more I think about it, the more excited I am about it." *'Not to mention, having a heart-to-heart with Jim before any decisions are made,'* thought Sue.

"I like that quilting idea, and if you want, you and I can do the first one with you 'memory clothes' to show them what you mean. Pick a day or a weekend, bring the clothes over, we'll park them in my back sewing room/pantry and get started."

"Thank you," said Sue as they began packing up the remains of the picnic. "I will let you know."

Sue and Abby dropped Moon and a reticent Joy off at Moon's bungalow, then headed to their own home.

"Did you still want to go to that movie tonight?" Sue asked idly.

"Yeah, I would like to see it before they change shows," Abby admitted.

"Do you have enough money for the show and snacks? Do you need an advance on your allowance?" Sue asked as they unloaded the car.

Abby looked up sharply. "What's going on?"

"Nothing," Sue assured her. "You've worked so hard today, I though you could use a treat, that's all."

Abby looked unconvinced but she wasn't willing to risk losing the chance to see the movie and maybe hang out with a boy she had a crush on, who seemed just as interested in her.

"No, I'm fine. You could maybe help me with some school clothes when the summer sales start," she suggested.

"I had planned on it," Sue agreed. "Early show?"

"Yeah, I'll grab a burger downtown and meet everybody at the theater after."

"Midnight curfew," Sue reminded her.

"Yeah, I know," Abby was gone before the door closed, leaving Sue alone in the house. First, she put the picnic things away and chose the ingredients for a simple cold supper. Then she checked the family engagement calendar and went to find Jim.

She found him in his study, going over the notes for his sermon that Sunday. Silently she stood in front of his desk until he looked up.

"Sue? Is dinner ready?" he asked.

"I have some cold chicken and potato salad; we still have some fruit and cheese for dessert. Before that, we need to talk." Sue took a deep breath going right to the heart of the subject.

"I know that we are facing some changes as a family, with Joshua going to college this fall, Abby in her junior year, your folks getting up in years, and now this new call is exciting for you: a fresh start in a new town closer to Mom and Dad Branwell, new challenges, a raise in salary and perhaps more benefits, but Jim…" Sue stopped, unable to continue.

"You have reservations." It wasn't a question, but a statement of understanding. Sue nodded.

Jim waited patiently. All his years of counseling had taught him that people would talk when they were ready. "Want to sit down?" he asked kindly. Sue shook her head.

"No, I'd rather stand. You are right. I have reservations. I understand why you want to accept this call, and I will stand behind and beside you wherever you go, but you are right. I really don't want to do this. I don't want to leave this house, this church, this town. It is going to be quite an upheaval for Abby, coming right in the middle of her high school years. Yes, she will adjust, Josh with be in college so he will be focused on his life there. And your folks need us closer. I understand and agree with all that, but I...I can't bear to leave here. There! I've said it. I promised myself that I would be honest with you and not just put on a fake smile, while I am crying inside. I really don't want to do this move."

Jim sat silently, watching, hearing Sue out without comment. When she paused for breath, he leaned back in his chair, steepling his hands in front of his chin. His hair was still a rich brown, but traces of gray were beginning to show at the temples. His horn-rimmed glasses were the same style he had worn since high school—they suited him, so he felt no need to change. Abby was always teasing him that he should get contact lenses, but Jim resisted, claiming he didn't want plastic stuck to his eyes. Thanks to braces as a child his smile, when he used it which was often was wide and white and even, without the enhancement of beard or mustache. Jim abhorred 'facial shrubbery' on his own person, even as he admired it on others. Josh had been experimenting that summer and was sporting a neat thin mustache that he was overly proud of.

Jim's long fingers remained unmoving, steepled against his chin. He seemed to be weighing each one of Sue's words. Finally, when he felt, she had come to a full stop, echoed what he was hearing.

"You see the benefits of this call, as well as the complications that will come with it, mostly the upheaval in Abby's life, and the wrench for you of leaving your home, because Sue, this place is and has always been your home. You grew up here and you felt rewarded when I accepted the call to your home church."

Sue nodded.

"You are willing to accept this new call with me, even though it is tearing you apart to leave here. You understand that this is part of the life of a minister's spouse, you will go with me if this is truly what I want to do, but you felt you needed to be honest with me about your feelings. I can't tell you how deeply I appreciate the courage it took to come here and tell me this. To tell the truth, I have been kind of wondering if and when you would because we have always made these kinds of decisions together-I almost felt like I was going it alone this time. I take it that Abby is 'otherwise occupied'?" he asked.

Sue nodded again. "I sent her to see that movie she's been going on about—midnight curfew so we have plenty of time to eat, talk."

"Sensible," Jim agreed. "Tell me, how long have you been feeling this way?"

"At first I was excited about the new call, about being closer to your parents, to be there when they need us more." Sue pulled up a chair and sat down across the desk from Jim.

"Then, the more I thought about organizing this move, changing Abby's school, winding things up here and packing, saying goodbye to everything and everyone here, preparing to start over in a new church, new town, different state, it just became overwhelming. When I went away to college it was an adventure because I felt I could always come home here. Mom and Dad passed away, my brothers and sisters moved on with their lives but never that far off and this was still home. You were called here—I really thought we would grow old and retire here, like Mom and Dad did. Silly, I guess, because that isn't how it works for ministers. And now it has happened, our time here is over. I admit, I don't relish telling Abby. There may not be a parsonage standing when the drama queen is done reacting," Sue smiled through tears that had welled up in her eyes. "Tell me, does Joshua know yet?"

"He does. I sounded him out as soon as I got the call. I must say, for all his reticence, his reaction was not much different than yours. And Mom and Dad were even more forceful about their opposition. They don't want us uprooting our lives on their account."

Sue looked astonished. "They don't? I thought they would be thrilled to have their 'favorite son' closer. Your brother is even further away and less able to be there to help."

"That is true. The State Department is not too flexible about assignments. Bud is a career diplomat. He will be stationed overseas probably for most of his working life. It suits him. There won't be much help coming from that quarter."

"Then, that settles it. Accept the call and let the council know at the next meeting," Sue sighed. "Abby and I will adjust—at least I feel better for telling you what has been going through my mind about this move. How big is the new house, so we know how much to take with us? How much time, do you think, we have to let our friends know, book the van and pack?"

"I would plan about…ten to twenty years. I declined the call." Jim spoke quietly, with just the hint of a smile.

"I am _not_ hearing this correctly!" Sue exclaimed. "You turned down the call? It's everything you wanted! Why would you do that? When did you decide? Why didn't you tell me?" Sue was openly crying now.

"Which question do you want answered first?" Jim inquired, rising from his desk chair to come around and offer his wife a hug.

Sue hugged him hard, then pushed away and swatted him lightly on the shoulder, wet with her tears.

"Ow! Domestic abuse!" Jim laughed. "Seriously, I decided last night after a long talk with the president of the church council. But I didn't actually decline the call until about an hour ago after he got back to me about some of my concerns. They are holding a special session of the council to vote, but almost everyone that he has talked to is on board with my requests: upgrade in insurance coverage, and a few other small perks in exchange for me staying put here in Jefferson. There are a few with concerns, but I am confident that we will come to an agreement that satisfies everyone. They have some requests of me as well, and I have no problem working with their ideas. As for Mom and Dad, they emphatically DON'T want us uprooting ourselves and moving out there just for them. They realize that Bud can't be counted on the way we can if they need help, but they also understand that we have made a home here, that Abby needs to finish her schooling and concentrate on getting into a good college. They are serious about not wanting to interfere with any of that. In fact, they have a better idea. They talked to Josh before they talked to me, voiced their concerns about us uprooting ourselves when they don't believe it is necessary yet, and he is more than willing to transfer after his freshman year to a college near Mom and Dad, finish out his undergrad work while living with them. He's actually happy with the plan. That's one of the reasons he stayed behind, to talk to the college there, figure out how to manage the transfer, and help Mom and Dad in the meantime. After Josh graduates college, Mom and Dad are planning on selling their place and moving here, to be closer to us.

"This is my home, too, Sue. I'm not sure I could easily leave my church and my people, even for a better offer."

Sue hugged him again. "You all came to this decision without talking to me? Have you formally declined the call, then?" she asked, her face buried in his shirt.

"I needed time to come to terms with my own thoughts first—I was torn, but the more I thought about it the more I was leaning toward staying here in spite feeling that to accept the call would actually be in everyone's best interests, for all the reasons you mentioned. Once I was on firmer mental footing about it myself, then I would have sat down to hear your take—although I pretty much knew you would say just what you did. I haven't been married to you for twenty-some years without knowing you pretty well, my dear!

"Knowing Josh's and my folk's thoughts made it easier to accept my own deeper wishes—to stay here at least a while longer. I don't feel that my work here is finished. I see so much more I can do for this congregation.

"Yes, I have called the president of their church council to let her know my decision, and I am drafting a letter to that effect, to be sent to them and to the conference office that put my name forward for consideration. I can't promise that this will be our last church, Sue, but I don't think this is the right time to leave, even if the offer is tempting. I trust you are okay with this decision and that we can now have supper? I am starving!"

"I didn't realize," Sue led the way to the kitchen to begin setting out supper, "just how much staying here would mean, and leaving here would hurt until that call came, and it seemed like accepting it was the only practical thing to do in spite of the problems that came with it." She stopped and looked him in the face. "I would have gone with you, Jim, you know I would, and I would have made a go of it. But it wouldn't have been easy, and I would have left a lot of my heart back here. I just wish I knew earlier what you were thinking—it might have made it easier for me to voice my own feelings."

"I know," Jim said simply. "I'm sorry. I really should have talked this out with you earlier instead of leaving you to struggle on alone for so long. I promise I won't make that mistake next time.

"And now that the BIG QUESTION is solved, would you like to let me in on what you, Joy, and Abby were so excited about earlier?"

Over supper Sue explained Joy's idea and Abby's fundraising suggestions. "It almost didn't make sense to pursue it if we weren't going to be here to see it through, but since we have decided to stay, I think a couple of things should happen. I think I should continue with the cleaning out and down-sizing that I had planned. We've been packrats for far too long. And I think we should really put some effort into this project of Joy's and Abby's. The Memorial Fund is a great place for the money raised by these Memory Quilts and I really think, if we present it right, that it will be a win-win situation!"

"Then I guess you all have your work cut out for you," Jim helped himself to seconds and looked expectantly around for dessert. He spied a plate of Abby's cookies on the counter that would do nicely for his sweet tooth. "This is what I meant when I said we had more we could do here. Let me close out this particular chapter with the council and I will see what I can do to help your efforts," he promised.

"Deal!" was all Sue could manage.

As Moon reviewed and deleted the older messages on her answering machine that night, she came across Sue's cryptic "War council?"

"I wonder what she wanted to talk about unless it was about the memory quilts. That doesn't seem important enough for a 'War council'—we always saved those for really big upheavals. I wonder if she got it all straightened out or if I missed something. Maybe she thought Joy's issues were more important, but nothing is more important than our friendship. I doubt that I would be here or in any fit state to deal with Joy's problems if it hadn't been for Sue's help. I will call her tomorrow and see what's up."

13

Tommy Investigates

Neil didn't remain a guest of the Jefferson police department for long. Charges were filed but he was out on bail by the time Moon and Joy returned home from her picnic. Thanks to some fancy footwork on Tommy's part, he never knew that Geordie was still hanging around the station, out of the public eye. It was interesting, Tommy mused, that Neil's bail had been paid anonymously with a TriCity State Bank cashier's check. Lacey? Richard? Geoff or Sherle? Someone else? There were several branches of the bank, it was almost impossible to figure out which branch issued the check.

The bottom line was that Neil was out of jail, possibly again a threat to Joy now that he knew she was living with Moon. Telling them was a priority, but should he move one or both of them? Tommy decided against it in case it spooked Neil and his associates. He could quietly increase security precautions and try to move his investigation along faster. His sergeant was solidly behind him as were the State Police, who were more than happy to allow him to assist in their own project. They had someone undercover at Fritz's but so far had been unable to make much headway. With Officer Williams and Geordie on board, things were likely to begin moving quickly.

The sooner Moon and Joy knew to watch out for Neil, the better. Tommy caught Moon early before she left for work.

"Thank you for letting us know. I'll pass the message along to Joy and also to the Branwell's. Joy wants to stay there during the day, so she isn't home alone. I didn't think you would mind."

"No, I think it's a good idea that she should not be left alone until we have this locked down better. I just don't want to take any chances. Are Josh and Abby home? I would worry about them caught in an altercation if Neil or his friends decide to use more persuasive tactics." Tommy was already trying to figure some way of protecting Joy without making it too obvious or destroying the department's budget.

"Josh is still out East with his grandparents stretching his last summer of freedom to the max, I assume, but Abby is home. Too bad we don't know any security guards," Moon said.

"Oh, but I do!" exclaimed Tommy. "A retired security guard who also put in some time on a police force when he was younger. I will call him, put him in touch with Rev. Branwell and see if they don't need some help around the church: maintenance, repair work, gardening, something to keep Pete busy with one eye peeled for trouble from Neil. He's well over six feet tall and muscular, kind of looks like an actor with his greying hair and mustache, but he is every bit as imposing a presence as he was when he was on the force: he'll be perfect to watch out for you and Joy. I will let you know what I set up, in the meantime yes, send Joy over to Branwells while you are at work, and make sure someone is looking out for Pansy. I don't want her caught in the middle of this either."

Pansy! Moon wondered if she should have the little dog stay with Ellen during the day or if she would be okay home alone. She decided not to chance it and scooped up the pup to spend the day with the Crawfords. Paul would be thrilled to have Pansy keep him company.

With Pansy and Joy both safe for the day, Moon felt better about going to work. She really couldn't afford to take off any time until her vacation began in a few weeks, and Moon was looking forward to spending the time off with Pansy and Joy. Moon hoped that Sue could help steer Joy back into the physical therapy work she had loved doing.

There was news about her bungalow waiting for Moon at work: a memo on her desk from the lawyers advising her that a motion to void the contract had indeed been filed, the judge was reviewing it, but the word was that it would likely be dismissed as a nuisance suit and there would be no other issue with her home. The lawyers promised that they would keep her informed about any progress or other developments. Moon sighed. She really didn't need this right now, but it seemed like it was being handled and she had been assured that she qualified to buy the little house outright immediately if necessary. Moon tucked the memo away in her tote bag to be added to the file at home. Nothing she could do now except get to work. Joy would be having lunch at Sue's, so Moon was on her own. Maybe something from the taco truck—something different.

She was packing up her tote bag in preparation for lunch when she heard the commotion in the bank lobby.

"I know she's here. I'm not leaving until I see her, and she tells me where my wife is!" Neil was demanding a teller to show him to Moon. Moon grabbed her bag and was just about to sneak out the back door while one of the secretaries called the police when she heard Neil remark, "If she keeps my wife away from me, you can believe she'll risk losing something valuable in return!"

'That sounds like a threat,' Moon thought. She was about to change her mind and confront Neil when she heard the teller remark "Thank God he left before the police came!"

Instead of leaving through the back door, Moon headed to the secretary in charge of personnel. *First Joy, now Neil. This can't keep happening! I will lose my job if my family keep disrupting my workplace!*

She arranged to change her vacation dates before calling Tommy to see if Neil could be picked up on Disturbing the Peace charges. Meanwhile, Moon decided she would finish out the day and get a fresh start on her vacation as soon as she got home. There were only a few loose ends to take care of—she would be set for two weeks of time away from work, perhaps out of town where Neil couldn't find her! Happily, Moon rearranged her appointments, called her clients to let them know that they would still be well cared for in her absence. She was about to pack up a bit early when her phone rang.

"Moon! I've been trying to get you for the past hour, but your phone is always busy! We don't know what to do! We don't know who to call and I'm afraid it may be too late!" Ellen Crawford was crying into the phone and her next word chilled Moon's blood.

"Someone drove by, up the alley, Paul was walking Pansy, Moon, they shot her!"

"Paul too?" gasped Moon.

"No, he's upset but okay. What do we do, Moon, she's bleeding!"

"Will call the vet and someone will come for her. Do the best you can…it will be okay. It has to be."

Moon disconnected the call and at once called Sue. "I'm calling the vet now, meet me there. Please?"

"I'm out the door already," was Sue's response.

It was too late. Moon was so afraid that it was too late for Pansy, but she was determined to do everything she could. After promising the vet that Sue was on her way with Pansy, Moon set off at a run. She was waiting when Joy brought the still puppy into the office, wrapped in one of Ellen's old towels. Pansy was barely breathing. The bullet had hit a lung and passed on through, she had nearly completely bled out. The vet took her into surgery immediately while Moon sat rigid in a waiting-room chair. Sue needed to get back, but Joy opted to stay.

"Who would do something like this?" she whispered.

Moon looked straight ahead. "Neil. He came to the bank earlier today—I was in the back room, but I heard him warn the teller that if I kept you from him, I would risk losing something myself."

"They play for keeps, Mom," whispered Joy. "And now the stakes are even higher."

"Joy, it's about time you tell me what you've gotten into and how we can get you out of it," Moon asserted. "As soon as we know Pansy…"

The vet was approaching with a sad look on her face. "We have done all we can do—it might be kinder to just let her go. I can't promise she'll make it anyway. The bullet did a lot of damage to her lung, she's lost much more blood that she can afford to lose. I'm kind of surprised she's still hanging on, to be truthful. Do you want to go in and say good-bye?"

Moon didn't answer. She couldn't.

"Isn't she the little dog from the humane society a year or so ago?" the vet asked. "I remember her, how many problems she had—a stray wasn't she? Someone covered all her medical bills and she fought so hard to get healthy. That was you, wasn't it? Sending in the money for her treatment?"

Moon nodded; Joy looked surprised. "Why would you do that, Mom?"

"Because no one else wanted her. Just me. I fell in love with her, and I vowed I would always be there for her." Moon looked up at the vet. "Can we see how she does through the night? She's a fighter, I want to give her every chance."

The vet looked skeptical. "Come back and see her, she's out of surgery and we did a transfusion to make up for some of the blood she lost. Come see her, then make your decision."

Moon knew it was hopeless, but she felt she owed Pansy that much at least.

"Mom. It's a dog." Joy began. Seeing the look on Moon's face she stopped. "Go. Say good-bye. I'll wait here."

"No, you will come with me," said Moon. "You and your associations are at least partly responsible for what happened to Pansy. You need to be in on the consequences."

Joy didn't argue. She quietly followed Moon back to the recovery part of the surgery.

Pansy lay on the examining table, wrapped in blankets, unmoving. At first Moon thought she was already gone, but she felt she owed it to the little dachshund to be with her one last time. She pulled up a chair next to the table, sat and began to stroke the little dog's head, thanking her for her love and trust, telling her what a good girl she was.

For a long time, she sat with Pansy, looking for some sign of life. She saw none. Finally, Joy put her hand on her mother's shoulder.

"It's time, Mom. Say good-bye. She's probably already gone."

Moon leaned down and kissed the little black head one final time before she turned to go. As she did, she saw just a flicker of the little dog's eye. Just a blink.

"No," said Moon to the puppy. "I don't think you are ready to leave just yet."

In response Pansy's ears twitched. "Muscle response," said the vet. "Not unusual as they leave us. Do you want me to give her something to help the process?"

"No," said Moon, "I want to know what the recovery protocol is? Does she stay here over night, should I take her home and watch her, what do you suggest other than putting her down?"

The vet looked skeptical. "We don't have anyone here over night to watch her and I don't know how wise it is to move her, but since I don't think she will make it through the night anyway..."

"Joy, call Sue. Ask her if she can come get us. Can you loan us something to transport her? I will return it tomorrow."

"If you are sure," the vet began, then turned away. "What the heck. We could use a good miracle around here."

Unnoticed on the exam table, Pansy thumped her tail. Just once.

Gently Joy and Moon carried Pansy from Sue's car up the stairs into Moon's little bedroom and place her, stretcher board and all, in the middle of Moon's bed. Moon brought in a chair from the dining room so she could sit by the bed; she wouldn't leave the little dog to struggle on alone.

"Go to bed, Joy, get some sleep. I will be here with her, she'll be fine, no matter what happens."

Reluctantly Joy changed into her pajamas and climbed into bed. She was exhausted and the revenge Neil had enacted against Moon on Joy's behalf made her sick to her stomach. The abuse she had taken from him almost since their marriage was on thing, this was a whole level of cruelty.

She didn't sleep. She tossed and turned, got up after a few hours, knowing it was a lost cause. The sun was just touching the far end of the alley, so Joy set the coffee to brewing for Moon and poured herself a glass of cold orange juice.

When she took Moon's coffee to her, she found her mother still awake, still stroking the little dog and talking softly to her.

"Any change?" Joy asked as Moon took her first sip.

"Not much, but she's still with us." Moon whispered. The vet doesn't open for a few hours but when they do, I'm going to call to see if they will come and check her over, in case she needs more medication or IV fluids. As long as she's holding on, we have hope. You didn't sleep either?"

Joy shook her head. "We will both need naps later today."

"Not until I know one way or the other." Moon said softly as the little dog stirred.

Crawfords called to enquire about Pansy, Sue called to check in, the vet didn't wait for a call from Moon but stopped by on her way to the clinic, declared herself surprised that Pansy was still fighting for life, and promised to send some meds with a vet tech as soon as the animal hospital opened: antibiotics and change of bandages, pain meds, anything to keep the pup as comfortable as possible. The vet then promised to check in with them on her way home.

Officer Williams came and took statements from the Crawfords, from Moon and Joy, and put out a call to pick Neil up for questioning.

While Moon sat with Pansy, Joy took Tommy to the kitchen, ostensibly for a cup of coffee, but really to tell him what he needed to know about Neil, about his business dealings including the names of others involved.

"I don't know everything, but I know enough that he won't want me out of his control. He will keep coming after me, keep hurting anyone who tries to help me. By now he knows I took my money from the cache, he knows where I am staying, it will be an all out war on Mom, you, and the Branwells. The best thing you can do is get me out of town somewhere he can't find me. It won't stop him, but it might slow him down. I tried it once before, remember, that's when he turned me in as a missing person. I...almost made it, too, until he found me and dragged me back here. Beware, Tommy, Neil won't stop with trying to force me to go with him or trying to kill Mom's dog. And, yes, he's roped Dad into this as well. The insurance didn't cover all of the medical bills and Dad was desperate to find a way to pay them. He sold his car and most of the things he owned but his girl-friend started seeing him as, well, more of a liability than the great provider she thought he was. Neil offered Dad a way out of debt, it was legit at first, and then it wasn't. By then everything was gone, Dad was broke and Neil practically owned him. That's why you have to shut Neil down once and for all. Put him away and don't let him out!"

"We are close to doing just that, and I will find a way to add charges for Pansy to the list," Tommy put his coffee cup in the sink, preparing to get back to work. "Are you staying here all day or going to Bran-well's?" he asked.

"Staying here, why?" Joy busied herself by rinsing the cups and set-ting up Moon's breakfast.

"Did Moon hire the painters yet to do the outside of the house? If she didn't, and you have the paint, I can send Pete over here instead of Branwell's. He's an ex-cop, and he agreed to keep an eye on you for me while finding odd jobs for the church. He can do that just as easily here. I don't want you ladies left alone. This is getting much too dan-gerous—I am happy that Moon is taking her vacation a bit early, with the scene Neil caused in the bank yesterday."

"Send Pete," was all Joy said.

All day Moon dozed fitfully in the chair next to Pansy. As long as the little dog was willing to fight, she wouldn't give up on her. By supper time, when the vet stopped by it was obvious that Pansy's chances had improved. Enough to warrant some fresh medications, and a new IV to keep her hydrated.

"I will stop by again in the morning," the vet promised. "I can't wait to see how she's doing. I would venture to say that if she makes it through tonight and if infection doesn't set in, she will recover. She may always have some issues with that lung, but, my God, she's a tough little pup! If they catch the shooter, I want to be the first to testify against them and put them away for good!"

"I'll call if there's a change," Moon promised. She rearranged the blanket over Pansy, keeping her as warm and comfy as possible.

"Or I will," Joy agreed, "because tonight we are taking turns. You sleep in my bed for a few hours while I watch, then we will switch."

"No, Mom, I mean it!" Joy emphasized as Moon tried to argue. "You are no good to Pansy if she goes into crisis and you are too tired to think straight. Let me help. Please."

"I give in!" admitted Moon. "I am going to put a hot dish in the oven for supper, there's fruit in the fridge. I trust you will look after our brave protector?"

"With pleasure. I found a book to read-—I may even read it out loud to keep myself awake. Do dogs like to be read to?" Joy laughed.

"I think Pansy does." Moon bustled about the kitchen. "She always seemed to enjoy the audio books I listened to. Nothing too exciting, mind!" she teased. "I just might treat myself and call a cab to take a big load to the laundromat—get all caught up on that basket of dirty clothes. Will you be okay with Ellen just across the alley? Or should I wait until tomorrow and call Sue?"

"You need to get your own washer and dryer here. Would you put it in the basement? Are there hook-ups for them?" Joy commented as she set the table.

"I didn't see any, and I would rather have the washer and dryer here on the main floor. I was hoping that 'pantry' off the kitchen where I have my sewing machine would be my laundry room too. No risk of falling down the stairs!" Moon brought in bread and butter to go with the casserole. She paused, listening for the timer.

"I want to wait until I own the house, not just rent it from the owners so I can make the changes I want. The stove and refrigerator are both old, I may have to replace them so that would come first."

Joy looked around the house. "You seem so much happier here than you were even when you were married to Dad."

"I am," Moon admitted. "This is MY place, MY home. I can please myself here the way I haven't been able to for years. As soon as I get either the lease or the mortgage settled, then I can do some more upgrades. For now, this is perfect for Pansy, me, and you as long as you want to stay. Did Sue tell you about the classes and possible jobs?"

"She did. I said I'd think about it." Joy looked uncomfortable but covered it up by going to check on Pansy.

"Mom! Come in here," she called softly. Moon rushed in to find Pansy trying to sit up and lick Joy's fingers. When she saw Moon, the exhausted pup lay back down, but her tail told all how happy she was to see them.

"Can we lift her carefully, bring her out into the dining room during supper? How clean is her dog bed, do you think? I wash it every week, but I haven't done laundry this week. Oh, I was going to do that tomorrow, wasn't I?" Moon was overjoyed at the progress Pansy was making.

"Towel, an old clean one on her dog cushion, should be okay." Joy went to check out the dog bed in Pansy's crate, leaving Moon to commune with her dog. "It looks okay, she doesn't have fleas so I would just put down some clean old towels."

"In a box in the pantry. I kept all my old towels from the apartment to use for rags, I never bothered to cut up some of them but everything in there is clean," Moon called.

"Found them!" Joy answered. She selected some larger pastel towels and spread them over the bed, tucking them in at the sides. "Ready!"

Moon carefully scooped up the pup who whimpered a little at being moved. She carried Pansy into the dining room and placed her on the covered dog bed that Joy set up in the corner by the plants. The timer was going off in the kitchen: dinner was ready.

"I have fruit for dessert," Moon noted as she washed her hands. "We will figure out the laundry after supper. But you are right, it would be lovely to have my own washer and dryer again. It's already on my 'house list'."

"You have a 'house list'?" Joy asked as she dished up.

"I have an entire notebook." Moon admitted. "I've been writing things down since I paid the first month's rent and prepared to move in. Sue and I came over the night before the move, cleaned everything, I measured, I planned, I dreamed. I knew where everything would go, and I had everything ready for the move the next day. Sue and the youth group loaded up Mr. Snow's truck; they did all the work while I was at the bank. By the time I was done with work for the day it was all set up. Sue even had dinner waiting for me in the oven: meatloaf with mashed potatoes and vegetables. It was like coming home. I _was_ coming home. I've been adding to the list ever since, crossing things off as I accomplish the task.

"The very first thing I changed was this room: I steamed off the old wallpaper in these two rooms and repainted." Moon didn't mention the upset in the alley that had spurred her to rent the steamer to work off her frustration with her daughter. "I bought curtains for the windows, plants, I found rugs and chairs at estate sales. Then there was the night the cupboards fell off the wall in the kitchen…"

"What? Were you hurt?" Joy looked like she might start one of her old rants but stopped herself in time.

"No, it was the cupboard with the old, mismatched pots and pans." Moon leaned back, remembering. "It came crashing down in the middle of the night while I was sleeping, woke me up, scared me half to death! It was just the pots and pans, nothing broken but the cabinet. I moved the dishes into the hutch here in the dining room and called the family the next day. Needless to say, they weren't willing to help, my problem, don't you know, so I called the Amish man who built this table and chairs," she smoothed her hand over the top of the oak table, "and hired him to build me new cabinets in the kitchen and shelves in the pantry. It's all a work in progress. One thing at a time. Now the family wants to break the contract—at least one disgruntled member does—so I don't want to do anything more until this is settled."

"Could you lose this house, after all you've done here?" Joy looked worried. This was a fear she had voiced when she heard about Moon's decision to move to a house rather than finding another low-rent apartment.

"I won't lie to you; it is a possibility. I talked to the lawyers, to the bank. I have options, I have the law on my side, but the fellow filed a complaint with the court and the judge is reviewing it. We should hear next week sometime. I really don't think it will go beyond that, but if it does, I can get a loan from the bank and convert the rent-to-own to ownership immediately. We will see. Until then, don't worry about it, please."

Joy nodded. She realized how important this house was to her mother. Moon wouldn't risk losing it. She had changed too much in the last year. She would never risk returning to the way she had lived at the apartment. In the meantime, she had her own issues to wrestle with.

"We will leave the laundry for tomorrow," Moon decided. "We'll gather everything up in the morning and do one big wash day. If Pansy is still doing ok, Ellen can watch her. I'm too tired to think about it now."

They washed the dishes in silence, not even bothering to turn on the radio. Ellen stopped by to see Pansy, who greeted her with thumping tail.

"Of course, I will watch her tomorrow if you like, but why go to a laundromat. Just this once, come use my machines. My wash is done, so you won't inconvenience anyone, you can be right on top of things. Please say "yes". That's what neighbors are for, and it will give Paul a reason to set up the grill—we can have a cook-out. Shame to waste this lovely summer weather, but Paul rarely bothers if is just the two of us!"

Moon looked at Joy. "That would be wonderful," she said. "Mom is lucky to have such good neighbors. May I bring a dessert to contribute? Do you need any help with the cook-out?"

Moon looked surprised. This was a very changed Joy, but she didn't express that opinion aloud. Well, maybe it was time Joy made amends for some of the upheaval she had caused.

"Bring dessert by all means," accepted Ellen. "I do salads, but nobody messes with the Mister when he's at the grill. I will go alert him and we will see you tomorrow morning, usual time?"

"Grandma's coffee cake, do you think?" Joy asked after Ellen left.

"Of course," Moon agreed. "Make a double batch and we will freeze some for a sweet Saturday morning or for guests."

"Or we could save some for Dad," Joy suggested.

Moon looked up in surprise. "For your dad?"

"He always liked that coffee cake. I think a slice would be a treat for him. Give it to Officer Williams to pass to Dad if you don't want to see him," Joy replied.

"Then it better be two slices or Dad won't get any. Remember Tommy stealing cookies? He still has a sweet tooth," Moon laughed.

14

Pansy

For days the little dog drifted in and out of wakefulness, always making sure that Moon was somewhere close. Her side hurt, it hurt to breathe, even worse than it had when she lived with all the other dogs, before she came to live here in this small comfy den, in the big building with the woman who brought her food, water, something to make the hurt go away, touched her gently and spoke kindly to her. Pansy had never known treatment like that before coming to live here. On the streets, her life was in constant danger, before that she had been largely ignored. After being caught and taken to the dog doctor, she had again been largely ignored except by one lady who came often to spend time with her before taking her home with her. Pansy wondered if it would be temporary, if she would be back on the streets or back in the building with all the strange dogs. When that didn't seem to be happening, she began to relax and place more trust in the lady who liked to sit and cuddle with her. She went away, she came back. She always came back, and she was always happy to see Pansy. No one had ever been really happy to see Pansy when they came back, and she almost always took Pansy out to explore the world. Such smells, such sounds, there was even a strange animal that called to her from the other side of a fence on her favorite part of their walk. Pansy loved answering the animal and carrying on a conversation of sorts. She would have liked to actually meet the animal, and she had the feeling that the animal would like that too, but the fence was solid and always kept them apart. Pansy heard the lady call the animal a 'cat', whatever that was. When Pansy heard that word, she knew they were talking about the friendly animal on the other side of the fence, and she was always eager to go back.

Now she hurt more than she had ever in her life. At first, she wasn't sure she wanted to wake up, it hurt less when she was sleeping. But that would leave her lady alone and Pansy knew she needed to be there to protect her. Something bad was out there. Her lady wasn't safe without her so each day she tried a little harder to wake up, to let her lady know that she was there to protect her. Each day, no matter how hard it was, no matter how tired she was, no matter how much she hurt, Pansy tried to tell Moon that she was there for her. Each day was a little easier, but not much. It would have be so much easier to just not wake up. If she hadn't come to live with the lady, if she was still on the streets, Pansy wouldn't have bothered trying.

From her clean bed in the dining room Pansy could hear Moon and Joy as they went about their chores. She could smell wonderful food in the kitchen, she knew Moon would try to tempt her to eat by putting a little sauce or egg in with her food, sometimes even a spoonful of plain yogurt that the vet said she could have. She didn't try to get up too often, it only tired her out more. Only when Moon or Joy carried her outside to do her 'business' did she stand and walk a little. Her routine was eat, potty, sleep, eat potty, sleep, and always Moon was close by. She didn't go away every day like before, she stayed home most of the time and Pansy was happy. Moon was safe.

Moon was pleased with the progress Pansy was making. All her vacation plans had been chucked in the trash—she couldn't take Pansy on a road trip, and she refused to leave her behind. Joy didn't seem to mind not traveling. She seemed to be settling in and Moon found that the two of them got on comfortably with few disagreements. She surmised that that might change once Neil and his cohorts were rounded up, but no one had seen or heard from him in days.

After confessing her moving scare to Moon, Sue had made a point of contacting people she knew about a job for Joy and schooling which would start in the fall. Joy seemed reluctant to take the next steps, but at least she was interested and not rejecting it out of hand. There was time yet to apply for the classes, if she missed the fall deadline she could still start in January.

Along with his other investigations, Officer Williams found that Joy's car had been sold by Neil without her knowledge and there was very little chance of getting it back, worse luck. Joy didn't seem to care, simply replying "It was more his property than mine. No loss. I'll get a better one later." Still, it would have been nice to have it now, for errands and trips out of the city even though by now Moon was used to not relying on automotive transportation. Joy didn't seem to miss it either. She bought a bicycle with some of the money she had taken from Neil's apartment, the last of her earnings at a PT aide, so she and Moon both had "wheels", but she rarely ventured far from the house unless Moon was with her.

Instead, she spent her days helping Moon around the house, caring for Pansy, reading, and sewing the quilt pieces that Sue brought over from the old clothes that she and Abby were dismantling, reviving skills she had learned in Girl Scouts as well as from her mother and grandmother. She had her eye on a knitted afghan pattern that she thought would be nice to tackle during the winter months, if she was still with Moon on Oak St. If she had to go back with Neil, well, then that would be a different story, as it would be if she were adrift somewhere on her own. Joy found herself more than half hoping that Moon would let her stay—at least a while longer.

Pete came every day to paint, repair, and keep an eye on Joy. Once the outside painting was done, he surprised Moon by finding some old shutters, painting them a soft green, and installing them on her windows that faced north and west. He was still on the lookout for some for the east and south windows. In the meantime, he cleaned up the grape arbor and donated some raspberry bushes from his own garden, as well as a bridal wreath bush to decorate the kitchen door.

"I got too many plants!" he declared. "You are doing me a favor letting me put some in over here!"

"Well, I do appreciate it," Moon assented. "We appreciate everything you do for us." Even Pansy thumped her tail in agreement.

"Say, would you like me to run plumbing and electric to that little pantry for you?" Pete asked. "I know the city codes and it will all be ship shape when the house is yours and you want to put in laundry machines. And while I'm on the subject, that fridge of yours feels hot to the touch. I would look at replacing it sooner than later, if I were you."

"Yes, I suppose you are right about the fridge. The stove needs updating as well. They were both here when I moved in—they are on my "Wish List". Now seems like good a time as any. I will check to see if there are any sales going on, and I will think carefully about the pantry modifications," Moon promised. "But I won't move forward with that until the house is in my name." She went and knocked on Joy's door.

"Pete says we need to replace the fridge. Any ideas? I don't think anything too fancy, maybe just a simple fridge/freezer combination?"

Joy put down her travel book on walking tours of Paris and considered. "I think you are right, the simpler the better. The big appliance store in Columbus should be running some sales soon, they usually have something going on. Maybe we could drive over with Sue to check them out? They deliver, so that shouldn't be a problem. Take a look at a new stove too, for future reference?"

"My thoughts exactly, but I really wanted your opinion. I will see when Sue is going that way next and ask if we can hitch a ride to check out what they have."

"Mom? Why does my opinion matter? I don't live here—I'm just staying here for the time being—until this is settled with Neil?" Joy wanted to know.

Moon sat down on the bed next to Joy. "Good point. Your stay here is probably temporary. But you are here now, for however long, and while I might not agree with every idea or opinion that you have, and I will ultimately do what I think best for my home, I do value your point of view and maybe you will see something I am missing. Have you thought about what you will do when Tommy finally breaks this business up and you are free again? Where will you go? What will you do with your life? No," Moon held up her hand to stop Joy's protests. "I don't want you to tell me. I just want you to think about your options, what I can do to help or even if you want my help. Just some points to turn over. Now, I'm going to call Sue, take some lemonade out to Pete before he collapses from heat exhaustion, and then Pansy and I are going to sit on the porch for a bit and enjoy this summer weather. They are talking about thunderstorms for tonight." Moon got up to leave. "Lord knows we need the rain!"

Moon's porch afternoon was postponed by the ringing of the telephone. While Moon answered the call, Joy got up and took the glass of lemonade out to Pete.

"I'm worried about that old fridge in the kitchen. It feels hot to the touch," she said.

"Just what I told your ma. Is she going to look for something new?" Pete took a long drink of the lemonade. "Oh, that hit the spot! Your ma makes it from scratch the way my ma did. That's the way to do it, not this powdered junk!"

"That's the way Mom always did things when she and Dad were together. When they split, she lost a lot of that for a long time. I'm sorry to admit that for the longest time I was ashamed of her. In this past year, since she found this house, she is more like the Mom I remember."

"You need to cut your ma some slack," Pete took another long drink of lemonade. "She's been through a lot in the past few years, and she is doing good. From what I hear, you are right, you haven't always been the most supportive person. You seem to have calmed down a bit."

"True. Sometimes it seems like my life is going down the tubes and I...I guess I lash out when I am scared. I took a lot of my fear out on my Mom when I had no business treating her like that. I don't quite understand why she has forgiven me for that..."

"Seriously? She's your ma! She loves you beyond belief—even more than she loves that pup of hers. She would forgive you almost anything and stand by you no matter what you need." Pete treated Joy to a long, penetrating stare. "Give her a chance to be there for you. Tell her sooner rather than later. Don't spring it on her and then take off. That will break her heart."

"Tell her what?" Joy looked uncomfortable.

Pete said nothing. He finished his lemonade, handed the glass back to her.

"Thank you." He finally said. "In your own time, as my grandma used to say." He turned away and went back to setting the raspberry bushes, leaving Joy to take the glass back to the kitchen.

Moon was still on the phone, taking notes on a pad of paper that she always kept handy, so Joy rinsed the glass and set it on the drainboard. She tried not to listen to her mother's side of the conversation, but it was obvious that it concerned the little bungalow. She wondered if the owners were truly trying to take the house back a year into the contract. *'Selfish people. They wait until Mom makes some improvements that they didn't want to make, then they want the house back. I hope her lawyers can squash this,'* she thought as she went back to her room. *'Maybe I can get her some nice dishes as a housewarming/I'm sorry/thank you gift,'* she mused. *'She deserves something better than those cracked, chipped pieces in the hutch, even if they are the ones I remember growing up. Something with a 1920's vibe would look perfect there.'*

Her cell phone was laying on her dresser with a message on the screen from Neil: "Pack your bags. We are leaving."

15

Lock Down

"**Pete!**" Joy grabbed her phone and ran for the back yard. Pete took one look at the message and ordered Joy back into the house. "I'll call Tommy. You and your Mom stay in the house and lock the doors. Don't let anyone other than me or Tommy in. Don't answer that message, don't answer your phone unless it's me or Tommy! Go!"

Joy barreled back into the house, slamming and locking the door behind her. Her next stop was the front door which she also locked after making sure that Pansy had not wandered out onto the porch.

Moon ended her call just in time to see Joy locking the front door. "Is something wrong?" she asked.

Wordlessly Joy showed her the message on her phone. "Does Pete know? Is he calling Tommy?" Joy nodded.

"Then we stay away from the windows and doors until Tommy or Pete tell us differently," Moon was calm but adamant. She scooped up Pansy, motioning Joy to follow her to the back pantry. It had the fewest windows and only one door—it was as close to a 'panic room' as Moon's home could manage. There was always the attic, but without the window fans that were still on her "Wish List" it was much too hot to stay there for long. The pantry would do fine, Pete would know where to find them when it was safe.

Outside they could hear Pete talking to someone. Tommy? One of the neighbors? Yes, Moon recognized Paul Crawford's voice urging Pete to bring the girls and Pansy across the alley to his house, before

201

anything got ugly. Pete seemed to be considering it. He stood outside the east window of the pantry room and spoke to Moon.

"What do you think? You might be safer there?"

"And put Paul and Ellen at risk also? No, Pete, we'll stay here. You and Tommy can handle anything that develops. We trust you."

"Got it!" They heard Pete thanking Paul for his concern but asking him to stay put until the situation cooled down.

"Joy? Keep your phone on, keep it charged in case I need to contact you, or you need to call 911. I kind of doubt that Neil will be cooperative." Pete moved out of earshot, leaving Joy and Moon wondering what the next step would be. Pansy snuggled close to Moon, content but alert.

"Good thing I grabbed this on my way out of my room! And who was that on the phone?" Joy asked as she reached over to plug her cell phone charger into the wall outlet.

"What?" It took Moon a minute to shift mental gears. Then she remembered the earlier phone call, before Neil's threat. "Oh, that was the lawyer about the case with this house. It seems the judge refused to hear the complaint, as we suspected that might be the case, but he said that the rent-to-own agreement might have to be scrapped in favor of an outright sale, so tomorrow I need to go to the bank and sign the loan papers to purchase this place. I really didn't want a mortgage, but the payments will be less than the rent and I can finally do a few of the things I want to it! The judge also ordered that I have first refusal—they can't sell to someone else unless I put it in writing that I can't buy the house at this time, which I certainly can. So, soon the house will be mine and we can have our own washer and dryer. Hooray!"

"You saw this coming?" Joy sat back down on the floor beside Moon.

"Not at first. I thought that when I signed the rent-to-own contract that I would have five years to decide if I wanted to stay here or if I could afford to buy it. Could I get a loan at that time? Would I still be working at the bank? Would I need more room? Less room? Would I be better off in an apartment or a flat? Then some shirttail member of that family that didn't want to be involved in the estate decided that he was being shut out now that the legal proceedings are closing out and that this house would compensate him for not being included. He said he wanted it for one of his children, but I doubt that's true. He probably would have turned around and sold it for more than I could afford. Good for him, not for me. So, when the realtor heard about his nonsense she gave me a 'heads up" warning, I right away went to talk to a lawyer, one who handles the bank's legal business, and I filled out papers with the loan department at TriCity for a mortgage, just in case I needed to purchase it. Joy, I am happy here, happier than I have been in a long time.

"A year and a half ago I looked in the mirror on my birthday, and I couldn't find ME. Just some fat old woman, living in a dump with a homicidal cat for a roommate, subsisting on junk food and not caring. The cat was healthier than I was, and I was disappearing into depression and flab.

"That was the day I found the eviction notice on the doorstep, and I realized that things had to change. Fast. I called Sue, we talked over lunch, she challenged me to begin figuring out what I wanted going forward, what I didn't want, how I was going to go about getting it. It was life changing, I will admit, and in a way, I wish I had done it a lot sooner. So, that day I called you, I wanted you to know you didn't have to worry about me, I was moving on in a good way and I wanted to let you know where I would be if you needed me."

"I am so sorry I screamed at you. I panicked. I didn't want you to know how bad things were getting. Neil was dragging me and Dad into his backroom dealings, I didn't know he was into selling drugs when I married him, just occasionally using them. I just wanted to get away from Dad and his girlfriends, from the tearing apart of my home. I thought if I had my own home, it would be like it was before. But it wasn't. I don't think it ever will be. But when I see how you have come back from it, Dad hasn't, I don't know what to think. I don't know how to move on the way you did! I hate it. And I'm scared!"

Moon sat quietly listening to Joy while stroking Pansy's ears, to give herself time. "Well," she said finally. "That certainly was a drastic response to your problem, but I see your logic and if Neil had been a more decent candidate, it might have worked. The thing is, I had support when I finally got shaken to my senses. Sue was there to offer advice when asked and to play 'devil's advocate' in order to get me thinking about digging myself out. I think this is your wake-up call. Neil is going to be spending a lot of time in prison if Tommy Williams had anything to do with it, not just because of his drug ring but because he put me and you in danger. You will need to decide where your loyalties lie and how to protect yourself in the future. What will your future look like? What do you really want to do with your life? You talked about loving your PT aide job until Neil made you quit, but you haven't signed up for classes or applied for that opening Sue found for you. I know things are on hold until Neil is behind bars but don't let this opportunity go by. Take this time to set some things in motion. What about those classes? You can still get in this fall."

"I don't think they will take a pregnant woman on as a PT student," Joy muttered. She glanced at her mother, expecting to see shock and disappointment. To her surprise there was none.

"They might, depending upon how far along you are and what the doctor says. You might have some restrictions later on, but it might be wise to do the schooling now, so you are ready to go to work to support the baby. Think about it. Talk to the school. Ask your questions. That way you can formulate a plan. And if you do have to wait until the baby is here, you can plan for that too. Does Neil know?"

Joy said softly, "You knew?"

"I suspected," Moon replied. "You weren't quite yourself, I thought there might be a good reason. Have you made any plans at all? Including or excluding Neil and the rest of us? Does Dad know?"

"I think Neil suspects, but he hasn't come right out and said any-thing. But I think that's one reason he's mad to have me back. Dynasty, sons carry on the family name, and all that. I don't want him and his people destroying this child's life the way he is ruining mine! And no, Dad doesn't have a clue. He's too wrapped up in his own woes. Vicki kicked him out so he stays wherever he can, usually on Fritz's couch. He helps out there when he can and of course Neil uses Fritz's for his business contacts because the cops don't come around that way too often."

"Interesting," Moon mused. "I assume Tommy knows about this?"

"I told him, he's on top of it. I just hope this isn't too big for him and gets him hurt. I would feel like it's my fault..."

"Tommy is a police officer this is his job. He would be going after Neil anyway, but you gave him more incentive. That cookie thief would do anything to keep you safe!"

The sound of voices raised in anger cut the conversation short.

"She's my wife, not yours. She's coming with me! Joy!" Neil yelled, "Get your ass out here or I will come in and get you. This is none of your business, Williams! And who the hell are you?"

This last must have been directed at Pete because a note of concern had crept into Neil's voice. Pete was an imposing figure at the best of times, with a gardening pitchfork in his hands he was definitely in-timidating! His reply didn't carry as far as the pantry window, but it must have made Neil take a step back.

"Fine!" he declared. "I'll stay out here. Joe here can go in and get her, whether she wants to come or not."

Neil motioned toward one of the men with him, but Pete stepped in front of him, and Tommy replied, 'Anyone sets foot on that porch gets arrested for trespassing. She doesn't want to see you, Neil. If she did, she wouldn't have called me when she got your text. Go home. Don't make this worse. I arrested you once for trying this, I will do it again, and your friends as well."

"Geez, Williams, look around you! I've got six guys here to your two, and this old codger isn't good for much more than punching practice, even with his dinner fork!"

Tommy just smiled and looked each man in the eye. He wasn't about to let them in on Pete's credentials. Let them find out for themselves. At once he caught the eye of a younger man who immediately turned away.

"Geoff! Listen to me! I don't want to see you go down with this crowd! I'll make you a deal! Get in your car and leave now, and I won't tell Lacey or Sherle that you were here, that you were a part of this. Your mother will have your hide if she finds out what you're doing!" Geoff Burnham looked uncertainly around him. "She...probably knows. She does what Richard tells her, so do I, and he told me to be here today," he finished defiantly. Neil laughed.

"Well said, my man!"

"Last chance," Tommy offered. "The same goes for any of the rest of you. This is between Neil and Joy, with me in the middle, so if anyone else wants to leave, now is an excellent time."

Nobody took Tommy up on his offer, but Joe turned and headed for the back porch. As soon as his foot hit the bottom step Pete had him on the ground and was zip tying his hands behind his back. At the head of the alley two squad cars pulled up to Moon's side lawn.

"Trespassing," Pete announced as he helped Joe to his feet.

"False arrest," Joe countered as he stumbled toward Tommy.

"Did I forget to mention that my friend here is a former cop? How negligent of me! And he still carries his credentials, keeps them up to date just in case. Sorry Joe. This one's legal. Anybody else?" he asked as one of the new officers took Joe into custody.

"I'll have you out as soon as I get Joy," Neil called to him.

"I don't think so," mused Tommy. "Neil Anderson, I am placing you under arrest for possession with intent to distribute," he announced. "Down on your knees, please, with your hands on your head!"

"I don't think so," Neil began but then he saw another officer standing by his open car with bags of drugs in his gloved hands. "That's illegal search!" he yelled.

"Matt?" Tommy called out to the officer who was holding the drugs, never taking his eyes off of Neil. "Do we have a warrant to search that vehicle?"

"We do," Matt replied. "Judge signed it yesterday afternoon. We were going to come looking for you tonight," he informed Neil. "But you just saved us the trouble."

"Gun!" informed a third cop, and immediately the other officers drew their weapons, including Tommy. Pete stepped up and began searching Neil while Matt called out, "Drop any guns, knives, any other weapons, down on the ground!" Each of the men were handcuffed and placed in the squad cars, except Neil.

"You will be riding with me," Tommy informed him. "There is no way I am letting you out of my sight until you and I have had a little talk."

Pete looked up sharply but must have been reassured by what he saw in Tommy's face. This was a cop who did things 'by the book' as Pete often said.

"How did you get a judge to sign a search warrant?" he asked curiously as he walked Neil and Tommy to Tommy's squad car.

"We had some reliable information that Neil would be meeting with his buyers tonight, I called a Judge that I knew was watching this unfold and got the warrant immediately. I just didn't think I would be executing it this soon. But when Joy called me, I knew we could clean a lot of this up right away. And Neil, here, is going to be a big help, aren't you Neil?"

Neil merely grunted as Tommy helped him into the back seat of the squad car. "Tell Joy and Moon they can come up for air," he told Pete as soon as they had stepped away out of Neil's hearing. "Tell her I will call her in a day or two as soon as things are more settled, but he's not going anywhere for a long time!" Tommy gestured toward Neil who was glowering at them.

"Do you mind sticking around here until we are sure we have everybody that is involved in custody? he asked Pete.

"No problem," replied Pete with a grin. "I got raspberry bushes to finish!" Whistling, he left Tommy to take Neil to the station as he himself headed back to the house to let the ladies know the coast was clear.

16

Loose Ends

Moon was surprised to see Lacey at her usual desk when she returned from vacation. She had no chance to ask about it or to speak to Lacey until lunch: her morning was spent catching up with clients, signing her own loan papers for her house, and moving into her new office. She didn't even stop for her usual mid-morning break except to call Joy to see how she and Pansy were faring at home alone.

"We are fine, Mom!" Joy sounded her former exasperated self, but Moon could hear the notes of laughter in her voice.

"Pete is here climbing all over everything with a measuring tape, the appliance delivery guy has been and gone with the old stove and fridge: the new one is up and running and full!"

"Full? We were down to our last eggs! I made sure we used up all the perishables so we wouldn't have to change things over until...oh, my Lord, it's grocery delivery day. Isn't it?"

"Relax. It's handled. Everything is put away, Pansy ate a bit of her food, I made coffee and sandwiches to keep Pete going, it's all good. He wants to know when you are planning to buy the washer and dryer?"

"Not until the papers are delivered and the house is in my name. I signed them this morning and they are enroute now. I will stop at the realtors on my lunch break to double check that everything is good, but there won't be a closing date since we already had the previous contract in effect. I guess the family is thrilled to get this done and over with. It's the last barrier to closing out probate on the estate and they want to put it all behind them. Even "Mr. Crabby" who made such a fuss about the house is fine with it. I don't care. It's mine now or will be by tonight. Do you want me to bring home something for a quick supper? Pizza?"

"No, there are casseroles in the chest freezer. I am thawing a ham/potato bake in the new fridge, so it is ready to heat up and we have fresh asparagus from Pete's Garden to go with it. He's hinting at a dinner invitation. Should I tell him 'yes'? I think we should, he's been working hard around here all day," Joy said.

"I agree. I don't have anything for dessert, though, how about apple pie from the bakery?" Moon offered.

"With ice cream or whipped cream?" Joy wanted to know. "We have heavy cream in the fridge, there's vanilla ice cream in the freezer."

"You choose," laughed Moon. "I'll have mine plain or I won't fit into my clothes again!"

"Oh, and I called the school, and I made an appointment with a doctor. Tell you all about it tonight." Joy hung up abruptly leaving Moon wondering '*Now what?*'

Instead of worrying, she went back to work setting up her new desk and filing system and getting used to her new office. At noon she checked her calendar, locked her door, and prepared to meet Sue at the diner for a 'catch-up' lunch. On her way out the back door, she stopped by Lacey's desk.

"It's nice to see you," she said when Lacey looked up.

"Is it?" Lacey asked. "Really? Or are you here to gloat?"

"No. I am not gloating," Moon replied. "How is Geoff doing? Did you get him a good lawyer? Someone who can extricate him from the rest of this business?"

"Yes," Lacey said shortly. "We found someone; I hope they can help. But I won't lift a finger to help Richard. He and your daughter's husband are the brains behind this whole thing, and I hope they throw them both away for good." Tears were making tracks down her cheeks, spoiling her make-up. Moon reached into her tote and handed Lacey a small pack of tissues.

"They will, if I have anything to say about it, but I hope Geoff only gets probation. He doesn't deserve to have his life ruined by the likes of those two," Moon said quietly.

"You tried to warn me. I wouldn't listen," said Lacey.

"I wouldn't have either, if the roles had been reversed. After all, I only had Geordie's word for it. And we both know how reliable _he_ is. I take it the wedding's off?"

"As If you have to ask? He's long gone but they'll catch up to him. He has a lot to answer for, the least of which is dragging the bank down with him. Did you know that he was using his position here to further his contacts for his drug dealings!" Lacey started to cry again. "And I helped!"

"You had no idea what he was up to, none of us did!" Moon declared. "I got taken in as well. If I hadn't missed his call that day he transferred, it might have been me rather than you, and you might be doing the gloating and telling me 'I told you so!' I'd say we both dodged a bullet on that one! You think?"

"I'd say you were right, but you _know_ how I hate to admit that, especially to you," Lacey smiled through her tears.

"Good luck," said Moon. "I mean it. You deserve a lot better than this."

Sue was waiting in their favorite booth when Moon finally joined her after stopping at the realtor's.

"The family had already been and gone, papers are signed, a copy of the deed and mortgage will be mailed to me as soon as they are filed with the courthouse, but for all intents it's done. The house is mine. The new stove and refrigerator were delivered this morning, just in time for grocery delivery and Pete is running around like a crazy man measuring for a washer and dryer to go in the pantry room. I may want to put linoleum down on that floor first, what do you think?"

Moon hardly glanced at the menu. All she really wanted was some vegetable soup and half a BLT sandwich with a diet soda.

"I's say you had one heck of a vacation!" declared Sue. "How is Joy holding up?"

"Fragile. She thinks she might be pregnant, but she hasn't been to a doctor yet because she didn't want Neil to know. That explains a lot of her changed behaviors lately. She said she made an appointment and called that school this morning about classes. So, we will see. And I do think l will go with sheet vinyl before I put in the washer and dryer. Maybe a woodgrain pattern? Or something livelier?" Moon signaled the waitress so they could order.

"What about you? Is Josh still planning on transferring next year?" Moon asked.

"Yes, he's looking forward to it. I don't think dorm living will exactly be his 'thing'. He's too private for that. It will be a good experience for him, but he will be better off living with Jim's parents in the long run, and it will be better for them as well. I can't tell you how relieved I am that we are staying here—at least for now. Who knows what will turn up down the line? So, Neil is in custody?"

"And according to Lacey, Richard Lemanski took off. They will get him, I'm sure. I always knew a man who liked cats couldn't be trusted!" Moon declared.

"So says the crazy dog lady. How is Pansy doing?" Sue sipped her iced tea.

"Up and around, thanks for asking. No signs of infection, she's healing well. She tires easily but each day is a little better, and she may always have an issue with that lung, but we will see." Moon thought about calling Pete about the linoleum when she got back to the office, decided to wait until that night at dinner so Joy could be included.

The waitress brought their orders. "Do they know who shot her?" Sue asked carefully.

"Yes, and I don't know what to do about it. If I press charges, it could really open a hornet's nest for me. If I don't then there is no justice for Pansy." Moon chewed her sandwich carefully.

"' Why on earth wouldn't you press charges!" Sue exclaimed. "They almost killed your dog out of spite, cost you hundreds of dollars in vet bills, why not go after them for all you can get?"

"Because Lacey's son, Geoff, was the shooter, on Richards's orders. Neil wanted me hurt and Richard used Geoff to do it. I'm not sure I can go after Geoff. I think I'd rather lay that one on Neil and Richard. I owe Lacey that much."

"You don't owe her anything!" Sue exclaimed.

"I feel like I do. There's been a lot of conflict between us over the years, we haven't always been very nice to each other. For a long time, Geordie was the pivotal point, then the job and Richard. Did you ever wonder why she named her son 'Geoff'? No, I don't think he's Geordie's," Moon amended quickly, seeing Sue's shocked expression. "But it was her sly way of telling him that she still had feelings for him. Without being too obvious. Maybe now that Geordie really needs someone in his life, he will turn to her."

"Not you?" Sue asked slyly.

Moon crafted her answer carefully as she finished her soup. "No. A couple of years ago, maybe, while I was stuck in that apartment and wallowing in depression. Maybe then I would have taken him back if it meant things would return to the way they used to be. Not now. Don't get me wrong, I want us to be friends, but I've come too far, worked too hard getting back to 'me'. That chapter is done. We will always share a connection in Joy, but he has to straighten out his life the way I had to straighten out mine. Joy will need both of us to support her if she is expecting, but how much involvement he will have is up to her. Did you know he cut a deal to help bring Neil and Richard down? He might not even be charged with any part in Neil's drug business since he was so helpful in shutting it down. I guess we will see that too." Moon pushed her empty bowl and plate toward the center of the table so Sue could stack hers on top. It was a habit of theirs to leave as little mess as possible for the wait staff to clean up.

"I need to get back. I have new clients this afternoon and I promised I would pick up a pie from the bakery for dessert. Pete seems to have invited himself to supper, he's contributing fresh asparagus, so Joy is thawing out a ham/potato casserole." Moon gathered her tote bag and left a tip for the waitress. Sue did the same as they took their bills to the register. "Sounds homey," she grinned.

"Don't get any ideas!" Moon cautioned as they emerged into the sunshine. "He's nice, he's handy, and I won't turn down the help. At least he doesn't own a cat! You can blame Tommy for setting this up. By the way, don't tell Joy but Tommy will be joining us for Sunday dinner. That's a romance I <u>will</u> promote."

"I understand if you don't want to make life harder for Geoff," Sue said, "so add that to Neil and Richard's charges. Ultimately they are the ones responsible."

"I know," agreed Moon. "I will do what I can, and hope Lacey understands. If not, then well, no different from what it has always been."

The two friends parted in front of the diner, Sue off to another committee meeting, Moon back to the bank, thinking about consulting with Joy and Pete about flooring when she returned home that evening.

Ann Larabee writes poetry, short stories, and novels. She is the mother of six children and six grandchildren. She currently lives in Wisconsin with her three Bassett hounds and a dachshund.